WEEPING
WATERS

WEEPING
WATERS

A novel based on a true story

Anne Maria Nicholson

HarperCollins*Publishers*

National Library of New Zealand Cataloguing-in-Publication Data

Nicholson, Anne Maria.
Weeping waters / Anne Maria Nicholson.
ISBN: 1-86950-617-0
I. Title.
NZ823.3—dc 22

First published 2006
HarperCollins*Publishers (New Zealand) Limited*
P.O. Box 1, Auckland

ISBN 10: 1 86950 617 0
ISBN 13: 978 186950 617 9

Cover design by Nadia Backovic Designs
Cover images: Woman and volcano © Photolibrary; Tangiwai rail disaster © Alexander Turnbull Library, National Library of New Zealand, reference number MP-0059-10-F
Typesetting by Springfield West

Words from the Neil Finn song 'Four Seasons in One Day' used with permission of Mushroom Music Australia

Printed by Griffin Press, Australia, on 70 gsm Bulky Ivory

In memory of my parents,
Jack and Mary

Acknowledgements

I would like to acknowledge and thank the many people who helped and inspired me with the research and writing of *Weeping Waters*.

Anne Lennox and Bruce Jensen who shared their true-life experiences at Tangiwai; Timi Te Heuheu and Martin Wikaira from Ngati Tuwharetoa; members of Ngati Rangi; Paul Green and Harry Keys from the New Zealand Department of Conservation; Steve Sherburn, New Zealand Institute of Geological and Nuclear Sciences; Tom Northcroft and Roly Buck; Christine Cole Catley; Stephen Stratford; Carol Jorgensen.

My daughter, Eva Westfield, who accompanied me on research trips including to the Crater Lake at the top of Mount Ruapehu.

The National Library of New Zealand for its great resources and the Coroners Court in Wellington for allowing me to examine all the postmortems from Tangiwai.

Katherine and Neil Owen, Mark, Paul and Christine Nicholson, Peter and Stephen Westfield, Linda Tizard, Denise Eriksen, Aniela Kos, Anthea Bulloch, Jane Dillon, Gay Murrell, Anne Jones, Gillian Thomas, Adrian Collette, Susan Patterson, David Hancock, Bronwen Reid, Nina Burridge, Diana Deeley, John Cameron and other colleagues at the ABC in Sydney, and Scott Roberts, who all helped in a myriad of ways.

The great team at HarperCollins, in particular Lorain Day, Shona Martyn and Anna Rogers.

Lastly, I wish to pay tribute to those who died at Tangiwai and to all the survivors and rescuers and their families whose lives were irrevocably changed. It wasn't until I'd finished the book I discovered that a relative I hadn't known of, my second cousin, Doris Workman, 41, was among the victims. Her body was never recovered.

Author's note

On Christmas Eve 1953, shortly after 10 p.m., New Zealand's largest overnight express steam train nose-dived into the swirling Whangaehu River at Tangiwai in the centre of the North Island. The train was packed and many of the 285 people on board were already asleep. Most of the passengers were families and young people at the start of their Christmas holiday. One hundred and fifty-one of them perished.

A torrent of water, a lahar, had gushed out of the crater of the nearby sacred volcano Mount Ruapehu and swept down the valley. It took all in its path and, minutes before the train arrived, weakened the railway bridge.

For the Maori tribes whose ancestors had populated the area for centuries such a tragedy was inevitable. The train track, they said, should never have been built across the path of the sacred mountain and Tangiwai, which means weeping waters, was named because it had always been a place of torrential flows and sometimes death.

But for those who live in the spectacular World Heritage area half a century on, memories of one of the world's worst train disasters drive them to look for ways to tame Ruapehu, where another lahar is building up in its crater.

Weeping Waters is a fictional work set between 1953 and the present. The story is based on true events surrounding the Tangiwai disaster and the real conflict that exists today about Mount Ruapehu. The characters and incidents in the novel are invented but many of the 1953 survival and rescue stories are based on true events.

AMN

The Passenger

I woke up drowning. Swirling black, cold water was enveloping me, filling my body and soul. In the liquid darkness I felt someone pulling my hair, pulling the long strands very hard, hurting me, connecting me again to life.

Suddenly I realised I was still on the train and I started kicking myself free of my seat. I'd always been a strong swimmer and a diver and instinctively I held my breath when I hit the water. I tried to open my eyes, tried to make sense of the carriage, tried to see David. But I couldn't see anything and the water hurt my eyes. I felt myself starting to panic as I flayed in the water trying to find my love. But the pulling was urgent and I succumbed to an invisible rescuer who was willing me away, clutching my hand, yanking me out of this watery grave. Somehow we found an open window of the carriage and one by one squeezed through. Together, we swam up into a swirling current.

We rose to the top, desperately took our first breaths, gasping and choking on sickly sweet sulphur fumes and oily water. As the water swept us away from each other, I caught her eye in the moonlight, saw her look of despair until she bobbed out of sight, lost in a sea of tiny waves. The river was full of branches, pieces of the train, suitcases and something, maybe a body, nudged me.

As I swam for the bank I could hear screams piercing through the roaring floodwaters. I think one of them was mine. I was gulping the foul freezing water and trying to force my way across the current. Feeling for the bottom, my toes touched sharp rocks beneath. I tried to grip them with my feet, realising for the first time my shoes and my jacket were gone. I was wearing the new dress I had finished sewing for the holiday only a day ago, on my birthday. The hem of the skirt had filled with river sand and formed a heavy hoop around me that was pulling me down. Slipping and retching, I scrambled painfully towards a large jagged object rising out of the edge of the river.

As my eyes adjusted to the light, I saw it was the smashed and twisted steam engine that had been pulling our carriages. Steam was still rising from the wreckage where the red-hot fires that fuelled the engine had been doused by floodwaters. I heard a cry. Behind me I saw the woman who saved me was struggling in the water. I reached out to help her up and she fell over me, coughing and sobbing. I saw for the first time she was about my age.

'My sister, my sister, I thought you were my sister. She's still on the train.'

I felt sick knowing I had been saved by mistake, a pretender. She had been searching for her sister who had long blonde hair just like mine.

'Come with me. You can't do anything.' Now I was the rescuer, urging her out of the river, begging her not to go back into the icy torrent. I thought of my fiancé and prayed somehow David had escaped the train too. I grabbed her hand and, using all my strength, pulled her towards the engine. We both fell against its side and climbed up onto it. I was shocked to feel it was still hot and the metal burned my skin. My throat and eyes were stinging, full of grit and oil. I heaved myself up higher, away from the water.

I didn't feel afraid for myself but I saw the girl was shivering uncontrollably and I worried she would die of shock and exposure. I wrapped my arms around her and urged her to call for help. I started crying out in a voice that I barely recognised as mine. As soon as I did, I heard another fainter call. There was someone below, trapped in the engine.

I heard more voices and soon I saw a group of men above us on the bank. 'Stay there, we'll get you off,' one said out of the darkness. 'There's someone still alive in the engine!' I called back.

For the first time, I looked around. Strangely, the night was clear. I could see people floating away in the current, others struggling to come ashore. Some had already made it and were lying on both sides of the river. I strained to see if David was among them but could not make out any faces. I thought of all the people I had seen on the train, the children who had been running up and down so excitedly just an hour ago. Carriages were poking out of a wall of dirty yellow water, some with just their roofs showing, another pushed onto its side.

Then I saw it. In the middle of the broken bridge, another carriage was dangling over the edge. In the seconds I watched, I could see it tilting slowly forwards. It lurched violently, and began falling, somersaulting into the river. Beyond it I saw for the first time the silhouette of the volcano.

I had been sleeping in David's arms when the train plummeted into the river. I never saw him again and his body was never found. My rescuer lost her sister. We were among only a handful out of fifty-six people in our carriage to survive. They never did find anyone alive in the engine. Both the driver and the fireman died.

Beverley Corbett, 19, a survivor of the Tangiwai disaster, 1953

CHAPTER ONE

It is still early when Frances Nelson steps off the plane in Auckland. She jostles among hundreds of other dishevelled passengers at the baggage carousel, looking for the one large navy-blue suitcase that contains all her essentials for the year ahead. It bobs towards her, instantly recognisable with its scratches and a small tear on the front, scars of previous journeys. As she hauls it off onto its wheels, she feels it pull hard on her tired body.

She adjusts her laptop computer bag on one shoulder, a small backpack on the other and attempts to walk away but a beagle blocks her way, brushing against her leg then sniffing her and her luggage. She knows it means business and resists a temptation to pat the dog as it lingers around the suitcase. Has it picked up a scent of the rocky wilderness she has left behind? Detecting no contraband, the animal quickly loses interest and pads towards a young woman with a Dutch emblem on her backpack.

Frances passes easily through customs and passport checks, glad her work visa is in order. There is none of the tension she felt in American airports on her way over; no guards with machine guns, none of the endless frisking and questioning that has become part of travelling post-September 11. The people around her look more relaxed too, a blend of softer faces from the Pacific and a faraway British colonial past.

After flying from Seattle to Los Angeles, she dozed intermittently on the flight to New Zealand, eating too many meals and downing a few too many glasses of wine as the plane moved through an endless day, a longer night and eventually into a fluorescent burnt-orange dawn. But as she walks through the terminal, Frances' tiredness lifts and she decides to forgo a planned night in a motel and drive the five hours straight to the mountain.

She finds a shower room at the airport and revives herself under the warm flow. Stretching her arms high into the air and standing on the tips of her toes, she lets the water cascade over her face, into her mouth and down her strong limbs that have been cramped for so long on the plane. She dries herself and combs her damp fair hair back off her face.

Catching her reflection, she is pleased with her new layered haircut, glad she had several inches cut off her long locks before leaving. Dabbing on some expensive moisturiser cream she bought impulsively on the plane, she screws up her face to see if there are any new wrinkles. She sighs when she spots one and doubts the new wonder cream will do anything for a complexion tanned and punished by years of mountain climbing. She slips on a new cotton bra and pants, a fresh pair of jeans and a fitted light-blue shirt before squashing her dirty clothes into her suitcase.

She has deliberately come a day early. On her way to join the investigations of the seismology team based in Taupo, she wants to fit in a visit to Mount Ruapehu alone. And there is a more compelling reason. As much as she fears it, she knows she has to go to Tangiwai as quickly as she can.

'You won't have any trouble this time of year,' the funky young man at the airport car-rental booth assures her. He dresses between two worlds with a spiky gelled haircut, a nose stud and a carefully pressed conservative company blazer. 'But give it another month or so and I'd have to make you take some chains for the car. Gets pretty icy up there.'

She watches him carefully noting the details on her American passport: Frances Tui Nelson, British-born, aged 36, fair hair, green eyes. He looks her up and down. She's used to that, especially when travelling alone. She waits for the inevitable question. 'Here for a holiday and a bit of adventure, eh?'

'Always like an adventure,' she teases him, 'but actually I'm here to work.'

He smiles at her. 'Tui's a Maori name. Funny name for a Yank to have, isn't it?'

'My mother's idea,' she says. 'What about Noah?' She nods at the name badge pinned to his blazer. 'Thought that was reserved for old men with beards and too many pets.'

'Touché,' he laughs. 'Yeah, what would we do without parents like ours? Listen,' he says, leaning towards her conspiratorially like a close friend, 'there's not a lot of traffic around there this time of year and we get a lot of tourists drifting over to the right-hand side of the road. We lost two Swiss people last year and two Germans this year. Cleaned up. Went home in boxes. They just forgot. So watch yourself, wouldn't want to see that happen to you.'

Heading south, Frances concentrates on driving on the left. The traffic is heavy but the roads are better than she expected and remind her of the trip she made so often south from Seattle down Highway No. 5 to Mount St Helens.

That's where she cut her teeth on this work. Triggered by an earthquake, the American volcano had erupted spectacularly in May 1980, setting off an almighty landslide. The landscape for miles around was still severely scarred when Frances joined a research team there a decade later. Acres of giant splinters were the only reminders of the once-mighty fir and cedar forests that had been felled in moments. Fifty people had died.

By the time Frances joined them, the scientists were beginning to regain a confidence shattered as severely as the mountain. The size and suddenness of the disaster had shaken them out of a complacency that they could predict what volcanoes would do. Now they were beginning to believe it was only a matter of time before they would amass enough data and new technology to make seismology an exact science.

This thought comforts her as she passes through Hamilton and continues south, following the route of the main trunk line. The traffic thins and the road narrows as it winds through small railway towns. The terrain changes too, from the damp green plains of the Waikato to the steep hilly sheep farms and forests of the King Country.

Despite a stop for a rest and a coffee, the effects of the long plane trip start to creep up on her. She yawns and fidgets, sips from a water bottle, chews some mints and tries to listen to the radio. But the reception is poor. There is just an annoying scratchiness so she turns it off.

The landscape changes again and there is emptiness all around. Frances feels a gnawing in her gut, her unwelcome companion for the last year. Then, suddenly, like a grand opera set revealed by a rising curtain, before her lies the volcanic plateau. It takes her breath away and sweeps aside her unspoken anxieties. She's spinning through the spiritual heart of the North Island where human and natural forces have interacted for many hundreds of years. Right in front of her, a trio of powerful volcanoes rise out of the austere earth like giant sentries — cone-shaped Ngauruhoe, the rambling slopes of Tongariro and, dominating them both, the towering grandeur of Ruapehu.

Frances knows the mountains' pedigrees stretch back 250,000 years. To see them again, rising up and piercing the bluest of skies, reminds her why they have earned their place among the earth's greatest heritage treasures.

The road rises steeply and Frances accelerates, pleased she's taken young Noah's advice to hire a powerful six-cylinder car. As she draws closer to Ruapehu, catching little glimpses as she winds around the steep road, she feels the tug of the mountain. It excites her, making her feel like a space traveller finally arriving on a distant planet after months of training on earth.

Just a week ago, in the comfort of her office on the other side of the world, she had watched live images of the mountain on her computer screen. The mountain had been puffing out huge clouds of acidic steam, ratcheting up the alert warnings. For the last five years Ruapehu had been playing up with momentous eruptions of lava and ash. Now it was threatening to expel a massive mudflow from the mysterious lake in its crater.

Frances wishes her colleagues were with her to see it. She smiles as she remembers their ribbing.

'So you're leaving us to conquer Mount Doom,' one said. Since part of The Lord of the Rings was shot here, vulcanologists often referred to Ruapehu by its cinematic nom de plume.

She rounds one more corner and the sudden sight of the mountain right in front of her is so powerful and overwhelming that she abruptly pulls over to the side of the road. Small plumes of steam drift over the summit in the late afternoon sun. Two decades have passed since she was here with her parents on their lonely pilgrimage. She feels compelled to get out of the car but shivers in the breeze as she remembers that time of grieving. The volcano's stark stony beauty, yet to receive its first winter white cloak, draws her in, just as it did all that time ago.

Although it is more than thirty-six hours since she has slept in a bed, the cool April crispness of the volcanic country sends a surge of energy through her. A month earlier, she had been working in her laboratory when she received the call to come here.

'Don't think this is going to be straightforward,' New Zealand team leader Theo Rush told her during their last phone conversation as she was preparing to leave the United States. 'A lot of people are terrified there's going to be a giant lahar. There's a big drive here to drain the crater lake to stop it happening. But the Maori people are pushing their belief that the sacred mana of the mountain is its unpredictability. They say nature should be allowed to take its course. So we're piggy in the middle.'

'So where does that leave me as an outsider?'

'I'm tempted to say between a rock and a hard place but really I don't want to scare you off before you get here. I'm just looking forward to some fresh thoughts from you and, don't worry, you'll get a warm Kiwi welcome!'

Now, utterly alone on a back road to this strange mountain, for a moment Frances can't believe she has come at all.

CHAPTER TWO

❧

Frances is struck by the barrenness around her. It must have been twenty minutes or more since she has seen another car. The only sounds she hears as she approaches the Chateau are the crunching of the tyres on the gravel and her own breathing.

She has forgotten how incongruous the hotel looks, stuck here on the lower slopes of the mountain in the middle of nowhere. With its bright blue-tiled roof studded with white chimneys and red brick walls interrupted by tiny-paned windows, it is an oddly European landmark for such a young country. It must have had the locals scratching their heads in amazement when it appeared suddenly in the late 1920s just as New Zealand, like the rest of the world, was plunged into the Great Depression.

As a teenager she was deeply impressed by the hotel's luxury and surprised by her father's unusual extravagance. 'It's just this once,' he had told her. 'Your mother needs a bit of comfort.'

Frances felt she needed it too, even though she hadn't wanted to come with them, hadn't wanted to leave her friends. She was used to a no-frills existence in a plain semi-detached brick cottage in Surrey, England. Although the purpose of that trip was a little unclear to her at the time, it was the closest she'd come to a holiday abroad.

As she pulls into the car park, she notices the telltale signs of the task that has brought her here a second time. Speakers on poles, instruction posters and aerials on some outbuildings, all are part of the early warning system that Theo Rush has told her urgently needs modernising.

Frances had worked with the team that had developed new acoustic early warning systems in Seattle. She had helped to put them to the test herself, first successfully in the States and later in other, wilder places. But she knows it won't be so easy here. Scientists are working in a much tighter timeframe. There could be as little as ninety seconds' warning from the build-up of a lahar in Ruapehu before it hit the upper part of the skifield. At best there would be one or two hours to move people out of the surrounding area.

When Frances put her hand up for this posting, she was still hesitant. Moving would be a wrench. She was frightened by the thought of it, even though it could be the emotional circuit breaker she needed. But when Theo phoned to offer her the job, her doubts dissipated and she knew instantly that this was what her life's work had been preparing her for.

She didn't mention that she'd been to New Zealand, to Ruapehu, before. Theo wanted her for her specialist expertise, her ability to monitor volcanoes, and she didn't want to give the impression that her return might be influenced by sentimentality.

'Had a long journey?' the red-haired receptionist asks, not waiting for a reply as she watches Frances dragging in her suitcase while struggling to balance her laptop and backpack. 'Leave your luggage and I'll have it put in your room,' she says as she checks her booking on the computer. 'We're not very busy and we've got you a lovely room with a view of the mountain.'

'Thanks. That's great. Has the mountain been clear for long?'

'Not much cloud around for the last few days. Where are you from? America? Canada?'

'Seattle . . . and England.'

'Well, enjoy. Dinner is served from six with lots of local delicacies and if you feel like a swim there's a hot pool on the basement level.'

Frances gratefully takes the key and lingers in the foyer. She is surprised how little the hotel has changed. Chandeliers still glisten from the ceilings and she smiles to herself when she has the same image she did as a girl, of Cinderella drifting down the elegant staircase. Thick woollen carpets lead her to the large lounge where guests with pre-dinner drinks are already settling into rows of plump sofas in front of an open fire.

As if in a familiar dream, she wanders over towards the large picture windows, framed with heavy velvet curtains. The mountain, soaring above, lit by the remains of the day's sunshine, seems to be telling her something. But the fatigue of her long journey is overtaking her and the thought fades as she sinks into an armchair. Her body finally relaxes and her eyes beg to close.

She hears it first, the unmistakable chop-chopping of a helicopter, and returns to the window in time to see it rising out of the cloudy summit's jaws like a dragonfly in search of its prey, hovering uncertainly for a few seconds, then determinedly flying off.

The Seismologist

I've been asked about the night of 24 December 1953 many times. The truth is, there was no volcanic activity or earthquake recorded on our equipment on that day or the days leading up to it. And we regularly checked it.

Ever since the series of major eruptions of 1945 we had been under severe pressure in the observatory here at the Chateau to keep a close watch on the Crater Lake. Until then many New Zealanders believed Ruapehu was extinct, although few of us in the scientific community ever shared that view. Four big bangs within months put paid to that theory once and for all.

With the war, of course, those were a trying few years. At the end of '45, conditions on the mountain were quite unbearable with the ash fouling the water supply to such an extent that it was almost like liquid mud. In addition, anything mechanical, such as the electric generating plant, was difficult to maintain with fine ash penetrating everything.

The war also put skiing on hold. The Health Department took over the Chateau to house patients of a psychiatric hospital near Wellington that had been damaged by an earthquake. But that didn't last long with the unhygienic conditions on the mountain. The female patients and staff were evacuated and they left on a special train three days before Christmas to go to a place up near Auckland. That certainly took the pressure off me.

Of course, we kept up the monitoring and we had a number of scientists coming and going. The eruptions created huge interest around the world and the photographs were spectacular so the place became something of a tourist attraction.

We had trampers constantly arriving and wanting to climb up to the crater. They tend to be a little gung ho, mad buggers some of them, and I always worried about their safety. And with good reason, it turned out. I remember a couple of them who camped in the snow near the crater, really copped it during the July eruption.

They were showered with hot rocks and badly burnt and one of them was knocked out. The mountain rescue got them down but they were very lucky to survive. The snowfields were wrecked, but mind you, after the war and with the first rope tows installed in '47, the skiers were back in droves.

After the explosions stopped, the crater looked completely different. I frequently climbed to the top to inspect it and take samples. There was a boiling lake surrounded by a steep-walled vent I estimated to be about 900 feet deep. Over the next three years it gradually refilled so by the end of 1949 it was approximately the same level as before the eruptions. We regularly saw small steam eruptions but not much else.

One day in March 1953, when I was up at the crater, I observed a lava dome had emerged from the lake and I could see occasional steaming puffs of ash coming out of it. It had clearly been formed by magma squeezing its way out of the vent in the crater and piling up in mounds. Lava had spread across the crater floor and pushed out all the water.

From then onwards there were regular powerful ash eruptions with the ash spreading out for hundreds of miles around. In May, I noticed a second larger dome growing. Later that month there was a huge explosion and we saw flames shooting up 300 feet high above the mountain. It was an awesome and terrifying sight!

Stories and photos of the eruption were all over the papers. We had our thunder stolen at the end of the month, though, by Mount Everest and Hillary. New Zealanders went crazy.

It was pretty quiet at Ruapehu for the rest of the year. On that Christmas Eve, we detected nothing on our monitoring equipment to worry about.

It was only after the disaster at Tangiwai, we were able to piece together what happened. We now know that some time after dusk, possibly as late as eight o'clock, a solid ash wall covered in ice inside the Crater Lake that had been acting as a dam barrier suddenly collapsed. This force cracked and shattered masses of ice and released a huge mass of water. It formed a cold lahar, a turbulent volcanic mudflow.

It washed out of the crater, pushing over the rim, and flowed down into the Whangaehu River. Moving with tremendous speed, it dragged everything with it: boulders, ice, large quantities of loose ash from the '45 eruption, trees, anything in its path.

The lahar flooded into the valley, depositing boulders and sand for miles around and it washed away six road and railway bridges. It reached Tangiwai at 10.17 p.m. Five minutes later, the train arrived at the bridge and plunged into the torrent, killing more than half the passengers.

As I said, we had no prior warning on any of our equipment about the impending disaster.

Geoff Andrews, 49, seismologist at Mount Ruapehu in 1953

CHAPTER THREE

❧

Look at this, the water temperature's definitely heading north.' His bright orange overalls and red hard hat clashing with the muted colours of nature, Theo Rush scrambles up from the edge with a thermometer and the small bottles he has just filled from the shark-grey waters of the volcano's Crater Lake. In his sixtieth year, he is still lean and tanned from a lifetime outdoors. He hands the samples up to the younger scientist crouched at the top of a heavily eroded ridge. 'That's the third time in a row we've had readings over fifty-five degrees and the crater level looks like it's still rising. What do you make of it?' Theo asks.

'It looks very dicey,' his companion replies. 'But then for the last six months it's been up and down, hasn't it, so I'm not sure. We'll have to weigh it up when we get the other measurements.'

The lake is the very pulse of the volcano. It is streaked with yellowish slicks of sulphur. Small clouds of steam and sulphur gas forced out from the hot magma deep within the volcano waft around the two men as they gaze at the thermometer.

A look of concern creases Theo's face. The colour of the lake tells him the mood of Ruapehu, from emerald green when cool, to sapphire blue when it is warming up. When the mountain dispenses with its jewel-like palette altogether and turns an even muddier grey than now, he knows the temperature will be dangerously high, above 60 degrees.

Far below them lies the valley where, for hundreds of years, dozens of gigantic lahars have swept down, wreaking havoc on the wild landscape. Ten thousand years earlier, rivers of molten lava spewed out of the core of the volcano. It was one of a circle of cones stretching from New Zealand across the Philippines, Japan, Russia, onward to the Aleutian Islands and the west coasts of both North and South America, all formed by the collision of the plates of the Pacific and the Indian-Australia oceans. Since the Asian tsunami, Theo and his colleagues have felt the pressure on them to be prophets and seers. It hasn't helped an already tense situation.

Sam Hawks packs the bottles into his backpack, placing them in special plastic bags already marked with the date. Hauling the pack easily onto his muscular shoulders, he begins to walk gingerly around the rim. For a tall man, he moves nimbly in his well-worn hiking boots, careful not to slip on the loosely spread scree.

'I'll take some gas readings. Then we'd better check the tephra dam,' he calls back to his boss.

At the end of an unusually dry summer and autumn, the snow has completely disappeared from the summit. Without its white cover, the craggy brownness looks unearthly, like the hostile surface of the moon. Only the lake stretching in front of them for some 500 metres interrupts the brittle, pocked surface.

Whenever it isn't freezing and they fly in by chopper, Sam lives in hard-wearing khaki shorts and shirt that seem to blend in with his freckled skin and corn-coloured hair. As a concession, he has packed a Gore-Tex parka in case the weather changes suddenly and lately he's begun to bring a hard hat and gas mask although, like today, he usually neglects to wear them.

He takes out the silicone tubing with attached thermometer and collection bottles to capture and measure the cocktail of gases that drift up from the very core of the earth. The rising waters of the Crater Lake have already filled most of the fumaroles, flooding the vents through which the gas leaks out of the mountain. But there are still a few on an exposed part of the crater. Sam crouches down beside the biggest vent, which is as wide as the length of his boot. Inserting a long piece of tube right inside its crusty lip, he gathers a heady mixture of water vapour, hydrogen chloride and sulphur dioxide.

'Getting some bloody good samples today,' he calls over his shoulder. As a column of steamy vapour hits him in the face, he reels back, choking. 'Fuck, that nearly knocked me out!' His usually steady legs tremble as he pulls a handkerchief from his pocket and noisily blows his nose. Tears stream from his eyes and for a few seconds he can barely see.

'Are you OK?' Theo asks as he climbs up to reach his partner. 'Maybe you should wear that mask rather than carrying the bloody thing. And for God's sake, put your helmet on!'

'You're a great one to talk, TR,' Sam grins as he mops the moisture off his face. 'Remember what you told me about the eruption you got caught up in.'

The older man laughs. He will never forget that day. He and the scientist he worked with in those days — it was 1995 — had measured an extraordinary 15,000 tonnes of sulphur dioxide on Ruapehu, the highest readings recorded from any volcano in the world. Theo had vomited violently, as sick as a teenager drunk on gin. He hadn't been wearing his mask either but that had been just the beginning of his trouble.

'Right, point taken. But we all should know better now, eh. Now let's get that survey gear sorted,' Theo says.

The two men walk halfway around the perimeter of the lake to the Dome Shelter, a hardy A-shaped shed containing the main seismometer on the summit, other monitoring equipment and emergency rations, packets of dried food and bottles of water.

The hardest task of the day still lies ahead. They want to detect any changes in the tephra dam, a large barrier inside the lake that has formed from deposits of ash, scoria, pumice and rocks thrown up during the last big eruption. It is now so enlarged that it sticks up like a fence across one side of the lake, blocking the natural outlet for the water.

Sam puts his helmet on and smiles when he sees Theo raise his eyebrows. He props his survey equipment on the side of the crater where the tephra rises out of the water and starts measuring the dam. He can tell immediately from the pegs they placed around the edge a month earlier that the water level has risen at least 20 centimetres.

'It's now one hundred metres long and eighty metres wide. I reckon it could be about eight metres deep,' he calls out. 'It's looking pretty precarious.'

Taking a sharp probe in his hand, he pushes it through the soft layers of tephra. It punctures them easily as if they are a packet of biscuits.

'The dam's under enormous pressure.' Sam looks back at Theo as he twists the probe through until it strikes the bedrock beneath. 'With these water levels, if it goes the lahar will be a monster.'

Theo frowns. This isn't the news he wants to hear.

Sam is quick to pick up his expression. 'After the uproar last time, maybe it's best we just shut up about it for a few more days and see if continues or drops back down again.'

'No, I'd better let the others know as soon as possible. They're nervous as hell about my last report and they want to hose down all the sensationalism that's been in the media. This won't please the politicians one little bit but I have to keep them in the picture.'

'Might be time to bring in the bulldozers after all,' Sam says.

'Pull your head in, Sam!' Theo snaps. 'It's not going to happen.'

Dr Theo Rush knows the moods of both mountains and politicians well. In fact he thinks they have a lot in common — lots of power, subject to whims of either nature or the voters and likely to erupt when you least expect it. After more than thirty-five years researching the volcanic plateau, he feels more comfortable with mountains, in spite of the fact that this one nearly stole his life.

He had just been recovering from breathing in gas when a sudden explosion caught him by surprise. Hundreds of rocks flew into the air like an uncoordinated juggler's load. One the size of a cricket ball smashed into his shoulder, catapulting him over a small ridge. He had crawled beneath an overhanging rock shelf where he lay for four hours, drifting in and out of consciousness, until eventually a rescue team arrived and airlifted him to hospital.

The close shave had done nothing to dim his awe of volcanoes, just notched up his respect levels.

'I'd rather die on a volcano than in a road accident,' he had told his wife Sue, who didn't care for either option. 'At the end of the day I can't really tell anyone when a volcano will erupt. No one can. When you walk on a live one, you take your life in your hands.'

Theo saw his work as an unequal contest between the unstoppable forces of nature and the human beings who were fiddling round the edges, playing the detective after the crime was committed and trying to prevent the next one. Another huge volcanic build-up could provoke an eruption combined with a hot or cold lahar, possibly twice the size of the one that caused the Tangiwai disaster. Either way, a giant mudslide was threatening to steal many more lives and destroy many hectares of property.

Too often these days, Theo feels he is being pulled between several irreconcilable groups, each looking to him to play God. But the volcano seduced him long ago, and he isn't alone. It is no puzzle to him why people continue to live under volcanoes even though they know, like him, their lives can be snatched away at any time.

From the top of the mountain, Theo breathes in the cool alpine air and surveys the expansive panorama around him. 'Never get sick of this,' he mutters under his breath. 'I sure as hell don't want to leave it.'

'Well, you're not, are you?'

Theo hasn't realised he was talking aloud and is troubled when he catches Sam glancing at him curiously.

The two men have worked side by side since Sam moved here from the earthquake research centre five years earlier. A highly qualified geophysicist in mid-career, he is ambitious to make a name for himself and Theo knows he is eyeing his job. The last thing he wants to do is retire, though he knows Sue, after the best of a lifetime in a small town, is keen for them to move back to the city.

'No, not for some time. Anyway, I need to keep an eye on things. Last thing we want is bulldozers up here!'

He watches as Sam ignores the jibe, shrugs his shoulders and starts packing away the equipment.

The two men are as different as they are alike. As he's got older and especially since his near miss during the eruption when the lake had disappeared altogether, Theo has been won over more to the Maori philosophy of letting the volcano be and stepping up the early warning systems.

Sam, more of an interventionist, thinks there are engineering solutions to the Crater Lake problem, like cutting into the tephra dam to ease the water pressure. He favours bringing in a couple of bulldozers to break into it.

Theo realises that Sam is probably on safe ground, tapping into the mood of some of the commercial interests and the up-and-coming politicians who, ever mindful of the lingering memories of Tangiwai, think it foolhardy not to take more direct action. There's a lot of nervousness in the mountain village of Whakapapa, partly because the ski operators dread another disastrous season that will keep tourists away. With winter approaching they are hoping for a boom season.

It is easy to unsettle the locals with dire warnings, but Theo feels obliged to keep everybody up to date with the best scientific information he can provide. But he is exasperated by their arrogance in wanting certainty from volcano forecasting. They have little time for cultural sensitivities. At least he has the alpine clubs on side. They're there for adventure, not profits, hardier types who have long co-habited with Ruapehu's moods and support the early warning system rather than drastic intervention.

Although he has caused him a few headaches, particularly when negotiating with the local iwi, Theo is still glad to have Sam Hawks on his team, and he admires his scientific skills. But he senses there may be further friction between them, especially with the arrival of the American woman. Sam was quite put out when he heard of her appointment.

Although he's not altogether confident that it will reduce risks to life, Theo has decided to push ahead with upgrading the early warning system, and he and Sam have started locating the best places on the mountain for acoustic microphones.

'We've got to finish off the location siting for the system soon,' Theo says. 'Frances Nelson arrives tomorrow so once she's settled in we'll bring her up here to see if she has any fresh views on it.'

'I'd be surprised. I think we've got it all covered. Sometimes I wonder why you put out the help call, Theo. We've got enough knowledge between us and with the other scientists backing us up at the universities.'

'Listen, Sam, do me a favour and make her feel part of the team. She's got a lot of talent and we're lucky to have her. The Americans really advanced the acoustic side of things and Frances has had first-hand experience. She's got a terrific reputation.'

Sam says nothing and Theo knows he's hiding his resentment. He has complained often enough that he can't see how a person without knowledge of the region's unique environment will be of much use.

The chopper pilot beckoning them down interrupts Theo's thoughts.

'We have to go, the weather's closing in.' Luke Gallagher is a tough Vietnam veteran who has flown in these mountains for more than two decades.

Gathering their backpacks, they scramble quickly down the slope: they know better than most how quickly the cloud can descend and envelop them. As they rise above the mountain, thick white pillows are already smothering the summit, becoming one with the steam plumes that continue to pump out of the volcano's throat.

CHAPTER FOUR

❧

B ugger, my watch!' Before Tori Maddison can stop him, one of the three men he has brought fishing, a rotund Melbourne media executive, jumps fully clothed into the lake and duck dives. As he plunges, the white soles of his sports shoes catch the rays of sun penetrating the depths of Lake Taupo. His companions on the boat sit helplessly as they see the clunky silver watch sink beyond his reach into the silky clear water.

Tori is alert, ready to peel off his cream sweater and toss off his boat shoes to jump in after him. But he holds back, counting to himself. Twelve seconds later the man surfaces, his dripping face pale and puffy. Tori's broad shoulders flex as he leans over to yank him out of the cold water.

'Bugger, that was a Rolex — cost me a bundle!' Denis Brown's normally booming voice is reduced to a splutter.

'Well, dive back in and get it, Denis,' the others tease him. 'What's wrong with you? It's only a few hundred metres deep. And get a big trout while you're at it, you mug.'

Denis scowls at them while Tori helps him out of his drenched clothes and hands him a dry T-shirt and a large towel.

'Well, if it's any consolation, your watch won't be lonely,' Tori says. 'There'll be plenty of others keeping time down there somewhere.'

The men burst out laughing and Denis, now shivering but slowly regaining the colour in his cheeks, joins them. 'Well, what are you waiting for, you wankers? I need a beer.'

As they sip from their cans, Denis trails his hand into the water again. 'Tori, mate, how deep is this lake?'

'Look down there and tell me what you can see.' He enjoys teasing his foreign fishing clients as they peer nervously down into the seemingly bottomless silvery-green depths. 'You're looking into the eye of the Taupo volcano that blew up nearly two thousand years ago. It was so big they saw it in China and it blocked out the sun in Rome. But don't fall in again, Denis, it could blow up at any moment.'

'Sure, and pigs could fly too!' Denis, his ego as large as his bulging stomach, snorts and his friends guffaw.

Tori lets them enjoy the moment. Today's group is typical: an Australian politician being fêted by Denis, and two of his friends — all middle-aged, well-girthed, well off and affable, at least when they're getting their way. Tori has earned a reputation as a canny fishing guide, not just because he knows all the tricks of outsmarting wily trout, but also because he makes himself indispensable to his paying guests. He takes them to out-of-the-way spots the other operators don't know about and they almost always catch a trout. And he has the gift of the gab. As well as the rods and reels, he has lots of stories to spin. One of his American clients was so impressed that he flew Tori over to accompany him on a fishing expedition to Canada.

Using his strong brown hands and smiling dark eyes, Tori slowly paints them a picture of the Taupo eruption.

'See those burnt trees over there.' He points to the edge of the now still lake. 'And next to them, the layers of pumice, ash and charcoal. They've been there since the eruption.'

For once the men are quiet, silently contemplating the evidence surrounding the vast watery wilderness where they're floating.

'So we're in a fucking crater — is that what you're telling us, mate?' Denis says at last.

Tori laughs. 'That's right. It's called a caldera. It's anything from a hundred metres to many hundreds of metres deep in parts.'

'No wonder those blasted trout have plenty of places to hide,' says one of the men, who has failed to catch a fish.

'And were you Maori here when this thing blew up?' Denis persists.

'No, not until a long time later. Apparently it's blown up many times but the last one was a helluva long time ago. It was in 186 AD and some say Taupo caused the biggest eruption the world had ever seen then or since. Much bigger than Krakatoa.'

'How long have you been here, Tori?'

'All my life, apart from a few years up north. It's my home. I grew up here on the lake and along the rivers. All my family did.'

'You got much of a family here?'

Tori laughs. 'You could say that. Too many sometimes. We have an extended family and I count hundreds of my tribe as cousins.'

'Boy, I wouldn't want to be shouting them all the time!' Denis mutters.

'Where did they all come from?' he asks a little later.

'I trace my roots right back to the thirteenth century, to the mighty Arawa canoe crossing from Hawaiki to Aotearoa, the land of the long white cloud, or New Zealand as the Pakeha called it.'

'You mean us white fellas?'

'Well, maybe your ancestors.'

'And who were your ancestors?'

'They came from three of the great tribes, Ngati Tuwharetoa, Ngati Rangi and Ngati Tahu. They broke away from the Arawa to find land of their own. They were led here by a powerful tohunga, a high priest called Ngatoroirangi. A lot of people died along the way, as you can imagine it was very rough country. Once they got here they claimed the mountains and lakes and then they built fortified settlements to protect their territory from other tribes.'

'So you grabbed the mountains too, eh?' Denis ribs him.

'That's right. But one of my ancestors gave them back for everyone to share.'

'How's that?'

'Well, because of the volcanoes, this was known as the land of fire. We've always revered the mountains as well as being afraid of them. In the 1800s there were so many others coming here — Maori and white men — who wanted to carve up the mountains that our paramount chief decided the only way to save the land was to make it a gift. So it became the first national park. This way the mana of our tribe, our power that lies in the mountains, is protected. Certainly my ancestors, and even some today, believe in supernatural forces, and many of our ancestors have been buried in lava caves in the mountains and have to be shown proper respect.'

'That's what we all want at the end of the day, a bit of respect. Even if you have to die to get it,' Denis adds with a chuckle. 'And what about the lake, do you own it too?'

'Again, yes and no,' Tori replies. 'Maori own the lake, but the lake bed belongs to everyone. There are rules — a limit of three fish, no live bait and so on — but they give the fish a fighting chance and make sure there's plenty of sport left for those who follow. You'd have to agree with that, wouldn't you?'

'Yep, nothing like a bit of sport,' Denis says, still shivering. 'Well, I think we'll call it a day. Whaddaya reckon? Feel like a hot shower and a few more beers.'

After four hours of trolling on the lake, Tori is pleased the working part of his day is drawing to a close. He's keen to do some more fishing alone, without interruption. He steers his shiny 8-metre charter boat with all the bells and whistles into the marina at Taupo. Just two years old, the vessel still gives him the same kind of pleasure he remembers when he was given his first bicycle at just five years old. He looks around at the other boats in the marina and feels pleased he no longer covets any of them. Not like when he had first come here, starting his business from scratch with an old second-hand boat and a motley collection of fishing gear. He edges close to the jetty and helps the men ashore.

'See you tomorrow. I'm taking you up the Tongariro River for some fly fishing. Don't drink too much beer. Remember I'm picking you up at five in the morning!'

CHAPTER FIVE

❧

Summer has given way to autumn and the adult fish are already moving away from the lake, starting their rigorous migration up through the turbulent rivers and streams to spawn. But Tori knows there's still good sport to be had with the mature rainbows and browns in top condition, fattened with the food from the lake.

He motors slowly away from the marina and accelerates as he hits open water. He heads to his favourite spot near his home on the western shore, a place where he never brings his clients. He slows almost to a stop when he approaches the mouth of a stream and props his rod at the back of the boat, the line dangling into the water behind. With the setting sun streaking the blue-green waters of Lake Taupo with gold, he knows this is the best time to try to snare a rainbow.

Before long, he hears a plink and turns around to see the unmistakable bend in the rod. Cutting the motor to let the boat drift, he leaps back to pick it up before it is pulled overboard. Adjusting the Polaroid sunglasses that allow him to see right through the water, Tori grips the rod firmly and leans back comfortably for the familiar contest. The veins in his neck strain when he feels the tug as the trout, now furious, runs out of line. It doubles back and leaps clear of the water to begin its fight for freedom or death. In the second it is in the air, the light dances on its pink-hued rainbow skin, long enough for Tori to figure it is the perfect size for dinner.

This battle between man and fish is in Tori's blood. His grandfather, who nicknamed him grasshopper because of the way he jumped up and down on the little tinnie, often took the boy out in his boat. He taught him patience as well as his fishing skills. He told him Maori secrets. 'Remember: the second and third days after a full moon, the end of the third quarter, the second day of the new moon and the second day of the first quarter — the best times to catch fish,' he'd say as the boy looked up in awe at his grandfather's lined brown face and snowy-white hair.

'You have to look after the land and the water,' he advised the boy gently, sometimes holding him in his arms, creased now with loose folds of skin. 'Look after it like it's your best friend and it will look after you.' Then he'd change the mood, make his grandson laugh by giving him a tickle before releasing him.

'Now stay still, little grasshopper,' the old man would say. 'Hey, don't rock the boat too much, you'll scare off that giant fish I've been trying to catch for years, eh?'

'Don't rock the boat . . .' Tori whispers the words aloud. 'That's exactly what I am doing now with the row over the mountain.'

The trout dives again, pulling the line until it stretches to breaking point. Tori feels it suddenly slacken. Seconds later the fish reveals itself again, hurling its writhing, shiny body into the air. Tori starts to wind in the line. Three more times the trout dives and leaps out of the lake, desperate to escape. But this is to be the man's victory and he reels the fish in with expert ease, raising the rod, winding in the line, centimetre by centimetre.

The exhausted trout now close to the boat, Tori leans over with his net and scoops it out of the water. Many a fish is lost at this moment, twisting away as the catcher loses a moment's concentration, the trout scoring an unexpected reprieve. As it wriggles and flicks in the net, the speckled skin, covered with its slimy coating, glistens in the last rays of the afternoon. Struggling to the end, it twists and heaves as Tori lands it onto the boat. Taking a chunky piece of kauri, Tori whacks the trout on the head, driving the last life out of it.

'What a beauty,' he thinks as he places the fish in a bucket. 'I'll cook that on the barbecue for the kids when they come over for dinner from Mum's place.'

Starting the engine, he slowly motors to shore, tying up to his mooring alongside the small jetty he shares with a few other locals. Out of the corner of his eye he sees the familiar white four-wheel-drive of the ranger.

'Hi, Tori, how's the fishing today?'

'Kia ora, Smithy. Pretty good. My fellas today went away happy. Most of them took one decent one each and threw the rest back. Just the way we like it, eh?'

'Having trouble with poachers,' the rake-thin ranger tells him. 'There are a couple of guys in a black ute been seen pulling out lots of fish. Have you seen anything?'

Poachers have been around Taupo almost as long as the trout and Tori sometimes turns a blind eye if it looks like just a couple of amateurs. But there's big money to be made from selling the fish and it's the organised thieves that everyone wants to get rid of.

'No, but I'll let you know if I do. Heard any more about the crater talk?'

'Yeah, lots of people are going crazy about it. They're being whipped up by some of the councillors who reckon we'll all be killed!'

Tori grins. 'Yeah, it suits some of those fellas to scare the shit out of everyone, if you ask me.'

'Well, I know where you stand but I'm not sure we should stand back and do nothing. Don't forget a big lahar could wipe out the fishing here. I've got to keep moving, Tori. See you later. Remember to ring me if you see those poachers. You've got my mobile number.'

Tori hears it faintly at first and then it comes quickly into sight, the helicopter used by the seismologists. Must have been up the mountain again. He's been on this chopper himself when he did a bit of deer hunting in the backblocks a year or two back. He's given that away — could never get used to that look in the eye of the dying Bambi.

He glances back at Ruapehu soaring in the distance and shudders as he thinks of what lies ahead. For a while, Tori had turned his back on his culture, his responsibilities. In his late teens, he followed the well-worn track of many young Maori out of town, drawn to the lights of Auckland. Occasionally, he wishes he had stuck things out in the city rather than taking on the burden of protecting the mana of the mountain.

'Don't rock the boat,' he murmurs. 'Maybe old Pop was right.'

CHAPTER SIX

～

W arm water flows over her, soothing jet-lagged limbs. Her body clock tells her she is still back in Seattle so Frances has risen earlier than usual to loll in the hotel's pool, its water pumped from one of the many hot thermal springs that dot the volcanic plateau. She has the place to herself.

She is dreading the morning ahead. Maybe she should skip her visit to Tangiwai. She could forget the whole thing and go directly to Taupo. That would be so much easier.

She is startled by a splash beside her. The plump Bavarian man and his equally round wife she encountered last night in the restaurant are circling in the water around her. Their vigorous splashing and the sight of bulging flesh that is testing the endurance of hot-pink and lime-green lycra costumes are enough to jog Frances into an early exit.

'Would you like to join us today if you're on your own?' the balding man asks her.

'Very kind of you.' Frances climbs out of the pool feeling their eyes all over her tall, contoured body. 'I've got a full day planned. Thanks anyway.'

They glide together to the edge of the pool and bob about like a pair of psychedelic seals. She catches them staring at her wistfully as she hurriedly wraps herself in a large white towel and heads purposefully towards the stairs.

Driving slowly down to the bottom of the mountain she is gripped with indecision. At a T-junction, she stops, unsure of which way to go, and sits there for a minute, squinting in the glare of the sun pouring through the windscreen. A car pulls up behind her and beeps its horn impatiently. She bangs the steering wheel with her fist. 'Coward!' she hisses as she turns right. Tangiwai can wait: she drives determinedly east.

Before long, she leaves behind the wild alpine vistas and the road descends towards Lake Taupo, its sparkling navy waters extending as far as she can see. Enormous pipes cling to the emerald hills, evidence of a massive labyrinth of tunnels belonging to the hydroelectric scheme fuelled by the waters of the lake. She knows that an eruption or lahar could destroy them. The road straightens and soon she is greeted by street after street of small nondescript wooden houses, soulless avenues leading into a town called Turangi. She recalls this was once home to thousands of Italians brought to this isolated place to tunnel into the mountains. The tunnellers have long gone but the project houses they inhabited seem to echo the loneliness of the immigrants.

Just past the town, Frances is startled by her first close glimpse of the lake — a vast expanse of blue water, mirroring an equally blue sky rippled with cirrus cloud. The road narrows and hugs the shoreline. As she winds around the bends through tiny fishing hamlets towards Taupo, Frances catches flashes of postcard vistas between stands of pine trees.

Rounding one corner she crosses a small bridge bearing the name Waitahanui. A long line of fishers, perhaps twenty or thirty of them, are standing waist deep in the lake, stretching across the mouth of a small river. She stops to watch them balancing in waders in the swirling water, casting their lines in and out of the currents. In their multi-pocketed fishing waistcoats over long-sleeved shirts and their floppy hats, they resemble a human picket fence, not about to let a trout pass through.

She soon arrives on the outskirts of Taupo where, on the lake's edge, every second building seems to be a motel. There's a small traffic jam as the cars travelling through the town are forced into a bottleneck. Following Theo Rush's directions, she easily finds the Office of Seismology, a small square faded building a few streets back from the main shopping centre.

Parking her car close by, Frances sits for a few minutes, taking in the faces of people with whom she will share this town, at least for a while. Walking into the building, she follows a sign pointing to the upper floor. Inside an office, she can see a genial-faced, tanned man in his middle years shuffling a pile of papers on a desk surrounded by a mess of boxes.

'Ah, you must be Frances. Great to see you've arrived here at last.' Theo surprises her by reaching out to give her a bear hug and kisses her firmly on the cheek. 'That's the welcome I was promising you,' he grins. 'Glad you made it safely. Had a good trip?'

Frances returns his kiss awkwardly, but is reassured by his confidence and the deeply etched laughter lines on his face.

'Yeah. Long trip, though. I feel like I've been travelling for weeks! It's not hard to believe I've come to the other side of the world.'

She sees Theo is sizing her up. 'Well, you look fit enough for the job ahead,' he says. 'You're going to need to be. It's pretty rough country. But then you're used to that, eh?'

'Yeah, no job too tough, no mountain too high.' She grins and flexes her arm to show a muscle.

'That's what I like to see, a positive attitude!'

A strong-looking man in his thirties bursts through the door carrying a battered brown leather briefcase in one hand and a backpack in the other.

'Ah Sam, there you are,' Theo says. 'Meet Frances Nelson. Just arrived.'

'Figured you must be the Yank.' Sam looks her straight in the eye. With practised carelessness, he drops his gear heavily onto a desk and turns to shake her hand. 'Don't have too many other scientists around here fitting your description. Most of them have beards.'

Detecting a note of aggression in his voice, Frances flashes him a brief smile. 'Shaved mine before I got here,' she says as she meets his gaze and feels his hand grip hers firmly.

'I just have to finish a few things then I'll take you to your motel,' Theo says. 'You might like to have a quiet night to settle in and we'll regroup tomorrow.'

Theo drives a dark green Range Rover that is worse for wear. When he pulls up alongside her car and motions her to follow, Frances sees the dust and scratches of a workhorse vehicle. He weaves in and out of Taupo's small CBD before stopping outside a motel perched on the lake's edge.

'You should be comfortable here for a while,' Theo says, handing her a business card. 'That's the real-estate agent I told you about. She'll show you some places to rent. You've come at a good time because it's off season and there's lots of choice.'

From her room Frances can see right across the water to the mountains. The sun is just setting and the blue of the sky is splattered with tangerine-tinted clouds. The light blue melts into navy and starts to blend with the darkening wash of the lake. She is reminded of Seattle, the beautiful water-surrounded city that was her second home for so many years.

Unpacking her bag, she finds a cable connection for her laptop and, after a lapse of four days, decides it's time to check her emails. Her inbox is flashing — seven new messages. For the first time that day, the gnawing returns to her stomach. The email she clicks on is the one she least wants to read but knows she can't stop herself. 'Hi Babe,' it reads. 'Hope you arrived safely. Miss you. Message me. Love, Damon.'

CHAPTER SEVEN

❧

She misses the intimacy. Their relationship was passionate for so long and in the early years they used to joke that the one way of preventing yourself rusting in Seattle was to avoid the rain altogether and spend the day in bed. They explored each other's bodies for hours at a time. He was a confident and considerate lover. Their lovemaking could be boisterous, Damon teasing her and calling her his Mount Vesuvius. At other times it was tender and they would drift in and out of a contented sleep, their limbs tangled together.

She had met him within weeks of arriving from England to take up a post-graduate university scholarship to do research on the Mount St Helens project in Washington State. During a lunch break at one of the busy cafés surrounding the vast parklike campus, one of her new friends, Olivia, grabbed her arm.

'Come and meet someone real cute, Frankie!' she whispered. 'He's the star in final-year architecture.'

He appeared to be holding court at one of the tables. Brushing back his fair curly hair, Damon Beresford displayed a brash boyish charm as he debated the merits of post-modern design with other students from the prestigious architecture faculty.

He beckoned them over. 'Ah, another of Olivia's coneheads,' he said, reaching out to touch her hand and giving her the once-over. 'Come and join us.'

They squeezed in next to him on a long bench seat. He wore a plain black sweater and jeans. She breathed in his earthy, masculine smell, grateful it wasn't overwhelmed by too much aftershave, which had become overly popular with a lot of the students she'd met.

Damon entertained the gathering with loud stories of architectural follies as they downed bowls of cheap and filling spaghetti vongole. Frances sensed his interest in her was more than passing as he included her in the talk and returned her glances with a sparkling eye.

'What do you think of Seattle architecture?' he asked.

'I haven't thought much about it at all really. Don't like the Space Needle much,' she said, referring to the quirky tower built for the 1962 World's Fair.

'That's heresy!' one of the other students interrupted. 'That's the finest edifice in the whole of the Emerald City.' The group burst out laughing.

'We get a bit sick of the Space Needle,' Damon said, rescuing her. 'It's an important part of our curriculum because it was revolutionary when it was built and it can withstand all the earthquakes we have around here. Right up your alley, I would think, Frances?'

'I'm told there's as many as six thousand earth tremors a year here and from what I've seen for myself so far with all the seismological activity it doesn't seem like an exaggeration,' she replied.

'I think you're right. So they drum it into us that our designs can be as unconventional as they like, as long as the engineering is there to stop the things from falling over. Anyway, I'm sure

Carl F. Gould would agree with you about the design, Frances. Pretty it ain't,' Damon said.

'Who?'

'Our great founder. He designed the university. He was the mover and shaker of architecture early last century. The trouble is too many of the money people around Seattle now still want buildings just like that.'

'But you're going to show them, right Damon?' teased one friend.

'You bet,' he said in a tone that left Frances in no doubt he would achieve whatever he set out to do.

'A few of us are going downtown tonight,' Damon called as Frances was heading back to the laboratory. 'Maybe you'd like to come. Do you drink beer?'

'Sometimes.' She hesitated. 'Actually, I love beer.'

'There's a great place near the waterfront where they brew it and you can drink it fresh. The Pike Pub. What d'you think?'

'Sure. I have to stay back a bit tonight, though. We've just installed some new microphones up in the crater. There's a bit of a buzz in the lab. But I could be there about eight.'

'Great,' he said, moving so close that she was looking directly into his blue eyes. 'It's on 1st Avenue. I'll be inside.'

'Fast mover!' Olivia, who had been waiting for her friend to catch up with her, poked Frances in the ribs.

'Yeah, hardly the shy retiring type. What do you think, Ollie?'

'A bit up himself. But, hey Frankie, very cute.'

The two women had clicked almost immediately. Olivia, who had moved north after researching earthquakes in San Francisco, was Frances' physical opposite: short, thick curly black hair and, although extremely fit, a little on the tubby side. Her infectious laugh and devil-may-care personality made her popular at the university.

When they reached the gushing Drumheller Fountain they paused, as they usually did, and gazed over towards the Cascade Range where they had been the day before.

'Look, you can see Mount Rainier really clearly today.' Olivia pointed to the spectacular cone-shaped peak on Seattle's horizon. 'It's so much bigger than Mount St Helens it's surprising it's not as active. I went up there once. Hell of a climb!'

'I'm still recovering from yesterday, that was hard enough. My thighs are aching,' Frances said.

Three of them had left shortly after dawn the day before to drive four hours to the research base at Mount St Helens. They were constantly developing a network of seismometers on and around the volcano which would beam back any telltale signs of activity to the university laboratory.

That afternoon passed slowly in the laboratory, although there was plenty to do.

'Ollie, look at this,' Frances called, indicating her computer screen. 'What do you think?' There were some curious peaks and troughs, showing something vibrating on the mountain.

'Helicopter,' Olivia said quickly.

'What?'

'A helicopter's landed on the mountain. It throws you when you first see one but the microphones are becoming so sensitive to vibrations now, they pick up everything. Look there and there — they're people walking, probably from the chopper. Listen, you can probably leave early, seeing you have a hot date. I'm happy to keep watch here. See you tomorrow.'

Frances heard the noise from the pub filtering along a street above the Pike Place Market. Once inside among the large crowd she could see the liquid amber of the beer bubbling through the clear pipes of the machinery behind the drinkers.

'Over here!' She saw Damon beckoning her to a table where she recognised a few other students.

'A pale ale for you, ma'am?' he asked after he had installed her on a seat next to him.

'Love one.'

She watched him push confidently to the bar and return with two pints of the beer, handing one to her.

'Cheers,' he said, downing a quarter of the glass in one gulp.

Frances followed suit, enjoying the cool crisp taste.

'Hungry? The food's on its way. There'll be plenty as long as you like fish. We're having a bit of a celebration to mark the end of exams so we're lashing out.'

Plate after plate arrived of the rich local catch: slices of freshly grilled pink salmon, crabmeat cutters, steamed mussels and fried oysters. They feasted and drank late into the night.

'So why haven't I seen you before today? Where have you come from?' Damon asked.

'I haven't been long in the States. I studied seismology in England but as you can imagine there aren't many volcanoes there any more. So I've been travelling a lot to Turkey and Italy and other shaky places around Europe,' she explained. 'I heard they were offering scholarships here so I applied *et voilà!*'

'Well, I'm glad you did, Ms Nelson. Hope we can do business together,' Damon said, clinking his glass to hers.

From that night on, they were an item. Frances had been staying in student accommodation near the university while Damon shared an apartment with two others. When one moved out it seemed natural for her to move in.

CHAPTER EIGHT

❧

The local newspaper's front-page headline spells it out: 'Mountain mudslide threatens to engulf Ruapehu region'. Frances reads the article while having breakfast. Though cool, the early sun from the west is warming a line of cafés facing straight across the lake. Sitting at an outside table, she gratefully sips a strong fluffy cappuccino, nibbles on some fruit toast and starts to digest the latest moves in the debate over the mountain.

The newspaper quotes from Theo's most recent report, describing the danger and explaining the instability of the tephra dam and the likelihood of a massive lahar when it collapses. He is promoting the new early warning system and other detection methods.

Frances almost chokes on her toast when she suddenly sees her own name in print: 'One of the world's leading authorities on the new acoustic monitoring systems for volcanoes, Frances Nelson from Seattle, will be joining the team in Taupo. Ms Nelson has had extensive experience with the technology at Mount St Helens in Washington State and at Pinatubo in the Philippines.'

As she reads on, it's clear that Theo's recommendations appear to have the backing of the government and national park authorities — but nobody else. A prominent opposition politician, Ian Carmody, is accusing the government of 'indulging in political correctness and bowing to Maori interests rather than taking responsibility for people's lives. "They have their spiritual values on Mount Ruapehu and I respect that, but public safety and property including railways, roads and hydroelectricity infrastructure and people's homes are paramount and it's vital that we overcome all opposition and do earthworks around the Crater Lake."'

A Maori spokesperson for the local iwi, Tori Maddison, is ruling out any suggestions of altering the Crater Lake. 'This is as sacred to us as a cathedral is to you. We'll resist anyone who tries to violate it.'

A local mayor says her council is lobbying the government to allow the tephra dam in the crater to be blasted or tunnelled through with the help of bulldozers. 'We believe our constituents' safety is far more important than cultural sensitivities. We're confident we can persuade the doubters to our side.'

When Frances opens the office door she can tell immediately that Theo is rattled. The same newspaper is spread across his desk and he is having an agitated conversation on the phone. His brow creased and speaking in what sounds like a barely controlled voice, he waves her over, pointing towards an empty desk.

Sam Hawks is already at his desk, one foot propped lazily on the edge. He nods at her curtly as she walks towards him.

'I've just been brought up to date by the local newspaper. Looks like we may be the centre of attention?' she says.

Sam winks at her. 'Sure you're used to that. See you made the paper yourself. Looks like you're out to make a big impression.'

Frances feels her face redden. 'Ah, that was nothing to do

with me. I found it a bit embarrassing really.'

She welcomes Theo's interruption as he walks determinedly towards her with a large box.

'The wolves are baying! You'll be right in the thick of it. Hope you won't regret coming. Here's your kit. There's a mobile phone in there too. We can't get by without them now. Supposed to keep the private calls to a minimum,' he says, throwing her a smile. 'Sam will take you through the data we collected yesterday and the options paper for dealing with the crater. I've got to prepare another report for the government that will take me a day or two and I'm getting a lot of calls from journalists. There's definitely a feeling of panic in the air. Let's catch up later in the day.'

'Come on then, I'll take you through our material,' Sam says.

Theo suddenly sticks his head back around the corner.

'Oh Frances, the local paper wants to do an interview with you and take your photo. OK?'

Frances catches a hostile expression in Sam's eyes. 'Sure, Theo,' she says evenly, 'but put them off for a bit. I'm not ready for that yet.'

'You'll be a celebrity before you know it,' Sam persists with a taunt in his voice.

'Give me a break, Sam. You can see it's out of my hands. Let's get on with the briefing, shall we?' she says as lightly as she can.

For the rest of the morning Sam shows Frances the readings and samples they've collected and briefs her on the computer system that processes signals received from the mountains.

She can tell instantly that in spite of his goading, Sam Hawks knows his turf well.

'The levels in the crater have been up and down all year and we've been trying to find out if water is leaking out. At the moment it's very high and we're worried about another big lahar like the one in '53. Have you heard of Tangiwai?'

The question has come sooner than Frances anticipated and she feels her heart skip.

'Yes, I've heard about the train crash,' she says, grateful that Sam seems to have missed her voice wavering.

'That accident might have happened a long time ago,' he continues, 'but it lives on here in everyone's consciousness. I'm convinced that unless something's done, the dam will collapse and we'll see a lahar much bigger than Tangiwai. Maybe twice as big. You'd better get your head around this.' He hands her a thick document. 'It will bring you up to speed about what we've been doing here for the last year or so.'

Frances thumbs through the report, then settles back to read it in detail. After describing the erratic changes occurring in the Crater Lake, it sets out all solutions and the risks they entail. At the extreme end is the idea of bringing in the military to drop thirty high-precision laser-guided bombs to break up the tephra dam. Another is for a bulldozer to excavate a huge trench through the dam. Further options are to pump, sluice or siphon off the water or build a concrete weir in front of the dam the same as they did at a similar active crater lake in Eastern Java.

Everyone has had their say. Frances smiles as she reads the views of the district councils and the mayors and some commercial ski operators who are advocating maximum intervention 'to remove lahar threat altogether'. Were it that easy, she thinks.

She flicks through to the section that details the Maori argument. She knew before she arrived that their position was important, but it's only now that she's seeing how much influence they wield. 'We must honour the mana of the mountain.' Frances traces her finger over the words. The mana. The power. She senses this will become a familiar mantra.

A railway logo catches her attention. It's attached to a submission from the company that currently operates the trains. 'No further action needed,' it argues, clearly not wanting to contribute any funds. The company claims it has already done enough by installing a lahar warning gauge upstream from the Tangiwai Bridge which is monitored by railway staff. Frances makes a mental note to check the system and the staff's ability to interpret the information.

The other threat outlined is to Lake Taupo itself. A large lahar could flow down several points of the mountain. Not only could it flood the Whangaehu River but also spill over into the Tongariro River and down into the lake. As well as jeopardising the lives of anglers, bushwalkers, farmers and anyone else caught out there, the wave of volcanic water could destroy the habitat on which the fish and protected native birds depend. The precious colonies of trout could disappear for at least a decade. Frances remembers the picket line of fishers.

She reads Theo's case for constructing a large stopbank to divert the swirling lahar back down the main river course to save Lake Taupo from pollution. But the local Maori are against even this minor intervention.

A grander scheme is described, though Frances thinks it is a contrivance and not a serious proposition: an elaborate series of earthen buttress dams across the streams and rivers where lahars would flow, to slow them down and reduce their severity.

Frances homes in on the favoured option: Theo's support for the acoustic warning system she will be helping them install. Unlike the existing system, which can detect the after-effects of an eruption or earthquake, the new one can pick up soundwaves from the crater inside the volcano during an eruption. It will also give more time for people to evacuate — only minutes, but enough to save many lives.

Putting the report on her desk, she turns to Sam, who is

loading some of the new data into the computer.

'Where do you stand on all of this, Sam?'

'Well, I'm not very popular around here for saying this but I think the Maori position is extreme and primitive,' he says, swinging around on his office chair and leaning back to put his hands behind his head. 'I mean we're in the twenty-first century for heaven's sake and all this carry-on about the gods in the volcano is a bit much, don't you think? I reckon we have to do everything we can to protect human life and if that means treading on some toes, so be it.'

Suspecting another agenda, Frances hesitates, trying to assess whether Sam is attempting to back her into a corner.

'Too early for me to have an opinion on that,' she hedges. 'But I agree you have to do everything to save human lives.'

'Good, I'm glad you're with me on that,' Sam says too quickly. 'At least someone else around here will have a bit of common sense. Just going to get some lunch — see you later.'

Thirty seconds later he is back in the office and leaning through the door. 'You could come with me if you like,' he teases her. 'I know the best café and if you're with me, they give us regulars specially good service.'

'Sorry, I have to meet a real-estate agent.' She smiles at him, surprised by his unexpected charm. 'Maybe next time. Thanks anyway.'

Frances inhales deeply in the fresh breeze blowing off the lake as she walks across the road to the real-estate office. She's looking forward to setting up house once more. Inside she shakes hands with Tammy Curtin, a plumpish blonde woman dressed in a cherry-coloured blazer and black skirt, who ushers her out through a rear entrance into the front seat of a new BMW.

They drive slightly too fast out of the driveway and into the traffic. Turning into a side street, Frances catches sight of Sam in the window seat of a café talking to a much larger man with grey hair and a pronounced double chin. Before she can see any more, Tammy accelerates, and they speed away from the town centre and into wide streets lined with row upon row of weatherboard and brick houses surrounded by gardens.

'Taupo has plenty of empty places this time of year,' Tammy says.

'I'd prefer an apartment rather than a house,' Frances replies. 'I'm on my own and I don't expect to be home much.'

'Normally good ones are scarce as hen's teeth,' the agent says as she adjusts her sunglasses and checks her make-up in the car mirror. Her lip liner sits heavily around her mouth but the gloss inside has disappeared. She quickly purses her lips and applies a fresh coat of bright red lipstick before adding, 'But it's off season and I have just the place, darls.'

They pull up outside a small complex of white brick townhouses just one street back from the lake. 'It's fully furnished and you can have it for six months.'

It's almost too easy, thinks Frances as she looks through what will be her new home. 'No need to look any further,' she tells Tammy, who is distracted by her constantly ringing mobile phone and seems to call everyone 'darls'. 'This will be fine. I'll move in after work today.'

Theo doesn't return until late in the day and looks wrung out as he flops down at his desk.

'I think we're in for a rough time with the politics of all this, but we're going to have to keep a close eye on things up there. We can't get the chopper for a few days. They're down one at the moment — one in maintenance and the other caught up in some rescue exercises. I thought you might need a good walk after all that sitting around in planes, Frances, and I certainly would welcome the fresh air. We'll walk up to the crater the day after tomorrow if you're up to it.'

Driving back to the motel to pack her bag, Frances tunes into the local music station. 'Four seasons in one day, lying in the depths of your imagination,' sings Neil Finn. She hums along, deep in thought. Up to now the mountain has seemed enough of a challenge: now she sees that the competing choruses of those in its grip may test her much more.

CHAPTER NINE

❧

Frances is still unpacking her suitcase when the doorbell rings. She opens her door to a barefooted woman in her late twenties wearing a tight-fitting pink blouse that exposes her taut midriff and a white short skirt that shows plenty of her well-shaped tanned legs.

'Hi, I'm Shona Jackson. I live next door and thought I'd welcome you to the neighbourhood,' she says, thrusting a bottle of white wine into Frances' hand and tossing back long blonde tresses that look as though they are regularly subjected to peroxide.

Although she's not feeling like company, Frances motions her visitor to the sofa.

'Aren't you going to open it?' Shona looks at her expectantly. 'We may as well get to know each other seeing we live so close.'

While Frances unscrews the bottle and fishes around for a couple of glasses, Shona loses no time in telling her short life history, her taste in boyfriends, her current one being an army sergeant, and why she loves her job as a masseuse in one of the hot-pool complexes that thrive in the town.

'You meet some good sorts around here and the money's good. Beats my last jobs as a checkout chick and being a dogsbody in a timber company. You're American, right? What do you do for a crust?'

Although a little taken aback by Shona's upfront manner, Frances enjoys the lack of game-playing and thinks she could do worse for a neighbour. She explains what has brought her to Taupo, then turns the conversation back.

'What's it like being a masseuse? What got you into that?'

'I used to think I'd like to be a nurse but I didn't want to spend years training for that. And I didn't want to wipe people's arses. I just drifted from job to job and then thought if I was going to get anywhere I had to take a course. So when I saw the advertisement to learn massage, I thought it sounded like me,' Shona says, twiddling the ring that is piercing her navel. 'I love meeting new people and you certainly get to know them very quickly,' she laughs. 'Every bit of them! Don't get me wrong. Lots of people think it's about sex, but it's not. Well, not mostly,' she giggles. 'I just love helping people relax and this is the quickest way and they pay you well for it.'

They manage to finish most of the wine and Frances makes her excuses. 'I've got a very early start and a long day of climbing ahead so I'm going to bed early.'

'That's fine,' Shona says as she gets up to leave. 'Come by the pool when you get back. It's the best way to relax your muscles. Everyone swears the water fixes all their complaints — arthritis and gout, broken bodies and even broken hearts. We're open until ten.' She winks, then sways out of the apartment.

CHAPTER TEN

❧

Tori shakes the water from his hair as he rushes dripping out of the lake wearing only a pair of black shorts. For most people the swimming season is over but he likes to swim as late into the year as he can bear. The cool water clears his mind like nothing else and lately he has had a lot to think about. He shivers as he looks for his towel and finds it blown into the grass beside the path leading up to his cottage. He quickly rubs it over his body, then wraps it around his waist and goes inside.

The newspaper article has prompted a flood of phone calls. Journalists, politicians and no small number of the iwi have been on to him about the crater lake. It's times like this when he begins to lament the loss of his old life, at least the fun parts of it. Strong and good-looking, Tori found it easy as a young man to get work as a labourer on building sites when he drifted north to Auckland. The money was good as well, although it slipped away too quickly on booze and dope. He met Cheryl at a pub and they made a wild couple, partying several nights a week, year in, year out. Even after they married and had a couple of kids, they thought the partying could last forever.

But a decade of that took its toll on everyone.

On a trip home, the lake beckoned and Tori decided to return. He remembers the moment. He was paddling in the shallows where he had just been swimming, enjoying the feeling of the sand and mud squelching between his toes and the cold water lapping up to his knees. It suddenly hit him, as if the lake was telling him something. 'Don't be a fool, Tori, this is your home!'

The family settled into a small-town routine where the kids flourished with lots of family around to help and he took up fishing again, this time for a livelihood. But after a year Cheryl grew restless and moody and one day she simply wasn't there any more. She had packed up and gone, leaving the kids with him and his mother. Tori thought of going after her but he was too proud, too scared of a second spurning.

It wasn't long before Tori was reeled into new relationships. There was no shortage of parties in Taupo where singles and would-be singles lived it up. For a while he enjoyed the easy sex on offer, savouring the sudden intimacy of a one-night stand here and there that made him feel desired and wanted. But gradually, he became less sociable, less approachable. Now in his thirties and immersed in his business, he rarely goes to parties, preferring a few beers in the local pub and an early night.

His work makes him feel appreciated and he's managing to save a few dollars. He's often grateful that he took the advice of one of his old teachers he bumped into one day in the main street of Taupo. In his seventies, the man was long retired, leaving Tori struggling to recall how this gentle-looking soul had terrified him at high school.

'I seem to remember you weren't that great with maths at school, Tori. Might be a good idea to study bookkeeping if you're going into business. I've seen a lot of dreamers around here go broke because they didn't look after the money side of things.'

Tori followed through, spending hours each evening poring over basic accounting techniques and finding his way around computer business-software programs. His hard work and attention to detail paid off quickly and he attracted many clients happy to pay good money, usually a few hundred dollars each for the day, in the hope of catching the big one. But it isn't without risks, with the weather often ruling out boating excursions for days at a time.

No, it isn't the work that bothers him. It's the pull on him by others that's taking its toll. Many of his contemporaries who left their tribal home for the city have never returned. The elders, many of them in poor health and burnt out from previous campaigns for land and fishing rights, are increasingly relying on Tori to lead them through a maze of new challenges.

He switches his radio on to hear the news. The crater story is leading the bulletin and soon his own voice fills his small lounge room, condemning any move to interfere with the volcano. He barely recognises himself and cringes at the sound, hoping he comes across better to others listening.

He fills the electric jug with water and watches as it quickly boils. As he pours it into a cup and dunks a tea bag, he thinks about Cheryl, how once she used to make his tea or pour him a beer. He's thought about her often lately since hearing she has moved in with another man in Auckland. It plays on his mind that maybe they had met when he and Cheryl were still together.

A yearning for her still visits him, usually in the quiet of the night when all he can hear is the soft repetitive rippling of the lake waters caressing the shore. He remembers her softness, her salty embrace. Feels the longing, the hurt, the loneliness.

CHAPTER ELEVEN

❧

It is still dark when Frances hears a soft beep outside her apartment. A cool wind off the lake blows right through her as she dashes to Theo's car. Sam is already in the front seat and barely acknowledges her as she climbs into the back. She tries to doze off again, resting her head against the door, but she is constantly jolted awake and soon gives up. She watches the unfolding of a magnificent dawn, a shining orb rising over the water from one direction with the last traces of the silvery moon still visible in the other.

It is a good two hours' drive up past the Chateau to Whakapapa. Theo seems distracted as he parks the car, almost reversing into a large power pole. 'Sorry, must have been the late night. Phone didn't stop ringing.'

They unload their backpacks and catch a chairlift to the upper reaches of the mountain. Downing instant coffee and toast at the last café, they make a thorough check of their equipment for the arduous walk ahead: mobile phones and pagers, gas masks, ice axes, crampons, survey equipment and temperature and gas recording instruments, bottles of water, dried fruit and nuts and sandwiches. Frances fingers two geophones, the small microphones that are the crux of the acoustic warning system she wants to install and start testing today. Dividing the load among them, they head up across the ridge.

'It will take us about four hours to walk up and back and we need to spend a couple of hours at the summit. It keeps me from going to fat, something you and Sam don't have to worry about.' Theo pauses, his mood clearly lightening the further he is away from the office. 'Well, not yet anyway,' he jokes.

Frances smiles at him but Sam's face shows no humour.

Sam leads the way up a rocky trail, followed by Frances and Theo. She is surprised to see the younger man wearing shorts but makes no comment.

'Sam always likes to flash a bit of leg,' Theo chuckles, as if reading her mind. 'Don't mind his manner. He's a bit prickly sometimes, especially since his divorce. It was, how shall I say, messy.'

It has been several weeks since she has climbed and Frances quickly feels the decline in her fitness. Although the morning is cool and clear, it isn't long before she warms up. She removes her parka and wraps it around her waist and puts on sunglasses to reduce the glare. The track rises sharply and within half an hour they reach the tree line.

As they scale a large group of rocks, Theo bends down to pick a small white daisy with woolly leaves and hands it to her. 'That's the only thing that grows up this high. We call it the North Island edelweiss. The botanists call it *Leucogenes leontopodium*.'

'I think I'll stick to edelweiss, thanks,' Frances says, tucking the little flower into a buttonhole in her shirt. 'I don't think I could even say the other name, let alone spell it.'

As they zigzag higher, the ridge narrows. Visibility is perfect and it's the first time Frances has seen the spread of volcanoes from this angle. As they stop for a rest, Theo points out the vapour curling out of Ngauruhoe, directly in front of them. A beautifully symmetrical black cone, it rises starkly out of the lower slopes of Tongariro.

'Not many people realise that Ngauruhoe is in fact one of several vents of Tongariro. They're actually the same mountain,' Theo says. 'There used to be other vents too but they've been obliterated in other eruptions.'

'When did it last blow?'

'About eleven years ago, wasn't it, Theo?' Sam asks.

'Yeah, but the last big one was back in '75. There were blocks of lava as big as cars flung out of the vent — an amazing sight. You could see the ash and smoke for miles around. People were pretty worried but even though it looks threatening, it doesn't worry us too much as it's very isolated. It's as much as ten thousand years older than Ruapehu but Ruapehu is still the troublemaker.'

'Has it always been active?' Frances asks.

'There was a big gap last century. The first settlers who farmed this area thought Ruapehu was dormant. Most of them came from England and Scotland and they tried to turn the place into a home away from home. They grazed flocks of sheep all around the mountains. It wasn't until the big 1945 eruptions that they had their comeuppance. It must have frightened the life out of them when the mountain first blew.'

'What happened? Why has it become active again?'

'Well, the mountain was partly formed by eight glaciers and when a huge amount of magma rose up in the crater and met the remnants of the glaciers, bingo, a whole series of eruptions.'

As they climb higher, the ridge divides in three directions.

'Watch your step along here,' Sam calls back to Frances over his shoulder. 'It gets slippery with all the loose rock and it's a long way down. Even trickier when we're surrounded by cloud.'

Frances feels exhausted by the time they reach the Dome Shelter, the emergency and monitoring hut near the summit.

Her shoulder hurting from the backpack rubbing against her, she drops the equipment with relief.

'Glad to see you've worked up a sweat too,' Theo says. 'We're at the highest point of the North Island now.'

Frances breathes deeply and looks around. She can see across to the horizon above Taupo, that magical divide between water and sky where the sun sets and rises, breathtakingly beautiful yet out of human reach.

'Leave the gear here for a bit and come and see the lake,' Theo calls to her. 'Sam, can you get the testing equipment ready while I show Frances around?'

Sam nods and ambles towards the pile of backpacks.

Few places on earth move Frances as much as walking into a crater. No matter how many times she does it, the feeling is always the same: the sense of danger, the feeling of landing on another planet, the niggling fear that you might never escape alive.

Steep-sided rock runs down to meet the still expanse of grey water before her. First putting on her hard hat, she negotiates the walk down carefully, not wanting to fall into the steaming acidic hot pool.

'It has its own kind of beauty,' she says, 'but you can see why everyone's freaking. Look how high the water level is. How worried are you really, Theo?'

'It was like this in the build-up to Tangiwai. And if I was a betting man I'd have to say the next one will be twice as big. But I can't be sure. We've got records of more than a dozen lahars flowing out of here both before and after Tangiwai. Lost some of the ski lifts and buildings in recent years. We found some diary accounts by one of the early settlers in the 1860s. He wrote about being near the banks of the river in the middle of summer when a wave of freezing water spilled over the area. There were blocks of ice, logs and a whole lot of canoes. Heaven knows what happened to the people in those. Then there were a couple of hot lahars caused by eruptions, floods of hot water and mud. But they were nowhere near as big as the next one's likely to be. Yeah, of course I'm worried.'.

As Frances listens to him, she understands how thirty years of scaling, watching and listening to this mountain have shaped Theo's passion for Ruapehu.

'And there are many other stories from long before I was even born about how different and clearer the crater used to be in the past,' he continues. 'The first person we know of who proved that this was the source of the Whangaehu River was an English bloke called Roy Sheffield — a bit of an adventurer who made quite a name for himself as a cricketer. He used to go tramping up here and then in the thirties he became a guide at the Chateau. Well, the story goes that he dived into the Crater Lake one day and swam down on the end of a rope. Down and down, he went, obviously with a strong set of lungs, until he found an underground passage beneath the ice cliffs. He reached a waterfall and this was the overflow down the valley into the river. Fancy a swim yourself, Frances?'

'You must be kidding!' she laughs.

'It's hard to believe I used to swim in this.' He points to the lake.

'Sure is. You wouldn't get me in there! It's pretty much an acid bath now. That would burn through all your orifices,' Frances says.

'Ah, that might be the case now, but in my courtship days it was the way to a woman's heart. Well, the woman I wanted anyway!'

'I didn't pick you for a romantic, Theo,' Frances replies, enjoying his familiarity. 'Who was the lucky one?'

'I used to come up here with my mates from university on field trips. One weekend I invited along a young lady who was studying social work. I have to confess I'd had my eye on her for a while. On this particular day, in spring, there was some early snow and the lake was at a very pleasant temperature. So after some strenuous climbing I persuaded her to join in when we all stripped off our clothing and went skinny-dipping.'

Frances bursts out laughing. 'You sly dog, she probably didn't know what to do.'

'Oh, I think she knew exactly what to do. To cut a long story short, our relationship heated up immediately and I ended up marrying her.'

'Damn, so I'm too late.'

''Fraid so. Mind you, if things go bad with Sue I might be back on the market.'

Frances throws him a grin. 'Is that likely?'

'No, I don't suppose it is. Seriously, I'm lucky I guess. We've had a couple of kids. They've grown up and left now. I think Sue's fed up with living here and wants to move to Auckland where the rest of the family is, so I might have a bit of a problem there. But we still love each other and in this day and age that seems to be a pretty rare thing.'

Theo watches Frances as she smiles back at him and says nothing.

'What about you? No man on the scene?' he asks her gently.

'Not now.' She pauses, surprised by a lump in her throat. Her smile fades. 'Well, there was for a long time . . . but not now.'

Theo puts a hand on her shoulder. 'Tell you what, if this bloody lake ever drops down in temperature, I'll take you skinny-dipping.' They both laugh, comfortable in each other's company.

'I can tell you what brought the skinny-dipping to an abrupt end. There was a serious eruption in '69. In the middle of the night, a lahar swept down here right into the Whakapapa skifield. It demolished everything in its wake. But amazingly no one died. All the skiers were asleep in lodges across the gully there. When they woke up they saw the extraordinary sight of a mountain divided down the middle, half black, half white like some exotic ice-cream cake.

'As for the lake, the acid levels went through the roof.'

Sam joins them with some thermometers and bottles to take water samples back to the lab. 'It's still over fifty-five degrees,' he calls, taking the first reading.

While Theo returns to the shelter, Frances turns away from the lake and climbs back up to the ridge. As she edges around for a better view to the west, down into the valley towards Tangiwai, her eyes follow the path that many lahars have taken on their destructive journeys. The pain of what happened that night stabs at her as strongly as the bitterly cold wind. Quickly putting her parka back on, she is startled when Sam suddenly appears at her side and grabs her elbow. 'Admiring the view? Everything OK?'

'Sure, just thinking about that terrible train accident. Long before I was born but I knew people who were on it.'

Sam raises his eyebrows in surprise. 'Well, you might want to try and help me talk some sense into Theo. I think he's taking too hard a line on the dam issue. Let me show you what I think we could do.'

She is relieved when he releases her arm and moves away.

'You can see how the build-up of the tephra is blocking the natural outlet of the lake. If that dam collapses, everything as far as you can see in that direction,' he gestures in a sweep from the west to the east, 'will be wiped out: roads, electricity pylons, bridges, houses, not to mention all the people who are out there. The warning system might give them a chance but I think we should be tunnelling into the dam to release the pressure and stop it happening.'

Frances can see the crusty wall of the earth's entrails spewed out by the volcano. It stretches right along one side of the crater and disappears into the murky depths.

'It looks pretty solid, doesn't it?' Sam says. 'But we've been probing it and it could just go. I think we should pre-empt that and tunnel through it to relieve the pressure. We could bring earthmoving machinery up here, either fly in small bulldozers or drive a large one up. Not easy but it's possible. We wouldn't need to drain the lake, just make a drainage channel so the water would stop building up. You'd have to say it's better than the alternative.'

'There would be a huge pile of excavated material. What would you do with that?'

'Push it into the lake — that would be the easiest thing.'

'I'm not sure,' Frances demurs. 'They've tried doing that in other craters. In Columbia they did all sorts of engineering works in the crater at Ruiz Volcano but in the mid-1980s it was all ruined by an eruption and there were several lahars and thousands of people were killed because they didn't know they were coming. So it was pointless. But at Pinatubo when we installed the early warning system, it didn't stop the eruption but everyone got out of the way. So I'm not convinced you can stand in the way of nature.'

Sam looks exasperated. 'Look, I could give you other examples where it does work. What about at Kelud where they've tunnelled inside the crater lake and Kawah Ijen in Java where they built the concrete weir inside the crater? There's an active crater lake there and it seems to have worked. I get sick of this attitude that just because we're in a national park and the Maoris are sensitive we should always back off.'

Frances turns and starts walking back towards the shelter. 'I'll give it some thought, Sam, but I want to focus on getting these geophones positioned first. That's what I came here to do.'

CHAPTER TWELVE

❧

At first she can't see Theo. Then she hears him call out to her from inside the shelter. He is down in a tiny concrete basement checking the sensitive seismic monitoring equipment.

'We keep this down here for protection. It's survived one big eruption and lots of little ones,' he says as he climbs out through the trap door. 'Everything's working OK. We should start working on the geophones.' Handing her a bottle of water, he steps closer. 'I see Sam was having a word to you up there about the lake. Did he persuade you that we should bring bulldozers up here?'

'Not quite,' Frances says, grinning, 'but I guess he'll keep trying.'

Theo shakes his head. 'I'm absolutely opposed to any of that nonsense. If you start playing around with things like that here in the national park you'll create a dreadful precedent right around the country. There are too many people out there who have simply forgotten or don't stop to think about how foolish it is to try and put a cork in a volcano. It's just not possible. I've been around them too long to know you've really just got to get out of their way.'

Frances is about to tell him that there could be a compromise, that maybe Sam has some valid points, but thinks better of it. Instead she turns her attention to the geophones. Choosing the right place will be crucial.

For around twenty minutes she walks all over the rugged terrain surrounding the shelter and the lake. The temperature is falling and she can see how hostile the summit could be if the weather turned. By the time she finishes Theo and Sam are waiting for her, their measuring completed for another day.

'We're going to have to be very careful with any geophone up here because it's so exposed,' she tells them. 'We can't afford to get them wet so they can't be out in the snow. The one up here will have to go into the basement and be linked from there. We need to back it up with another one further down the slopes and another one again at the base of the mountain.'

Sam takes one of the geophones from her and looks at it closely. 'So they did the trick for you before?'

'Yeah, but because there are no lakes in the craters at Mount St Helens and Pinatubo, the volcanoes are much more exposed to the atmosphere and the magma much closer to the surface. It's different at Ruapehu with that huge volume of water in the lake, but I'm confident they'll still pick up the subaudible frequencies underneath. It's another complication but we've experimented with this in the lab and it should work well.'

Sam hands back the geophone. 'Hard to see how it will make that much difference,' he says dismissively.

Resisting the urge to tell Sam to take a hike, Frances climbs into the cramped basement and works side by side with Theo to install the first geophone. They place it alongside the seismometer that measures volcanic tremors.

'OK, let's switch it on and see if it's working.'

Frances turns on the tiny switch, initially fumbling with it until she hears it click. 'Seems to be working. Let's phone the lab to see if they're transmitting properly.'

Theo takes out his mobile phone and hits the office number.

'Yeah, it's working fine,' he says, after talking to the technician. 'Good on you, Frances. Let's hope we get the system as near as perfect before the ski season.'

Closing and locking the trap door, they start to pack all their equipment for the descent. When Sam joins them outside they take refuge from the biting cold behind the shelter and share packs of sandwiches and bottles of orange juice.

'We're going to have to make sure the system is maintained extremely well,' Frances says. 'When the microphones work, they do give you extra time to spread the alert but that depends on the personnel around to do that. What plans did you have for that?'

'All of us have pagers and so do all the rangers and lift operators on the mountain,' Theo replies. 'We'll link it in with our loudspeakers I showed you earlier around the mountain. It doesn't give a lot of time, just a few minutes to warn skiers, snowboarders and everybody else on the slopes get out of the path of the mudflow and head for higher ground. Then we have to worry about all the other people who might be in the path — trampers, army people, farmers, tourists.'

'It's ambitious because of the different features up here. At all the other volcanoes I've seen, including Pinatubo, there was a longer lead time to get the hell out of the way,' Frances says.

'Yeah, it can all happen very quickly here as we've found out the hard way. But every minute counts. We can only do the best we can and then worry about what the volcano will do next. We should get going.'

'I'll scout around for a place for the other geophone on the way down,' Frances says.

They finish packing their gear and load their backpacks onto their shoulders.

As Theo leads them down the summit, wafts of cloud encircle them. Unfamiliar with the track, Frances stays close to the other two, knowing one wrong step could be fatal. It is a sharp descent and her thigh and calf muscles start to ache as the pace quickens. She knows her joints will give her hell the next day.

'We can't install the other geophone in this,' Frances tells Theo. 'Can't see a thing.'

'Don't worry,' he answers, 'we'll come back when the weather clears.'

Driving back to Taupo, Theo breaks the silence brought on by the exertion of the day's climbing. 'By the way, while you're both here I wanted to ask you to come to a public meeting next week to explain all the things we're doing up here.'

'Oh great, more of the Christians-into-the-lions'-den stuff!' Sam complains.

Theo shrugs. 'Just part of the service,' he says grimly. 'Anyway, please do your homework because we might all have to answer questions.'

'What do you want me to talk about, Theo?' Frances asks.

'If you can concentrate on the monitoring system, that would be great. Sorry to drop you in this so soon.'

Sitting in the front seat she feels Sam's hands on her shoulders and his breath is warm against the nape of her neck as he leans towards her from the back seat. 'You'd be happy to fight a few lions, wouldn't you?' Frances shakes her head and decides not to reply, pushing his hands away. She closes her eyes and tries to sleep, unsettled by her ambivalent feelings towards him.

Something about Sam reminds her of Damon: he has the same dangerous attractiveness. As she has so many times before, she tries to retrace the events that led to her sudden realisation that Damon was two-timing her. She had pressed Olivia for more information after the split. At first, her friend was not forthcoming. Only later did she suggest that this wasn't the first time he had been caught playing around. Olivia told her he had been seen with several other women in bars during the previous year. The news had shocked Frances to the core. She had started going back over the weeks, trying to work out how many times he had fooled her.

CHAPTER THIRTEEN

✧

She treads on the piece of pink writing paper as she opens her front door: 'Make sure you come to the pool. It's the best cure for tired limbs. See you there.' It is signed, 'Your neighbour, Shona.'

Tired and dirty, Frances tosses up between collapsing on her bed or accepting the invitation. She opts for a quick shower and soon is making the twenty-minute drive to a bush-enclosed pool complex on the outskirts of town.

For a weeknight, Frances is surprised by the number of people soaking contentedly in the steaming pools while their more energetic children are swimming and jumping in and out. She finds Shona in the massage centre chatting to a solidly built Maori man in his thirties with a crew cut. His broad shoulders and well-developed pectorals bulge beneath a black rugby jersey with an All Blacks motif.

'Come in, Frances,' Shona beckons her. 'This is Bill Harp, my very special customer.'

Bill shakes her hand, his smiling brown eyes engaging hers.

'Bill's coming over for a drink later if you'd like to join us.

But you should have a swim now. We're closing in an hour.'

Frances sinks into the warm waters, breathing in the sulphur fumes, which she finds pleasantly therapeutic. She can feel her tired muscles relax. Leaning her head against the rail around the pool, she closes her eyes, shutting out the quiet chatter of those around her.

'Penny for your thoughts.' She starts as a hand brushes her shoulder beneath the water. Sam Hawks is floating beside her, his face uncomfortably close to hers, his breath tinged with beer.

'Small world,' Frances says, masking her annoyance.

'It didn't take you long to find the hottest place in town. Would you like to have a drink afterwards?'

Frances grapples for an excuse. 'Not tonight. I'm here with a friend and I'm going straight home after the pool closes. Maybe another time.'

Sam lingers next to her in the water, clearly not wanting to leave. His eyes travel from her lips down her shoulders to the rise of her breasts visible above her red bathing costume.

'I could drop around for a drink,' he persists.

'I don't think that's a good idea, Sam. Let's try and keep things on a professional level. I'll see you in the office tomorrow.'

With sure strokes, she swims away, leaving Sam looking after her, his face flushed.

As she leaves the pool, she is pleased to see Shona beckoning her over.

'I've twenty minutes to spare before closing. Fancy a quick head and shoulder massage?'

Frances dons a robe and lies on the table on her stomach. With sure hands, Shona kneads her scalp, moving to her neck and shoulders. 'You're holding a bit of tension,' she tells her. 'You'll have to loosen up.'

Succumbing to the pressure, Frances starts to let go. Closing her eyes, her mind wanders back to the Crater Lake. What mysteries are hidden there? Can she really ever hope to discover its moods? Lost in her doubts, she is surprised to hear someone calling her name.

'Frances, time to go,' Shona is saying. 'You nodded off for a minute or two. At least you were relaxed!'

Feeling disoriented, Frances sits up and laughs apologetically. 'Must have needed that. You've got a great touch.'

'Glad you think so. You should book in for a full hour next time. Think you need it, girl.'

The Family

We were in a bit of a flap when we arrived at Wellington Station to catch the three o'clock overnight express train to Auckland. Eric wasn't able to take the day off from his job as a postal clerk because it was the day before Christmas and he had to work till lunchtime. I had to pack our bags and get Valerie organised on my own for our first holiday away as a family. My mother had sent her a teddy bear from England so I gave it to her early to keep her happy. She just loved it and wouldn't let it out of her sight. I dressed her in a new blue dress I'd made for her and the gold chain bracelet with the little heart that had been her christening present.

There was a real festive air at the station with a huge Christmas tree in the middle of the main hall with shiny decorations dangling from the roof of the large cavernous building. I liked the grandness of it all. It reminded me of the holidays I'd had as a child with my parents in London when we headed off from Victoria Station south to Brighton before the war.

Eric carried Valerie because like all toddlers, she always dawdled. I carried our two bags along a platform that seemed to go forever. The great steam engine was fired up and ready to go and we were forced to breathe in the fumes drifting along the platform. But we didn't mind. In fact it made it all the more exciting. Finally, we were on our way.

We found our seats in Carriage C in second class, two seats facing forward and I crossed my fingers that we might be able to have the two facing towards us as well so Valerie might be able to lie down and we might all get a bit of a rest. As she wasn't quite two, we didn't have to pay for her but she'd only have a seat if there was a spare one. As it happened the train was fully booked but we were able to have the seats for more than half of the sixteen-hour journey when some other passengers would board further up the track.

This was a special time for Eric and me. Things had been a bit of a struggle since we had immigrated to New Zealand three years earlier.

London was still in a shocking state after the war and we wanted a fresh start to our lives in a new country. But I was terribly lonely in Wellington, a pretty enough city but one that could shut you out as coldly as its roaring forties winds if you didn't know anyone. I missed my family and friends very much and longed to have a baby.

At first I couldn't get pregnant and I used to go to this beautiful monastery overlooking the harbour and sit there and pray for a child, even though I'm not Catholic. It must have worked and so when Valerie was born, we were both overjoyed. At last, someone of our own!

When we heard the new Queen was coming to New Zealand on her first royal tour we decided we would plan our first trip north to Auckland to see her. Elizabeth was just 27, three years older than me, so I was always watching to see how she would go and often dreamed how wonderful it must have been to be a princess. I used to cut out all the pictures of her from the magazines and put them in a special scrapbook. There were pictures of her wedding, of her coronation and of her babies, first Charles and then Anne. And my mother had sent me a tin of biscuits with a photo of Elizabeth and Prince Philip on it. I loved it. It always reminded me of home and I used to keep it filled with peanut brownies. And of course I had to have my hair styled just like hers so one day I took the tin along to a hairdressing salon and said, 'There, that's how I want my hair done!' All the girls there gathered round to look and when the stylist finished my hairdo it looked quite a lot like the Queen's. Well I thought so anyway, even though Eric didn't seem to agree.

There were more than 200 passengers on board when we pulled out of the station and as the train moved north we took on more at each stop. There was a lot of excitement with people looking forward to Christmas. Many were going home to see families or on holidays and there were quite a few others like us who had decided to see the Queen.

Valerie was enjoying herself but she was always trying to escape, running up and down the carriage, charming the other passengers.

She had such beautiful blue eyes and blonde curls. Eventually though, she fell asleep with her teddy bear and we were all able to have a bit of a breather. When we reached Taihape Station around ten o'clock at night, Eric went to the refreshment rooms to buy us a cup of tea and a piece of fruitcake. We'd already finished the sandwiches I had made earlier in the day and of course some of the brownies I'd packed.

We lost our spare seats to two young men who were heading to Auckland and when Eric returned, we had to lift Valerie onto our laps while trying not to spill the large heavy white cups of hot tea.

Once Valerie was asleep, we all dozed off. Suddenly I was awake, sensing the warmth of Valerie leaving me. Instantly, I was thrown forwards so violently that I felt as if I was flying through the air. Everything was black and people were screaming and I was falling out of control until I crashed into something. I felt fast-moving water rising around me and I desperately called out to Eric and Valerie. I couldn't see or hear them. 'We're in a river!' I heard someone shout. I think it was one of the young men who had just got on the train.

Our carriage must have tipped on its side and the man pulled me up towards a window. I tried to go back to find my little girl and Eric but I was pushed through into the water. I just prayed they were together. It was then I heard Eric calling both our names and I feared the worst. I looked back to see him crawling out of the side of the mangled carriage that was now nearly completely underwater.

He swam towards us on a wave of water that washed over us and then lifted the carriage away into the current. Some of the other passengers who had escaped from another carriage had formed a human chain to the bank and I was pulled along it.

The current was so strong it washed away most of our clothes and I was left wearing just my bra and pants. I begged them to let me go and swim down the river to find my baby. But they held me back, pushed me forward. I wept and prayed. But I knew she was gone. Nothing was ever the same again.

Ada Nelson, 24, a survivor of the Tangiwai disaster

CHAPTER FOURTEEN

❧

I'll be back tonight,' Frances tells Theo on the phone. It's Saturday morning and she knows she can't postpone her visit to Tangiwai any longer.

'But why do you want to go there on your own?' he asks. 'I could take you there one day when I have a little more time.'

'It's OK, really.' She hesitates before continuing. 'Theo, there's something I'd like to tell you. It's about Tangiwai. I do have a special reason for wanting to go there and I'd prefer to be on my own. You see, my parents were on the train and ah . . . they survived but knew others who didn't.'

'You're full of surprises, Ms Nelson,' Theo interrupts her. 'Here's me thinking you're an academic seismologist but you've been bottling up all that emotion. Nothing like a passion to keep you going in this business. Trouble is, you never know where it will lead you.'

'Ain't that the truth. Sometimes I think I'm already all passioned out,' Frances replies.

She has woken early on her first day off and at first pretended to herself that she could stay in bed all morning. But like unfinished homework, she knows she won't rest easy until she has visited the scene of the disaster.

Shortly after eight, before the Saturday shoppers have emerged, she drives out of the still town and heads south, retracing her way back towards Ruapehu. Ever changing in the late morning light, the mountains seem to mock her as she heads for Taupo. As she steals glances at them they almost seem alive — she swears she can see faces. Too much time worrying about ghosts.

She passes the turn-off to the Chateau and heads west towards the township of National Park, then south again. There is little traffic as she drives into Ohakune, a small town rescued from oblivion by a skiing boom when the Turoa slopes were opened up on the western side of Ruapehu. She smiles as she wonders what Shona would say about the giant sculpture of a carrot she glimpses on the side of the main street, a proud phallic tribute to the local produce.

It's dead quiet and when Frances drops into a café there's just one other customer there. Over her passably good cappuccino and a salad sandwich with too much carrot, the waitress, a dark-haired woman in her forties, tells Frances how the town was thrown another economic lifeline when a horde of people arrived to film scenes for *The Lord of the Rings*. The tourists had followed, hot on the Tolkien trail.

Enjoying a new audience, the woman recalls how, during filming, the few small streets of the town looked like something out of *Gulliver's Travels*, filled with very tall and very short people specially picked for their height extremities.

'Lots of people around here were extras in the film. They did it for the fame and the glory, certainly not for the money,' she explains. 'My son got a bit part but it was so cold up the mountain, I went out and spent a hundred and fifty dollars on thermal underwear. Then the wardrobe people had to slash it to bits to get the costume to fit. I think he made a loss out of it. Came back freezing to death but had a good laugh!'

Frances continues driving south, winding through harsh countryside. She has been told the turn-off to the accident scene is easy to miss so she scans the road closely. Soon she sees a small sign and pulls into a lane. Surrounded by rough farmland, she can see the metal spans of the replacement Tangiwai bridge ahead. At first glance, the place is indistinguishable from many other lonely outposts.

The few cars travelling along the main road flash past, oblivious to the dark history they are bypassing. In front of her, a man and a woman on a motorbike stop just ahead and walk over to a tall black granite obelisk. Beyond them is the bridge and rising behind it, partly obscured by grey cloud, is the volcano. The middle-aged riders, wearing black leather jackets emblazoned with their club motif 'Growing Old Disgracefully', remove their helmets. Frances can hear them discussing the memorial, which is decorated with the doomed steam locomotive's original red and black number plate, KA 949. The woman, who has unruly plum-coloured hair, nods to Frances in acknowledgement as her grey pony-tailed partner studies the inscription.

'This is for those poor buggers who went down with the train,' he says, reading the date on the side. 'I'd forgotten how many people died. God, this place gives me the creeps.'

'Yeah, me too. Let's get out of here. Nothing more to see,' his girlfriend replies as she moves aside to make way for Frances.

Smiling at them, Frances edges closer to see if the names of the lost are recorded. She is both relieved and disappointed that they are not. Sometimes, she thinks, seeing the names of the dead eases the grief. It makes the deaths real, not just a locked-away pain, nibbling at the subconscious.

Walking towards the river, Frances is affronted by its smallness: in parts it's reduced almost to a trickle. The clear shallow waters of the Whangaehu flow over submerged boulders, snaking around little islands of river sand punctuated by metal-grey stones. It moves around bends fringed with poplars already stripped of their leaves, dark-green pine trees and the wispy, straw-coloured fronds of toetoe. Layers of black sediment stain the banks, hinting at bygone floods and lahars.

Coming back here fills her with memories of her parents' still raw grief, the droop in her father's shoulders and his sad eyes, her mother's carefully arranged expression. It was the first time they had been back to New Zealand since their abrupt return to England following the train crash. They told her they wanted to come back just once more, to remember the dead and thank God for their lucky escape. They always seemed to be locked into a past of unresolved grief, which annoyed Frances — after all, they had survived. They said they knew people who had died but would never elaborate. Frances watched them exchange glances that concealed secrets.

As the unexpected arrival in her ageing parents' lives, she had always felt out of place.

'You don't know how lucky you are if that's all you've got to worry about,' her father would chide whenever she went to him with some childhood complaint, some grievance from the schoolyard. She dreaded time alone with her father, whose moodiness she learned to avoid. She stuck to the monotony of small talk that they all felt comfortable with. By the time she was 12, Frances had stopped confiding in her parents completely. Instead she would store her hopes and disappointments deep inside her like the red squirrels she saw hoarding their winter supplies of cones and nuts in the forks of the large trees on the edge of the local common.

She walks towards the river and trembles as she remembers the memorial service, the sad circle of mourners standing on this very spot. Her parents slipped into the group and she reluctantly followed. The survivors had moved from youth to middle age, losing hair and gaining girths, yet many recognised each other instantly.

At the end of the ceremony came the two sentences that changed Frances' life forever.

'Ada, it's so lovely that you were able to have another daughter. It must have helped you get over losing your baby girl.'

The lines were delivered innocently by an elderly woman who had also survived the train crash. But Frances could only stare in disbelief at the faces of her parents.

'Let me look at you,' the woman said, stepping back to appraise the girl as if she was a work of art.

Frances stared at the stranger whose words hung in the cool still air. 'Another daughter.' Frances felt her heart beat faster. She caught her mother's dismayed expression. She looked across to her father and saw him shaking his head, incapable of further speech.

It wasn't until Frances screamed that her mother ran to her and held her. Her father didn't move.

'Why didn't you tell me?' Frances cried out. 'Why?'

'I'm sorry,' her mother said, holding her close now. 'We thought it best you didn't know. Thought we should start over. Valerie . . .'

'Valerie?'

'Yes. Her name was Valerie. She wasn't even two. She was swept away. We found her body . . . someone found her body a couple of days after the crash.'

So much had suddenly fallen into place for Frances. Looking back on her childhood, it felt like an old black-and-white movie with her as some sort of imposter.

'Frances!' Her mother rushed to her as she tried to escape her grip. 'Wait. I'll try to explain.'

Frances had stopped but she could not release the words that were shouting in her head. She could not express the shock — she had had a sister, she need not have been an only child.

Her mother grabbed her arm. She held her close and stroked her head. 'I'm so sorry we didn't tell you. We couldn't bear to,' she whispered at last. 'We've never recovered from her drowning here. We couldn't even talk about it ourselves.'

Pulling away again, Frances ran to the river. She stared into the water and imagined her baby sister tumbling like a rag doll down the muddy torrent. She was overwhelmed by a sense of loss for the sister she never knew. Nightmares about her drowning plagued her sleep for years to follow.

Standing here again, the images flash back, horrible pictures of her sister's tiny face distorted beneath a watery crystal mask. She feels the loss even more keenly now. As a child, Frances had always thought of her parents as old. They were certainly older than many of her friends' parents and they lived a life without much excitement, seeming to avoid the company of others. Frances is jolted by the realisation that she is now much older than her mother and father were when they were caught up in the train crash. Then they were in their early twenties, full of hope for the future.

At last, she grasps why their lives were so suddenly shattered that night. Tears stream uncontrollably down her cheeks as she thinks of those who drowned and the lives they were deprived of. Of the sorrow and anger their deaths caused to those who had to keep living. Of the guilt those survivors had to suppress because they were still in the world.

CHAPTER FIFTEEN

✎

After that day on the riverbank, Ada started to tell Frances stories about Valerie, as if she had suddenly been given permission to grieve. She showed her the tiny white dresses and hand-knitted pastel cardigans, a small pair of black patent leather shoes with silver buckles and a bracelet, taken back with their breaking hearts when they returned to England. The little clothes rested in a bottom drawer like ghosts in shrouds of tissue paper, hidden away, the most sacred of family relics.

Frances had often fantasised about having a sister. As an only child, she had badly wanted someone to play with. The belated knowledge of Valerie's short life made the loss worse, left Frances feeling cheated and now sharing the unspoken burden her parents carried with them and had unwittingly passed on to her.

When Frances left home to attend university, her mother gave her the gold chain bracelet, pressing it into her hand, as if she was releasing both daughters.

Reaching into the recesses of her bag, Frances touches it now. She feels the precious gold links and the tiny heart, lumpy through the thin silk pouch she carries it in. It has become her talisman, the piece of her sister that survived the nightmare. Still attached to her tiny wrist, the bracelet helped her parents confirm the identity of their baby. There had been so many small bodies lined up that day in the makeshift morgue.

Her father still resisted talking about the past. 'It's best it stays there,' he'd say, refusing to look up from his newspaper in order to discourage further questions.

Over time, her mother told her about the crash, the rescue and the search for their daughter. Frances pushed her more and more for the detail until she could see it all for herself in her mind's eye.

Eric broke his arm in the fall into the river and spent a couple of days in the army hospital. Ada escaped physical injury, but her wounds were far worse. She was given a bed in the home of one of the forestry workers and his family who lived near the river. His wife's name was Tui, a Maori woman who, like many other locals, was also searching. Her cousin had been on the train, one of many young men leaving the city and coming home for Christmas.

Tui had been her mother's strength when she was staring into a well of despair. On Christmas Day, stinting on her own children's demands, she embraced Ada's despair, cradling her for hours in her plump brown arms. The weather had turned foul, raining incessantly, soaking the countryside. The two women huddled together as they squelched in gumboots through the mud along the bank, searching the sad faces of the rescuers, returning with the bodies, hoping to see the one they knew, dreading they might.

The forester, pale and skinny, was a friendly sort. Without discussion, he willingly took over his wife's tasks, lighting the worn coal stove that heated the water and cooked the food in the bare kitchen with the faded linoleum-covered floor. He prepared a simple Christmas dinner of roast mutton, kumara, potatoes and freshly picked silver beet from his well-tended vegetable garden.

The bereft young mother was urged to eat, to keep her strength up. She picked at the food, unable to swallow, longing for her missing child.

That night, Ada sat numbly with the kindly strangers in their remote home. She listened to their young daughter tapping out 'Twinkle Twinkle Little Star' on a painted miniature wooden piano she'd received that morning and tried to shut out the ghastly images that she was conjuring up of her own little girl. Another gift sat unopened on a varnished wooden sideboard. The small box, wrapped in white paper with a piece of fake holly on top, glowed in the soft light. A tiny card read: 'To Rawiri, Wishing you the happiest Christmas'. Tui saw Ada staring at the present. 'It's for my cousin,' she said. 'A packet of cigarettes and a glass ashtray. Real flash. He usually rolls his own.'

A crackling Christmas message from the new young Queen Elizabeth sounded out from a large wooden wireless set in the middle of the small living room, the family's most valuable possession. They hushed the child, gathered closer to listen.

Ada gripped her hands tightly together and bit her lip, trying to concentrate on the thin, high, girlish voice.

'And now I want to say something to my people in New Zealand,' the Queen continued. 'Last night a grievous railway accident took place at Tangiwai which will have brought tragedy into many homes and sorrow unto all upon this Christmas Day. I know that there is no one in New Zealand and, indeed, throughout the Commonwealth, who will not join with my husband and me in sending to those who mourn a message of sympathy in their loss. I pray that they and all who have been injured may be comforted and strengthened.'

Ada could hold back her tears no longer. Rushing out of

the house into the cold darkness, she found the toilet, a small wooden outhouse, and pushed open the squeaky door, sat down and wept. Half an hour must have passed before Tui came for her, pulling her to her feet and leading her inside to bed. Humming a Maori lullaby, she stroked Ada's brow and covered her with a rough grey woollen blanket. The young English woman curled herself into a ball, clutched a pillow hard into the pit of her stomach and rocked back and forth, back and forth until eventually sleep overtook her.

Ada and Tui woke early to resume the search. For four hours, they walked through drizzling rain up and down the river, stopping to talk to rescuers, many of them farmers and workers from around the district. They had brought their sons to help and their wives and daughters to ply survivors and rescuers with cups of tea and sandwiches and fruitcakes they had made themselves. All of them had a new look in their eyes, one that betrayed their feeling of shock that their quiet lives had been so violently shaken apart.

It was on the second day that one of these farmers' sons found the baby. Valerie was buried under sand on a riverbank, her body battered by the violent voyage that had dumped her there. Her clothes had been torn off but she was still clutching her teddy bear, the beloved toy held fast under her arm.

Ada was back in the cottage when she heard someone talking to Tui at the front door. When Tui came to her and reached out to hold her, she said nothing. The two women hugged each other tightly. Tui looked into Ada's eyes and gently nodded. Ada felt surprisingly calm as her friend led her to the door where the messenger, a tall young man wearing an oilskin, was waiting for her.

He said little as he drove Ada to the army camp. 'I'm sorry,' he muttered eventually, his clear bright eyes not leaving the road ahead. She glanced over at his dirt- and tear-streaked face that had seen so many unwanted sights since the train crash. 'I know you are,' she said and put her hand on his shoulder.

As they drove through the camp's gates Ada could see Eric standing by the side of the road, his face stiff and unsmiling, his right arm awkward in a sling. She told the young man to stop and thanked him quickly. As he walked away, she called after him. 'What's your name?'

'Trevor,' he said in a hoarse whisper and hurried on.

At first she felt distant from her husband as she walked over to him, wishing they hadn't been forced apart since the crash. But as they held each other, Ada started to cry and he tightened his grip and, for that one moment, their intimacy was complete.

Together they walked into a green-painted weatherboard building that served as the camp hospital. There were dozens of people milling around inside, some crying, others comforting. A woman behind a desk beckoned them over. They told her their daughter's name and she scanned down an appallingly long list. Ada watched as she located the name and tapped it with her finger.

'Yes, yes. That's her. I'm sorry.' She motioned them to take a seat. Almost immediately, a nurse appeared and asked them to follow her.

Beyond the reception area, they caught glimpses behind screens of other nurses, some still teenagers, tending to a line of bodies on the floor, cleaning the faces and trying their best to give them back some of the dignity the volcano had ripped away.

The nurse led Ada and Eric into a hall decorated with fading streamers and half-deflated balloons left over from a Christmas party. A row of small white coffins lined one wall. Inside them were the shrouded figures of babies, toddlers and older children.

Ada started to shake, not sure she could continue. Eric took one arm, the nurse the other. Like the chief mourners in a funeral procession, they slowly approached the third coffin along. The nurse pulled back a fresh white sheet.

Valerie's tiny face, framed by moist curls, was as still as a portrait photograph. Her mother traced a gentle finger down a cold little cheek. Her child's body still held traces of volcanic silt, although the young nurses had washed off as much as they could. They had crossed her arms in front of her and put her new teddy bear, now looking many Christmases old, under one hand. On one wrist was her golden chain bracelet.

The father squeezed his wife's hand in wordless grief. Ada began to sob but then bit her lip to make herself stop, wanting one last time to be the mother. Leaning over, she kissed the little girl's forehead, shocked by its coldness on her own warm lips. She stood there for as long as they'd let her, staring at her beloved child.

Eric undid the bracelet, clumsily using his left hand. He kissed it and handed it to Ada. 'You should keep this. To remember her by.'

The nurse whispered to Eric and he nodded. 'Time to go, love. We have to say goodbye now.' She stalled, not wanting to go. Other families were coming and going around her, numbly identifying their own lost sons and daughters, nephews and nieces.

'Come on, love, we must . . .' Ada walked reluctantly away, repeatedly looking back over her shoulder, desperately wanting to scoop her baby up, hoping she would cry out and they could all just leave this place together, a family once more. But the cry never came.

That night, Ada returned to see Tui. The women prayed together in the tiny house, each contemplating a different God. Ada clung to her friend, momentarily a child once more herself.

Eric, his arm now in plaster, and Ada, unable to speak, travelled back to Wellington, again in second-class seats on a train. Their baby was in the tiny white coffin in the goods van at the rear. Two days later, they buried her in the vast Karori Cemetery in Wellington where she would rest forever alongside the passengers with whom she shared that final journey. A few months later, a childless couple once more, they returned home, still silent, trying to think of something, anything, to say to each other.

Six months elapsed before Tui's cousin was identified. His body had washed up 20 miles down the river a week after the crash. The water and silt had cruelly stripped him of his familiar features and his body was among a group hurriedly loaded onto a train to Wellington. There were also bags of blackened body parts, too damaged to piece together. They buried the bodies in a mass grave. Months later, when the weather had cooled, they were exhumed. From a missing persons list with details of jewellery and body markings, the pathologists were able to confirm nearly all their identities. They located a tiny tattoo of a heart pierced with an arrow on Rawiri's left arm and his family could at last put the young man to rest.

Ada sent Christmas cards to Tui for many years until one was returned with 'address unknown' stamped on the envelope. But she didn't forget her and when Frances was born, she gave this unexpected new child her friend's name.

'Too-ee, too-ee,' her playmates would call, amused by this strange name. But Frances didn't mind the ribbing. Strong and independent, she sometimes thought she lived in a parallel world to the other children. She pretended to them she was named after a Maori princess and didn't bother to tell them that Tui was really the name of a little New Zealand native bird whose song haunted the wet forests around a faraway mountain.

When first she stood here before Ruapehu, she felt angry and cheated by what it had taken from her, without mercy. Later her rage became obsession: she wanted to outwit volcanoes, understand how they could penetrate the cracks in the earth and in the human heart, learn how to protect those who found themselves in their path.

The Guard

It started off just like all the other journeys on the three o'clock Wellington to Auckland Express except the passengers were a little more excited than usual with it nearly being Christmas. We left on time.

The stations and towns we passed were decorated with coloured lights and streamers for Christmas and there were lots of families and young people getting on the train all the way along the line. When we reached Taihape there was a changeover of crew with a new engine driver and fireman. But I was not changing until we reached Taumarunui, about another hour away.

We were running on time and I remember passing the Tangiwai Railway Station, just a little place where we didn't stop. We were travelling at the normal speed for this area, about 45 to 50 miles per hour. I was sitting in the guard's van at the back of the train when I felt a sudden jolt, which must have been the driver trying to brake.

I was thrown forwards as the train stopped. When I checked my watch, it was 10.20 p.m. I picked up my torch to see what was going on and I saw someone waving a torch at me outside. I couldn't believe it when this man said, 'Half your train is in the river.'

He came with me and we walked through the carriages, checking to see if the passengers were all right. It wasn't until I got to Car Z, one of the first-class carriages, that I was able to look out the north-end door and saw the river lapping just a few feet below the rails. I realised the engine and rest of the train had gone in.

I quickly told the passengers to hurry back out and not to panic. Seems a funny thing to say in the circumstances, I know, because I was bloody terrified and trying not to show it. But as I reached the middle of the carriage everything started to sway. We were tilting towards the river and lots of people started screaming. Suddenly the lights went out and I grabbed hold of a seat, then the luggage rack just above it. We seemed for a moment to be flying through the air into blackness. Water started pouring in everywhere. I couldn't see a thing but I realised we were now in the river. The water was up to my armpits and I clung to the rack as the carriage rocked and bounced.

While some people were crying out, most of the passengers were surprisingly calm, hanging on to things and keeping their heads above water. I could feel we were floating downstream like a boat, except the water was washing over us. Abruptly we stopped and I felt I was falling as the carriage tipped over onto one side. We had run aground and for a few seconds I was submerged. But the river level had dropped and the carriage was half underwater and half out. I managed to open one of the windows and climb out onto the upturned carriage. Everyone was following, pushing open other windows and helping pull people out. There was a lot of shouting as family members tried to account for each other.

Strangely, by this time the river had subsided almost completely. When I slid off the carriage into the water, it was just over my ankles. We grouped together and herded everyone to the edge of the river and onto the bank.

It wasn't until later I found out we had lost one young girl in our carriage. She was 14 and had been travelling alone. No one realised she was still trapped in the darkness of the carriage under a seat. How could I ever forget it. But we fared better than all those in the other carriages that had gone in when the river was torrential.

Neither the driver nor the fireman stood a chance. They'd only left their homes and families less than an hour before. But the force of the engine smashing into the bank was incredible. I don't think they would have even realised what was happening. Most of the survivors were in the last three first-class carriages that never left the track.

The loss of life was devastating. It affected all of us on the Railways very much. I never felt the same about working again. There was also a lot of bad business going on about the safety of the bridge in the first place and we all thought the fire that burned all the records after the crash was just a little too coincidental. The volcano got the blame but we were all very unhappy about what happened later.

Fred Walters, 48, guard, New Zealand Railways

CHAPTER SIXTEEN

A force she can't resist prods Frances, wills her to discover more about this place of death. She wanders towards the bridge, a humble construction with silhouetted steel-framed sides balanced on concrete piers that dig into the riverbed. It is completely deserted. After scrambling up a bank and climbing carefully over a barbed-wire fence, she lands heavily on rough gravel lining the tracks and looks around her. Stands of thickly grouped pine trees stand guard along the track opposite her. To reach the bridge she must walk along the railway tracks. Ignoring warning signs of danger, and her rapidly beating heart, she picks her way over the wooden sleepers and along the narrow silver gauge. With each step, she looks for a spot where, if a train should come, she can leap to safety.

Her stomach tightens as she glances ahead. She nears the middle, only 100 metres or so from where the doomed train, with her family on board, had reached the bridge. Beneath her the water flows more swiftly than further downstream. She tries to imagine the terror of that night when the huge wave swept right over the place where she is standing. Further along the track she can see the bend the train had rounded just before the bridge gave way. As the engine and the first carriages went onto the bridge, the massive concrete pylon in the middle collapsed into the floodwaters.

Dizzying images of the crash start to resound in her head: the enormous hulking steam locomotive smashing into the bank, the carriages washing away, the terrified passengers, her parents panicking and searching . . . And again, those nightmare images of Valerie's face trapped beneath the water.

Feeling nauseous, Frances turns back, needing to get away. She balances on the silver rails, trying to cover the distance faster, to escape the sight of the water below, but her legs are failing her and she keeps slipping off onto the sleepers. Forcing herself to slow down, she walks on towards the end of the bridge. Just as she reaches the end, she slips onto the sharp gravel and cries out in pain as her knee buckles under her. Pulling herself up again, she fights a dizziness that is enveloping her. She thinks she can hear a train coming and uses all her strength to throw herself against the fence. Panting for breath, she lies there listening. The dizziness subsides and she strains to hear. But there is no train, only a soft whistling as a breeze blows though the pines. She climbs back over the fence, now dragging feet that feel like lead weights, and walks slowly back to the memorial.

The bikers have gone. But an elderly man wearing a tweed jacket and felt hat is standing staring at the memorial. He glances up at the flushed and sweating young woman before him.

'Been for a bit of a walk?' He looks at her knowingly. 'You shouldn't go up there. Could get into all sorts of trouble.' Frances sees he's looking at a fresh tear around the knee of her jeans.

She touches the hole, pushes back escaped damp tendrils of hair and tries to smile reassuringly. 'Got a bit carried away,' she says apologetically.

'Where are you from?'

'Seattle . . . well, sort of. I was born in England.'

'This was a bad business. I saw you went for a closer look at the bridge. You're brave.' He grins at her, revealing two gold-capped middle teeth. 'But there are hardly any trains these days so it's not too much of a risk. Not like the old days. Used to be about thirty a day. They called it economic rationalism when they sold the railways off. Bloody robbery if you ask me.'

He snorts in contempt then pauses to look more closely at Frances, who is shifting uncomfortably in her thick leather walking shoes and rubbing her knee.

'You wouldn't pick it now but this little river can be a torrent. It was that night . . .'

'Did you see it? Did you see the train accident?' she quickly interrupts him.

'Sure did, well, certainly the aftermath. I nearly got swept away myself. My farm's just back up around the bridge a bit and all of us heard this roaring sound and saw the river was right up. It was damn peculiar as it hadn't even been raining. But it's that volcano up there. You know we call this river Sulphur Creek? It often pongs from the chemicals.'

Frances sniffs the breeze, detecting the odour.

'Can you remember much about that night?' She encourages him with her eyes, eager to hear more.

'I'll never forget it, love. Nothing like that ever happened here before . . . or since. The train was in the river and there were lots of people hurt and . . . and bodies . . . bodies everywhere. My wife was here and all the farmers around, helping pull people out. Bringing blankets and cups of tea and the like. A very bad business.'

'There were so many people on the train. How did you rescue them?'

'We worked in small groups, got out all the ropes and horses from the farms. We went for miles up the river. We found half a carriage six miles downstream. There are steep cliffs along the river further on, very hard to search. Some of us kept going for days . . . you just had to do it. Had to keep going.' He pauses. 'Are you sure you're OK?'

'Yes. Thanks.' Frances hesitates. 'Actually my parents were on that train and my baby sister . . . she drowned.' She blurts it out, not knowing if she can trust this stranger with information she usually keeps locked away inside herself.

For a moment the man says nothing, just looks at her. 'I'm really sorry about that. Nearly everyone around here was affected,' he says at last. 'It's like that in a small place — everyone knows someone who was involved somehow. It changed everything.'

'Do you know others who saw the accident, were there on the night?'

'Quite a few. I even know a woman who was on the train, someone we found on the riverbank. We've kept in touch with her but she won't come anywhere near here for love or money.

'Then there's Trevor Atley. He was only a lad at the time. Well, I suppose we all were! He was here helping for days. Had a big impact on him. For years after, no one really wanted to talk about it. It was too terrible. But everyone gets together for the odd anniversary now. We make more of everything in the past now, don't we? Except for Beverley, she'll never come here.'

The old man bends down to pull a few weeds that are pushing up through the gaps in the cement surrounding the memorial.

'I like to keep my eye on things, make sure this doesn't get vandalised. It's happened before. A lot of bloody idiots around. So what brings you here?' he asks, brushing away the loose soil.

'I suppose I'd like to know more about what happened. But also I'm a scientist, so I'm interested in what's going on in the volcano.'

The man lifts his eyes in surprise and rises awkwardly to his feet, complaining about a sore hip. 'Well, we need people like you here. Pleased to meet you. I'm Cedric Morton,' he says, holding out his hand.

'Frances Nelson. Pleased to meet you, Cedric.' She grips his thick weathered hand and feels fingers distorted by arthritis.

'Come on, I'll show you around.' They stroll away from the memorial towards the river where they can see the mountain clearly. 'There's a lot of us around here who are worried sick it will happen again. Some of the scientists say this time it will be even bigger but no one seems to be doing anything to stop it. I understand they could do things in the Crater Lake to prevent it. Trouble is the Maori around here are against it and so are a few others — the greenies, some of the government people.'

'Yes, I've already heard the arguments. I'm working on a new early warning system so at least people like you will know when to expect an eruption or lahar.'

Cedric laughs. 'Well, give us a call and we'll run like hell! That's if I can remember how to run with this blessed hip of mine.'

'Hey, give me some credit.' She laughs with him. 'It does help to know when to run. It worked in the Philippines. I went there a few years ago with a group of scientists from many countries when we were still experimenting. We knew Mount Pinatubo was threatening to erupt and, unlike here, there were thousands of people living on the surrounding slopes. We installed an early warning system there and believe me, it worked.'

'I'm glad you're on our case,' says Cedric. 'We all worry like mad that we'll have another Tangiwai disaster.'

Frances takes a small notebook from her bag. 'Can I have your number? I'll let you know how it goes.' She also writes her own on another page and tears it out to give to him. As she turns to leave she calls back to him, almost as an afterthought, 'If you find any numbers of others who were there that night or afterwards, could you let me know? I'd really like to talk to them.'

The Policeman

It was just after one in the morning on Christmas Day when I got the call. I was on duty at the Wanganui Police Station, the biggest one in the area. I had to drive the three or so hours to Tangiwai, to take charge of the operation. Other police were called out from some of the smaller stations and along with the army were doing their best to put some order into a shocking situation. It was nearly light when I arrived.

I saw the railway bridge had collapsed. The wreckage of the train was strewn everywhere in the river and on the banks. There was a massive concrete pier from the bridge lying in the middle of the river. The water level had dropped but it was still muddy and there were large quantities of silt and sand all along the river. There were many bodies and bits of bodies, including heads. My job was to prepare a temporary mortuary at the Waiouru Military Camp just a few miles away.

Over the next three days, 114 bodies were brought in. Of all the bodies, sixty were found more than 10 miles downstream from the accident. Some bodies were swept along the river by the silt and we believe out to sea, a distance of more than 80 miles. Some were never recovered. By far the greatest casualties were in second class where only twenty-eight passengers survived.

We had to do our best to put the bodies back together with the help of the army, local volunteers and lots of nurses who came from local hospitals to help.

The Prime Minister arrived early in the afternoon with some of his government ministers. They had come from Auckland where they had gone to welcome the Queen and Duke of Edinburgh. So we were also taken up with helping them inspect the site. By this time, there were also a few journalists and photographers arriving and the Prime Minister was giving interviews and sending messages of condolence.

Then some of the families started arriving from many parts of New Zealand. My constables, the medical staff and many others had to show them the bodies of their loved ones for identification. In all my years as a policeman, I've never experienced anything like this. Many of the bodies were in bad shape and we had to clean them up as best we could before the families could see them. There was one poor fellow who had to identify his brother, his sister-in-law and their three kids — all girls aged three, six and nine. None of us knew what to say really. We felt that bad about it. Most of us had kids ourselves.

There was a special area where we laid out the children's bodies. It was a room full of Christmas decorations where the army kids had their Christmas party on the day of the crash. It was the saddest thing I've ever seen. At the end of three days there were still forty bodies that were unidentified.

Quite a number of the victims were from other countries. There was a young Dutch couple from Amsterdam, both of them in their twenties, who had only been in New Zealand for two years. He had been working as an optician in Wellington. There were many young single people from Britain, Australia, Canada and Ireland. Contacting relations overseas was difficult, especially as it was Christmas time and many people could not be located.

We had to put them into coffins so they could be returned to Wellington for postmortems and identification. We loaded the coffins onto a train, including many where families had already identified their loved ones. They went back down the track the way they came but this time in wagons with white crosses chalked on their sides. We all gathered along the railway platform and bowed our heads as the train left on its journey all the way back to the mortuary in Wellington.

Senior Sergeant Robert Andrews, 42, policeman at Tangiwai

CHAPTER SEVENTEEN

❧

It's the first Sunday of the month so Beverley Corbett is preparing to go to church where she will play the organ. She checks she has her sheet music, her hat, her glasses and a handkerchief in her small white handbag. A neat woman in her seventies, she stopped going every week years ago. Not like when she was growing up, when she would never have missed a single Sunday. But this is another life, another time. And she is another person. In spite of her struggle with her faith, the new Beverley goes to church, just in case.

For the last dozen or so years, since retiring from her job as a bank clerk, her life has been completely ordered. Not that it wasn't so during her work years — it's just that now there's even less chance of anything unexpected happening. That's the way Beverley prefers things to be: safe and predictable, with nothing left to chance.

So on this cool autumn morning, she is unusually agitated, a feeling she hasn't experienced since, well, since she finally moved away from all the do-gooders who wouldn't let her be.

It was the phone call from Cedric that did it. He called her on the Friday and it has been bothering her off and on ever since.

'There's an American woman who'd like to meet you,' he told her. 'She's a scientist, come over to look at Ruapehu. But her parents were on the train. Wants to know more about the accident. Seems OK. Shall I give her your number?'

If she didn't have so much time for Cedric she'd never have agreed. But he sounded keen and was a hard man to refuse. He and Pauline were her last links with that other world of hers that ended that night. They were the first to help her after the men had carried her off the engine and deposited her on the riverbank. They found her there and took her and Betty, the girl who had rescued her, away in blankets. They filled them with hot cups of tea, a glass of rum and Christmas cake, not that she wanted to eat anything. In fact she hasn't been able to face fruitcake since that day, although for some perverse reason she bakes one every year and donates it, fully decorated, to the church fête.

They put the two women up in their farmhouse for a couple of nights while the rescue went on. She and Betty shared a lumpy double bed with a sunken wire base and every time one of them twisted or turned, trying to find solace in sleep, they would roll into each other.

Beverley didn't like to think too much about that. It made her squirm. She remembered thinking Betty really resented wasting her efforts on her. After all, she was groping around in that horrible darkness for her sister, not her.

On the Friday morning after Cedric's phone call, she could not concentrate at all on her weekly game of bridge. Her partner noticed straightaway because it was so out of character and she was secretly pleased when Miss Perfect made two mistakes. Beverley was a star player with a reputation for having a short fuse if a less competent player held things up. So in the tea room when they brought out the sandwiches and biscuits each had prepared that morning, they grinned at each other knowingly as they whispered to each other that she had, for once, been the one to hold things up.

Beverley's lack of concentration continued all through Saturday. Her sole companion, the latest in a succession of tabby cats, all called Marmalade, meowed incessantly and it wasn't until eight that night that Beverley realised she had forgotten, for the first time, to feed her.

Dressed in her lavender best, her hair immaculately combed, shoulders back, hymn music tucked under her arm, Beverley slowly but determinedly begins the short walk to church for the nine o'clock service.

She could find it with her eyes closed, she's come this way so often. As she passes worn white wooden fences holding back unruly gardens, she rubs a small shiny scar on the palm of her left hand with her thumb. The burn from the engine that never completely healed is her only tangible link with crash. She touches it automatically whenever she thinks about David. They never did find him or the girl's sister. But Cedric kept looking for days after the others stopped. Then, when they were given up for dead, he drove her back to her hometown and they had kept in touch ever since.

Beverley stops to admire a large white cat that is sleeping in the sun. It starts when it hears her hand scrape the fence and meows loudly. But it doesn't budge and they stare at each other. Beverley loves cats — so self-detached, so independent. That's how she decided to become. She remembers how neither she nor her rescuer wanted to see each other again. Too much pain. Too many ghosts from that night together.

For years afterwards she resisted efforts by her family and friends to bring her back into the old life.

'What would they know?' she whispers at the cat. It blinks.

'They weren't there, at the river. They didn't know how such a thing changes you forever. They didn't see the bodies. My four best friends. We were just beginning to taste our freedom.'

The cat yawns, closes its eyes and resumes its nap.

Beverley walks on. She can see them laughing together on the train, so excited to be travelling together for the first time, partying, on their way to a camping holiday for young Christians.

She rubs the scar again. She can see his face so clearly. They had been going out together for more than a year and had talked about getting married.

Beverley can still faintly recall the desire that spread through her body after they kissed more deeply than ever before on the train. How he slipped his hand beneath her bra to stroke her breast and how she yearned for more. It was a sensation she hasn't felt with anybody else since that night.

She searched for him for two days, meeting the rescuers near the river, looking into their eyes, glancing at the contorted shapes they were depositing behind a makeshift canvas morgue on the bank. Then she was led away, told to wait at the army camp with the others for a more formal, clinical process. She saw them sifting through pathetic piles of possessions, waterlogged suitcases and a few watches forever telling the time at 10.22 p.m., the moment when the water came.

She was there when grieving friends and relatives started trickling into the army camp on Christmas Day to try to identify their loved ones. David was missing and after a while, missing, presumed dead. She stayed on, hoping, praying, disbelieving. For her, he would always be just missing. She would always be waiting. Secretly, at times, she wished that girl hadn't pulled her out by her hair. She had cut it all off the next week. Always kept it short after that.

It became so bad at home that Beverley decided one day

she had to move away, just to be on her own. She was tired of blind dates set up by well-meaning friends, visits by the local minister, constant offers of outings by the family. And she had to see David's family too: in a small town she was always bumping into his parents or sister or brother. It got so difficult that they began crossing the road to avoid each other.

So as a 25-year-old who could have passed for someone ten years older, Miss Beverley Corbett successfully applied for a transfer to another branch of the bank in Taumarunui, a comfortable distance away to the north. And here she found a safe haven without questions or demands or a past. The years drifted by and Beverley finds it hard to believe that she has passed three score and ten and is starting to worry about the spiritual void she sees ahead.

That's what's bringing her here today, to the pretty wooden church. She props herself on the raised stool at the organ and plays a few notes of the opening hymn as the faithful and the doubting file in.

On a good day, about a dozen other elderly women, three or four families and one man in a wheelchair will gather to hear the word from Pastor Warwick Fowler. Today he preaches on the evil of coveting one's neighbour's wife or goods, gazing down from the pulpit, hawklike, trying unsuccessfully to catch the eye of anyone in his tiny congregation. It even brings a smile to Beverley's stern mouth that hasn't been kissed by a man since David disappeared; adultery was never an option, let alone a desire.

The minister nods at Beverley.

O God our help in ages past
Our hope for years to come
Our shelter from the stormy blast
And our eternal home.

She plays without thinking as the singing fills the church. Her mind drifts. For once she doesn't feel angry with God — if indeed there's a God out there who cares anyway. She finds herself in a rare state of curiosity.

CHAPTER EIGHTEEN

❧

A nd what do you fear most, Frances?'
'Snakes and rats,' she had trilled back instantly as the
teacher had probed the phobias of his ten-year-old charges.

Such simple fears, Frances thinks as she lies in bed, not able
to summon the energy to get up. She has spent most of the day
there, her strength sapped.

'Betrayal and abandonment,' that's what I would answer
today, she thinks as she pulls the sheet over her head and cuddles
a spare pillow.

Since her return from Tangiwai, she has dwelt on her sister's
death. She knows it is completely unreasonable to think Valerie
abandoned her and yet Frances feels the pain of loss keenly.
Her thoughts turn back to Damon and she toys with the idea
of replying to his growing number of emails. Out of habit, she
wants to share her experiences with him.

So many nights in Seattle they'd link arms through the
streets towards the university district to 9th Avenue and share
their day over a pizza at an Italian trattoria that traded twenty-
four hours a day. Then they would return to bed, wrapped around

each other so tightly they became as one. For the first time in her life, Frances had felt safe, protected and contented. She thought they would always be together.

A part of her wants his reassurance and to hear what he's doing. She knows returning to Tangiwai has made her vulnerable. But she resists the urge. It was too easy for him to skip over the hurt he caused her, to pretend it hadn't happened. While she suffered, he seemed untouched.

Although they hadn't spoken for three months, the longest gap she can recall in their long partnership, he rang her the week she was leaving and suggested they should get back together. She rejected the notion, but the emails showed he wasn't going to let her rest.

She remembers when everything between them began to unravel. It was after the massive earthquake that shook Seattle to its bootstraps. The city convened a conference of scientists, planners, architects and environmentalists in the mop-up to analyse how they had weathered the tremor and what they could do better to prepare for the next one, which would inevitably arrive.

As she walked into the room her eyes were immediately drawn across to the other side where she saw Damon talking to a dark-haired young woman in a tight-fitting black trouser suit. It hit her immediately, their familiarity. They stood close together, the gap between them narrower than it would have been if they were strangers. He hadn't seen her and when she walked up to them, he stepped away from the woman, startled.

'Frances, I didn't expect to see you here.'

'All of our team is here,' she said, looking from her lover to the other woman with a question in her eyes.

'Ah, this is Joanna,' he said, looking embarrassed. 'She works in our firm as an intern. Joanna, Frances.' He paused. 'I've just got to catch up with someone from the university — I'll see you later.' He turned abruptly on his heel, fumbling a folder in his hand as he escaped, leaving the two women standing together.

Too shocked to talk, Frances muttered that she too had to meet somebody, and retreated to the foyer.

She had scaled the world's most dangerous volcanoes, but Frances had never felt as insecure as she did at that moment. Stunned, she made her way to a bathroom. As she sponged her face with cold water, searching her face in the mirror, she asked herself whether she was simply imagining a betrayal.

She always thought she would marry Damon, perhaps have children with him. But somehow, like so many other twenty- and thirty-somethings they knew, they didn't get around to it, not seeing any need to hurry. They were a close couple and the years just passed by as they happily pursued their careers.

Damon was working his way up through a large city architectural firm. Competitive and testing, it was a long haul, but with Seattle embracing the push for post-modern buildings, his experience and ideas were highly valued. Their professional paths crossed occasionally: with Seattle on a fault line, an architect and a seismologist made comfortable bedfellows. Certainly, Damon often consulted Frances about the ongoing seismic monitoring and predictions, knowledge that undoubtedly won him more than a few points when he was discussing earthquake proofing of buildings with prospective new clients.

Frances returned to the conference where she sat with Olivia and another researcher. Her eyes searched the room until she saw Damon, staring intently at a folder on his lap. The woman was seated several rows away from him.

The speakers came and went but Frances may as well have been sitting alone in an empty room: she heard nothing of what they had to say. At the end of the session, she followed Damon out and, brushing his arm gently, asked if he had time for a coffee before returning to work.

'I'd love to, babe, but I've got a lot to do,' he said, avoiding her eyes. 'Have to run. See you at home tonight.'

It was at that moment she recognised the change in him. She had failed to notice the first time he did not look her in the eye, failed to connect with her. The way he had become evasive, secretive.

Her work filled the gaps, taking her away frequently, both around Washington State but also south to California and occasionally much further afield to Hawaii and the Philippines. For a scientist with her talent, there were plenty of opportunities.

No longer able to concentrate, she left work early that afternoon, picked up some fresh salmon and greens and a bottle of her favourite Australian fruity white wine with a name she liked, Madfish, and returned home to prepare dinner. As their careers had flourished, they'd moved away from their basic student digs and rented an attractive apartment with views over Puget Sound.

Dialling Damon's direct line, she went cold when it clicked over to voicemail. She didn't leave a message. She tried his mobile number. It too switched to the message bank. She pretended to herself nothing was amiss and started preparing dinner, anticipating he would be back around six-thirty as usual. It was not until nine that she heard the door click and Damon walked in, looking flushed. She could see he had been drinking.

'Don't ask me where I've been.' He pre-empted any questioning. 'I'm not in the mood.'

'I was trying to ring you . . .' Her voice faltered. 'Have you eaten?'

He said he was hungry so they sat at the table and ate

together, not far apart but separated by an unbridgeable abyss.

'That woman today?'

'What woman?'

'The one you were talking to at the conference when I arrived.'

'She's just someone from work. No one important.'

'It's just that it looked more than that . . .' Unused to the role of the victim, Frances heard her voice trail away.

'Well, it's not. You're imagining things.'

Later they lay side by side in the bed they had shared for at least a thousand nights, not touching, not daring to speak. Frances had experienced loneliness as an only child, but that night was the loneliest of her life.

They both left for work at eight next morning, planning to meet for dinner downtown. Around three o'clock in the afternoon as Frances was sorting through the monitoring schedules for the coming quarter, her phone rang.

'I've left home,' he told her in a strangely cold voice. 'I've been back to pack my things. I need some space.'

Gripped by nausea, Frances struggled for words. 'What's happened?' was all she could muster. He mumbled that he'd be in touch and hung up.

Making an excuse to leave the office early, she ran to her car and drove over to the office block in the city where Damon worked, needing to see him, not believing what he had just told her, hoping to change his mind. She chanced parking her car illegally on the opposite side of the street. Then she saw him: he was sitting in an outdoor café with the woman. The space he craved had a name — Joanna Bishop, trainee architect, fully qualified cuckoo.

Frances felt her gut tighten and wrench. Resisting the urge to confront them, she returned home. There she paced the floor of the apartment, then lay sobbing on the bed until waves of nausea overtook her and she crawled to the toilet and vomited.

Hours later she awoke, her head on the bathroom floor, her cheek strangely comforted by the cold. For a while she lay there, mentally counting the number of tiles — anything to block out unwanted thoughts. She crawled to her bed and lay there staring uncomprehendingly at the ceiling in that half-world before dawn. Sleep finally claimed her again and she awoke with a start, later than usual at eight o'clock, to a new world, a new reality.

Looking at herself in the bathroom mirror, she saw a face she found it hard to recognise: swollen, reddened eyes, a sad mouth and a pallor of grief so marked that she reached out to trace her hand over her reflection. Then she switched into automatic. Cleaned her teeth, showered and washed her hair, dressed in a warm red suit, applied her make-up and blow-dried her shoulder-length hair, wearing it loose to cover as much of her face as she could.

Mumbling a few words to her co-workers, she sat at her desk, switched on her computer and then sat staring at the lab's home page. She was amazed nobody had noticed that a different Frances had entered the room. Her mind was screaming in pain, yet she remained silent.

For the next six months, Frances threw herself into new projects. Single again, she renewed lapsed friendships but there was no space in her life for romance. Damon had rung her a few times after his new relationship faltered. They met a few times for a drink or two. He suggested reconciliation.

'You're really the one I love, Frances,' he said, matter-of-factly, as though nothing had happened, nothing had changed between them. She was tempted, frightened of letting go of her partner forever, but she decided to let things drift for a while.

One morning she arrived in the office to hear a buzz of

excitement. Olivia called her over. 'My God, Frankie, look what's happening in New Zealand!' They gathered around her Internet page, staring at the images of Mount Ruapehu, hissing steam and smoke. 'They might need some help down there!'

Frances gazed at the screen for a long time without speaking. In that instant, she knew she had to return.

CHAPTER NINETEEN

❧

'They want to bomb the crater.' Theo has edged his way through the crowded hall to where Frances and Sam are sitting. 'One of the local mayors is itching for a fight over this. And he's got the backing of that former bigwig in the government who's stirring things up. We're in for a top night,' he grimaces as he moves back towards the podium where he's part of a panel that will be fielding questions throughout the evening.

'The odd bomb mightn't be a bad idea. Short and sweet. Save a few lives.' Sam nudges Frances and grins as he sees her wince. 'See that group of Maoris over there. They represent the local iwi. Trouble, if you ask me. Don't be surprised by anything you see tonight.'

'I'd like everyone to take their seats, please.' A grey-haired woman calls the meeting to order. She is a manager of one of the government branch offices in the area. Frances met her earlier that evening and doesn't envy her the job of moderating such a disparate group.

About three hundred people are squeezing into the hall. Many huddle in groups until gradually they take their seats.

Wearing a pair of metal-rimmed glasses Frances hasn't seen before, Theo is sitting on the stage poring over his notes. He removes his glasses as he stands and walks to the microphone, then puts them on again as he shuffles his notes and starts to speak. He looks awkward and nervous.

'When you live around a volcano the first thing you learn is that you can't control its behaviour, you can only try to predict what it might do so you can prevent anybody getting hurt,' he tells the crowd. 'I and a team of scientists have detected a significant danger at the moment with the Crater Lake and tonight I want to tell you about the action we've proposed.'

He starts to describe the options, explaining why he doesn't want to bulldoze or bring other heavy machinery into the crater but to install a sophisticated new warning system instead. 'I believe this system will give everybody enough time to get out of the way if a lahar does eventuate. The bottom line is you can't control nature, you just have to learn to live with it.'

He singles out Frances, inviting the audience to ask her questions about the system after the addresses. Sitting next to her, Sam squeezes her arm and whispers, 'Are you brave enough to disagree with the boss?' Frances jabs him with her elbow and avoids looking at him. He has a disturbing effect on her. She finds him physically attractive — the first man she has felt like this since her relationship with Damon foundered — but there's also something threatening about his manner that makes her very cautious.

A beefy, middle-aged man dressed like a gentleman farmer in a checked sports coat, cream chinos and leather riding boots rises to his feet, indicating he wants the microphone.

'Who's that?' Frances whispers to Sam.

'Ian Carmody: loves the limelight.' Frances feels his hot breath on her cheek. 'Some think he's the bully boy in the opposition party. But he's effective. Watch him wind people up.'

Carmody now draws himself up to his full height, his double chin pointing upwards in a peculiar angle. Something about him is very familiar, but Frances can't place where she has seen him.

'This government is guilty of neglect. Those buggers in their ivory towers in Wellington are risking your life and mine.' His voice booms across the room as though he is in Parliament rather than a country hall. But he knows how to win a crowd's attention and he is rewarded for each gem of rhetoric with a smattering of applause.

'I believe what we have here is an administration that is a slave to political correctness. Too frightened to upset the greenies, the ferals, the anti-this and the anti-that groups. And let's call a spade a spade here, to upset the Maori. A lahar could wreck this place. It could do millions of dollars worth of damage to the roads, the houses and shops and, let's not forget, the railway. They would rather all of us got killed than offend their namby-pamby friends.'

'Order, order,' the chairwoman calls as half the audience cheer and the other half start yelling abuse. 'Mr Carmody,' she says with pursed lips, 'it might be helpful to all of us if you could be a little less emotive and more objective in your language.'

Frances can hear Sam snigger beside her. He leans over to her again. 'Carmody learned his bullying tactics in the front row of a first fifteen rugby team. He loves this and he's not about to let her deprive him of his few minutes of glory. He's just warming up.'

'What we're talking about here is the choice between common sense to fix a problem with a few bulldozers or, better still, a few very safe bombs dropped into the crater, and a gutless group of pathetic arselickers who are trying to tell us we should just stand here and wait to be drowned like all those poor buggers at Tangiwai.

'I have it on good authority the military could easily drop in around thirty high-precision laser-guided bombs and they would instantly excavate the crater and we could all sleep easier in our beds.'

The hall erupts as Carmody's supporters cheer him on and his opponents shout at him to sit down.

Frances sees Theo struggling to control his temper, putting his glasses on and off. His face is drained of blood and she detects a slight trembling of his hands. He calls for the microphone and rises to meet a mixed reception of applause and interjectors.

'I'd like to address Mr Carmody's plan to bomb the crater,' he says. 'It's true this has been looked at but it would be a very dangerous course and it's culturally abhorrent. If you dropped explosives into the crater it would create shock waves that would weaken all the rock beneath the crater rim. This could have a catastrophic effect of making the whole summit collapse. Also all the natural material up there would be contaminated by chemicals and fragments from the missiles. It would be a disaster.'

'What about bulldozers or teams of men digging it up?' Carmody yells from the floor.

'My reasons for opposing bulldozers up there are the same as for bombing. It's too risky and anyway if the mountain blows, it would be pointless. As for digging by hand, we've looked at that too and it's totally impractical. You'd need hundreds of people working up there for more than a year to do it. We think that's impossible.'

A thickly made-up bottle-blonde rises to her feet.

'Now there's a piece of work,' Sam mutters to Frances. 'The deputy mayor, Careena Price. She knows what side her bread's buttered on. She campaigned on opening up the national park for more development. She got heaps of dough from the firearm and four-wheel-drive lobbyists to get her to the town hall. The gossip is she's extremely close, if you know what I mean, to a lot of her, er, backers.'

'I think I get your drift,' Frances whispers.

Smoothing her short skirt, the woman calls on those at the meeting to demand that the government immediately starts excavation works on the summit. 'I'm extremely disappointed in this government,' she says, her voice wavering. 'They don't care what we think. We're the ones that have to live here and I think we have to demand that the threat is removed completely. They're hell-bent on letting this mudslide, this lahar, just do, just do whatever it likes . . .'

Some of the audience titter as the fledgling politician nearly falls off her platform heels.

'You can laugh all you like!' she screams, jabbing her finger at some of the environmental representatives as she sits down, 'but we're not going to take it.'

Theo moves to the microphone again. The blood is rising up his neck and his tanned face is reddening and sweating.

'I'm sorry this meeting has become so divided. I just want to emphasise that some of the speakers here tonight, in my view, have been recklessly alarmist. Once the early warning system is installed there'll be no chance of a repeat of Tangiwai. While we of course took into account opposition from Maori, that wasn't the only reason we have chosen this course. I for one would not want to see bulldozers at the Crater Lake. And of course this would severely jeopardise the World Heritage listing of the park and quite frankly that would benefit nobody.'

'Sit down, egg-head!' somebody at the back yells.

Frances, sickened by the disrespect, wants to go to Theo to show her support but makes herself stay where she is. She glances at Sam and is surprised to see he is smiling to himself, seeming to enjoy Theo's discomfort. Something about his expression reminds her of Carmody. Then she remembers: he's the man who was in the café with Sam when she drove past with the real-estate agent.

'Madam Chair, can I have the floor?' Just as she is about to challenge Sam, she hears a new speaker. A tall well-built man with short black hair emerges from one side of the hall and walks to the microphone.

'I would like to tell the meeting about the Maori position,' he says, looking directly at the audience. 'My name is Tori Maddison and I've been asked to speak on behalf of the local iwi. For centuries we were the sole custodians of different parts of this region of Aotearoa–New Zealand. Ngati Rangi on the southern reaches of the mountain, Ngati Tahu the north-eastern reaches, and extending to the western and eastern boundaries, the ancestral domain of Ngati Tuwharetoa.'

Tori uses his hands to emphasise his words and Frances is immediately taken by his strength and confidence as an orator.

'We revere these mountains as we revere our ancestors. Like our ancestors, we believe these mountains symbolise nature's authority over us. They are ageless and beside them, man is puny and insignificant. We have the duty to protect the total environment as all life originated from the same parents, from Rangi of the heavens above and . . .'

'Sit down, we know what you lot think — all hocus pocus talk and no action,' says one of Careena Price's supporters to the cheers of a group around him. 'What about Tangiwai? Do you just want to let it happen again?'

'Please don't interrupt the speakers,' the chairwoman says.

'As I was saying, we must protect the total environment from Rangi of the heavens above and Papa the earth mother below. Ruapehu is a symbol of the power of creation and is of great spiritual importance to us. While we respect the Pakeha view, we state most strongly that we will resist any moves to interfere with the mana of Ruapehu. The Crater Lake is the most sacred place for our people. We oppose any machinery being used up there or any alteration of the natural landscape of the crater rim.'

When the chairwoman asks Tori if the iwi support extending the early warning system and building a dam to divert lahar waters away from the trout catchment, Frances watches his expression.

'We support the early warning system in principle and we'll sit down and talk about other solutions as they arise.' She's relieved to hear his response but notices that each time he makes a statement he glances for reassurance to the group of his friends observing him closely from the aisle. 'But we will never agree to bombing or bulldozers on the mountain summit. And can I remind you all that one of our ancestors, the great chief Te Heuheu, gifted these mountains to preserve them for the national heritage for generations to come. I quote for you from the Book of Proverbs: "Ki te kahore he whakakitenga, ka kore te iwi e tupato — Where there is no vision, the people perish".'

As he leaves the microphone, the audience again divides itself between cheers and abuse.

'He's a real troublemaker,' Sam whispers to Frances. 'Give him a wide berth.'

Before she can reply she hears her name called out. Although used to delivering lectures on her work, Frances is apprehensive, but when Theo motions her forward and introduces her to the meeting, she knows she can't back out.

'Thank you, ladies and gentlemen . . .' As she begins her address, one of the hecklers yells out, 'Sit down, we don't need any Yanks telling us what to do.' He is rewarded with some supportive guffaws from his cheer squad but otherwise the audience is paying attention to the newest recruit.

Feeling her heart thumping, but determined to finish the briefing, Frances continues. 'I've personally seen the effectiveness of acoustic microphones monitoring volcanic activity on a number of mountains. They give the most advanced warning ever of an eruption or a lahar. I'm confident they'll work very well on Mount Ruapehu and give vital extra time for evacuations. The system won't prevent these things happening, but it will give us time to warn anyone who might be in danger to evacuate the area safely.'

'I've heard there could be only a minute or two's warning. How can you expect people to evacuate that quickly?' a voice calls out. 'Ski like a bat out of hell!' another yells and the audience starts to laugh.

'In the event of an eruption or a lahar, we have a comprehensive network of people who will be involved in contacting everyone in the region. The new microphones, or geophones, give us extra time. There are loudspeakers all over the ski fields and safe areas to gather on the slopes. For the wider area, it takes a couple of hours for a lahar to travel as far as Tangiwai and I understand that's enough time for people to react and leave the immediate area.'

'What about the train? We don't want another Tangiwai disaster.'

'No . . . I'm sure. No one wants that, least of all me,' Frances says, trying to control her now quavering voice. 'The railways have assured us no train would venture onto that line if there's a lahar. There would be plenty of time to stop any train.'

'Miss Nelson . . .'

Frances is startled to see that Tori Maddison has risen to ask her a question and is staring at her intently.

'I would like you to tell us what your opinion is about further intervention at the summit. Do you support bulldozing, bombing or suchlike?'

'Ah . . .' Frances hesitates, struggling to find the words, trying to appear composed when her mind is full of doubts. She feels both Theo and Sam staring at her and wishes she could be anywhere but in this hall. 'No . . . that is I agree with Mr Rush. That is our united view. No intervention. Better early warning systems and monitoring.'

She sees Tori sitting back and whispering to one of his Maori friends. As she returns to her seat she tries to avoid eye contact with Sam, whose face is wrinkled with amusement. She ignores him when he mutters to her under his breath, 'Your first lion attack!'

She catches Tori Maddison watching her but he quickly averts his eyes.

The meeting ends in an impasse and the crowd drifts out into the darkness. Packing his briefing papers, Theo thanks Frances. 'Sorry to put you through that. You performed well.'

'You looked pretty upset, Theo. Is it always like this?'

'Whenever Carmody is on the block it is. He never worries about twisting a few facts if it suits his purpose. He's been working behind the scenes to try and railroad the government's decision not to intervene.'

She is about to mention seeing him with Sam but Theo is already heading towards the door. 'I'm sorry if I have to dash off but I'm feeling exhausted after this week and Sue's getting annoyed by all the long hours I've been working. I'll see you tomorrow.'

A few minutes later, after answering a few questions from a woman who approaches her, Frances leaves the hall.

She hears them before she sees them. A short distance from the door in the half-light she sees Sam pointing at Tori Maddison, who is backing away.

'Is everything OK?' she asks, walking over.

'Nothing for you to get involved with, Frances. I'm just telling this guy here to come into the twenty-first century.' As Sam turns to leave he offers to drive her home.

'No, I have my own car,' she says as he storms off.

Tori is looking at her and suddenly she feels uncomfortable about being associated with Sam's behaviour.

'I'm sorry. It's Mr Maddison, isn't it? I'm not sure what I've just walked into here.'

'You're obviously not from around here. Don't worry, we're used to those kinds of insults. As you've probably guessed, Sam Hawks and I go back a bit. We have a history. He's come to some of our meetings before and, how can I say, we agree to disagree.'

'Well I'm sympathetic to what you were saying there,' Frances says, 'but I know very little about Maori beliefs and I know a lot about the Tangiwai disaster. I can understand why people are afraid. I suppose I'm also a little bit on Sam's side because no one wants to see a lot of people killed if we can prevent it.'

'Ah, someone else who thinks they have the power to match the mountain.' His deep brown eyes stare at her with mocking amusement.

Frances shifts uncomfortably. 'No, I don't think that at all. But there may be a middle ground. Do all your people agree with each other?'

'Mostly . . .' He hesitates. 'The ones that think deeply about it, at least. But we don't agree on everything. For example, the bund, to divert the waters away from Lake Taupo. Some of them don't want that either. They see that as interference. I'm not sure about that myself.' Tori sees he has her attention and is enjoying the moment. 'Maybe I could be persuaded,' he says.

'Well, I'd like to learn more about your beliefs. Maybe we could swap some of our expertise one day,' she laughs, easing the tension.

He chuckles. 'Maybe, maybe not. I'll probably see you around.'

He walks away with what she thinks is a bit of a swagger to join his friends who are waiting quietly for him by the road. He looks embarrassed when he turns back and sees she is still standing there. They pile into his four-wheel-drive, and as the night swallows them Frances feels like she has just had the tiniest glimpse into another world.

CHAPTER TWENTY

❧

The trouble is none of them want to work. They just want everything handed to them on a plate, don't you agree?' On her way home from work a few days later, Frances is hoping to slip past her other neighbour, Iris, but the pensioner is on the driveway where she is planting bulbs in time for a spring flowering. Once Iris learned Frances was working on the crater problem and involved in consultation with Maori, she saw her as a conduit for her prejudices.

And she wasn't the only one: Frances has noticed a division in the town in attitudes towards local Maori. 'I'm not racist, but . . .' was often the opening sentence to a stream of vitriol about land ownership, government grants, fishing royalties and other rights won back after decades of colonial dispossession.

She is especially anxious to escape her neighbour this evening. She has invited Shona over for drinks with Bill who has just arrived on leave for a few days from the Waiouru Army Camp. Minutes after she is safely inside she hears Bill's vehicle pull into the driveway and smiles as Iris' pained expression follows him up to Shona's place.

A few minutes later when Frances opens the door she is taken aback to see Tori Maddison standing there next to Bill and Shona, his hands buried in the pockets of his fishing jacket.

'Hope you don't mind one extra, Frances,' says Shona. 'This is Tori, Bill's cousin. They were just catching up with each other while Bill was in town and I said you wouldn't mind him joining us.'

'No, not at all,' she says, ushering them in. 'Actually we've already met, haven't we?'

'Yep, it's a pretty small town. Hope you're OK with this, Miss Nelson?'

'Please, call me Frances. Of course, come in.'

Bill hugs Frances warmly and immediately throws himself into a soft padded armchair, exhausted from a week of training new army recruits. Tori accepts the offer of a beer and sits tentatively on the edge of a chair on the other side of the room.

'You should see the latest lot!' Bill scoffs. 'Some of them had dreadlocks, others shaved heads. Most of them can't run to save themselves. Can't see them sticking it out.' Raising his beer to his lips, his bulging arm muscles twitching beneath his fitting shirt, he starts cackling. 'And the piercings. Pierced this, that and the other bloody thing when they arrive. I made them whip the lot out. One of them even had something called a Prince Albert through his dick.'

They all roar with laughter as Shona presses for more information. 'And what is a Prince Albert?'

'Well,' Bill says, gathering them in as he puts on a conspiratorial voice, 'you've seen those rings they put through bulls' noses. It's like that. Poked through the end of the penis with a chain attached to it to pull the male member to the left or the right. Named after the original prince who, I've heard on good authority, liked to dress left.'

'Always thought those royals were kinky,' Shona says as she

sidles up to Bill and grabs him around the hips. 'And what about you, Sergeant, where do you like to let your little fella go?'

Bill spins her around laughing. 'I like to let the big fella go where he wants to. And don't you know it!'

Frances catches Tori's eye as the couple kiss each other passionately. He can see her blushing and rescues her by asking if she'd like him to pour them another drink.

Bill asks for another beer, then downs a second pint of cold Waikato Bitter in one long swallow. 'Needed that, haven't had a beer for a week.'

Not to be deterred, Shona persists with her tease. 'I've had a bit of a drought for a week too,' she says, provocatively licking her top lip. She sits on his lap and pulls at a greenstone pendant around his neck. Within minutes, the pair make an excuse to leave and soon Frances and Tori can hear shrieks of laughter through the walls. Frances is furious with her neighbour but helpless to do anything about it.

Struggling for something to say, she puts on a CD and the music drowns out the rising sounds of passion next door.

'Hope you're hungry?' she asks. 'I've bought food. Looks like we'll have to eat this on our own.' When he nods, she starts to unwrap packages she has picked up from the delicatessen: cocktail onions, fresh pâté and crackers. She adds kalamata olives, sticks of carrots and celery and urges him to eat.

'Good kai,' he remarks, popping an olive into his mouth and plastering some of the pâté onto the cracker.

'Good what?'

'Kai, food,' he smiles at her. 'Good word for you to learn, especially when you're hungry.' He eats the cracker quickly and has another. 'What is it?' he asks.

'Duck pâté. What do you think?'

'Well, I've shot a few ducks in my day and eaten a few but none of them tasted like this. Not bad.'

She shows him a bottle of wine, labelled Mission Sauvignon Blanc. 'Would you like to try some? The man in the wine shop told me this is made in some old monastery in the North Island. Do you think that's true?'

'Yeah, I'll try some,' he says and sips from the glass. 'Could be true,' he says. 'Though I don't know if there are many monks left.' He sips some more then pauses and starts to laugh as they hear a loud thump through the wall. 'Mind you, I'm feeling a bit like one myself at the moment.'

Frances laughs and for a moment envies Shona her casual attitude to sex.

Although she knows so little about him, Frances feels oddly at ease with Tori. 'You're at an advantage,' she tells him. 'You know what I do but I don't know anything about you — just your ancestors,' she adds with a grin.

'I'm a fishing guide. Pure and simple.'

'I suppose I could have guessed you'd be a man of the land — or at least the water.'

'Well, it wasn't always that way. I guess I've come full circle. I used to fish for fun but now it's a business as well.'

'What did you do beforehand?'

'For years I lived in Auckland, in the city, away from here. I always seemed to be working hard. Too hard.' He punches his other palm as he relives the days of hard manual labour. 'Construction and road jobs. It was like a prison and I thought, I don't want to get to fifty and still be working like this. So when I came back here I thought about a fishing business. But although I knew about the fishing I didn't have a clue about running a business. So I took some courses and here I am.'

'You look pretty relaxed. It must be a good life.'

'It's so much of my life. I used to live to work. Now I can work to live. If I don't feel like working I don't have to. But when I do there's always people who want me to take them out fishing.'

'Why is there so much resentment to Maori ways here?'

At first he doesn't reply. He swirls the wine in his glass and says, 'This isn't too bad. I'm more of a beer drinker myself, but I've got to say I could get used to this.'

Then he looks at this outsider, who has taken him by surprise.

'It's just some people. They can't relate to our culture, our way of doing things,' he says at last. 'Yet the same people's kids might be on the dole or they're getting some fat superannuation as a handout but they always point the finger at Maori as if they're bludgers. It's true a lot of our young generation, the mokopuna, might be a bit laid back to work too much. But I don't blame them. I was like that myself when I was a teenager. I think you have to work hard but there's more to life than that.'

'You mean balance?'

'Yeah, I suppose so. We have a phrase — te ao hurihuri: it means the changing world. It's our way of saying that everything in our life, the way we do things, the things we believe in, our connections to the past and our tribes, to the land, our place in the world, our relationships, if you like . . . they're all bound up together. But that's enough about me. What about you? Why are you interested in volcanoes?'

'Once you've been close to one, it's like an addiction. I came to New Zealand as a teenager and I have to say I was overawed by Ruapehu the first time I saw it.'

'How come you were here?'

'On a holiday with my parents,' she hedged. 'When I went home to England I became obsessed with geology and volcanoes and read everything I could find about them. I remember going to sleep at night, calculating how, if I was a wizard, I could fit the twelve giant pieces of the earth's jigsaw all back together again — the east coast of South America fitting into the west coast of Africa, Madagascar could pop back into the African mainland, the Antarctica part of Australia's south coast and so on. I used to imagine pieces of the earth floating over seas of rocks, constantly moving and colliding.'

'You've missed your calling — you should be a storyteller,' Tori says. 'Tell me more.'

'I was an only child,' Frances feels the words catch in her throat, 'so I spent a lot of time on my own and I would escape in my mind. I used to sit in our little garden at the back of the house and I would calculate what would happen if I drilled a hole in the flowerbed on and on for thousands of miles, through the cool rock of the planet's crust, deeper and deeper, and the more I drilled, the hotter it became. Then into the centre of the earth, the engine room where the sheer heat and force of the molten layer moved the huge pieces of jigsaw around the earth in the continental drift.

'And I remember the first time I heard about the ring of fire. It sounded so romantic. It fascinated me and, as you can tell, it's become part of my life and I've followed it all the way down the coastline of the Pacific Basin until I landed back here in New Zealand.'

'Well, you've certainly taken on a job and a half, Frances, and if you can convince everyone the early warning system works, I for one will be very grateful.' As if he suddenly remembered an appointment, Tori stands up abruptly. 'I'm sorry if I barged in here. I wasn't expecting this to happen. I certainly didn't expect the others to leave.'

'Please don't worry. I haven't known Shona long but nothing really surprises me. I'm glad you came by.'

As they walk to the door, Frances turns to him. 'I was serious about wanting to learn more of Maori culture — all I've heard is second-hand information.'

'Fine. As it happens, I'm climbing up one of the other mountains for a special ceremony with some of my iwi on

Sunday. Maybe you'd like to come along.'

'Sure. I'd like that,' she tells him. She fetches a writing pad and watches as he writes directions to his house in bold printing with a little map and lots of arrows pointing towards the lakefront.

'It's about an hour's drive away from Taupo, near the lake. Wear some strong shoes and warm clothes. It'll be a long day.'

CHAPTER TWENTY-ONE

❦

I can skim it more times than you — I'm better than you!'
The boy runs three steps, stretches his arm back as though
bowling a cricket ball and throws the stone with all the might
of his ten years. The small grey missile skips across the lake,
bouncing once, twice, three times before dropping out of sight.
The morning sun captures the ripples billowing out in large
circles from the spot where the waters of Taupo swallow it.

The taller slender girl beside him laughs. Ignoring the taunts
of her younger brother, she selects a larger, flatter stone from
the shoreline. Rather than running, she stands, barefooted with
her jeans rolled up to her knees, in one spot on the wet sand,
strokes the stone and passes it from one hand to another. Then
setting one foot in front of the other, she brushes back her long,
straight, black hair with one hand and with the other, she aims
the stone at the water and throws it with a sideway spin as hard
as she can. It bounces a full four times before sinking.

The boy's eyes widen and his chin sets determinedly. 'Let me
have another go! I'll beat you this time!'

Enjoying their play, Frances approaches the children and asks if they know where she can find Tori Maddison.

'Dad's just coming now,' the girl says, eyeing the woman in her well-fitting beige jeans, polished brown leather boots and pale-blue parka.

Frances looks back to see Tori sauntering out of an old green weatherboard house with a small satellite dish on the roof about 50 metres back from the shore. It is surrounded by a number of sheds and a large concrete water tank. Wearing what looks like a well-loved black T-shirt and denim jeans, he comes towards her, his handsome face creased in a smile.

'Glad you could make it,' he says, holding out a large hand that reveals a life of manual work. 'Hemi, Moana, this is Frances. She's the scientist I was telling you about. She's coming up the mountain with us today.'

The two children nudge each other and giggle.

'Sure you want us to come, Dad? Maybe we'll be too crowded,' his daughter says, setting off her brother into another round of giggling.

'She looks brainy, eh Dad?' Hemi adds.

'Come on, you kids, we haven't got all day,' their father says, looking embarrassed. 'Have you packed up the chilly bin yet? We need lots of cold drinks and sandwiches from the fridge. There are no shops where we're going. Leave your car here, Frances, and we can all go in the four-wheel-drive.'

They drive for less than an hour before pulling over to a clearing in the foothills of Mount Tongariro.

'This is the end of the comfort part of the journey,' Tori says. 'Everyone out, we have to walk from here — just a four-hour stroll up and back. Let's see what you Americans are made of.'

Frances is feeling better than she has for months.

'I'm getting used to these so-called mountain strolls,' she jokes. 'The one I did last week was five hours and I can still feel it here,' she says, leaning down to rub her calves.

They pack the drinks and food into a backpack and the four of them walk briskly along a track pushed through brown tussock and dotted with pumice stones.

'Is that heather?' Frances asks as she reaches down to pick a purple flower.

''Fraid it is,' Tori says. 'It's a legacy of one mad Scotsman who spread tonnes of heather seeds here in the nineteenth century. He was trying to recreate his lost highlands. He'd been planning to go another step and introduce grouse and woodcock to complete his creation of a new Scotland downunder until it was realised all the native plants and birds were dying. But the Pakeha introduced lots of other animals that have taken hold here — possums, deer and pigs. Good hunting but not great for the environment.'

As they continue climbing, the landscape changes dramatically, first to open green scrubland and then to a rich damp forest of centuries-old native trees. They slow to a dawdle as they enter the forest, a last remaining remnant spared from the rush to clear land and harvest the magnificent trees to build ships, houses and furniture. Moana calls out the names of the wooden giants to Frances: rimu, totara, kahikatea, matai, miro.

The air is cool and moist and they can hear the trickling of hidden streams. A moment later the silence is broken by beautiful birdsong.

'That's a tui,' Moana tells Frances. 'It's our nightingale.'

'I'd love to see it. Where is it? Tui's my second name and I've never seen the bird.'

They scan the branches of the trees that rise up around them, looking right up to the canopy screening the sky, following the melodious call. Then they spot it, a small, dark, shiny metallic purple and green bird with two tufts of snow-white feathers at its throat.

As Frances cries out in delight, the bird flies away and is instantly lost in the arboreal gloom.

'How come you have a Maori name?' Tori looks at her curiously.

'My parents were caught up in the Tangiwai disaster. They were on the train with my sister. She drowned in the river, a long time before I was born, and a woman named Tui looked after my mother while they were searching for her. So, when I came along, she gave that to me as my second name.'

'Well, it's a beautiful name — it suits you. You're full of surprises. No wonder you want to tame that mountain. Have you come to grips with the loss of your sister?'

The question takes her by surprise. 'I suppose so,' she stammers. 'It's hard to deal with the loss of someone who is linked to you and yet you never knew.'

She follows Tori closely as he strides ahead.

'Tui have always been important to us,' he says over his shoulder. 'They actually like being around people and I've seen some of the old people train them to sing certain songs on the marae. That's in our settlements.'

When he sees her sceptical glance Tori slows down until she is level with him. He's laughing. 'Would I lie to you?' he asks. 'Maybe we can track the other Tui down — we're probably related. A lot of my aunties have that name too. You'll meet one of them up the mountain today. She would be too young to be the same person but she may know who it was.'

As they continue walking, the old forest gradually thins. The thick green underlayer of shrubs and moist ferns disappears and gives way to red and silver beech. Eventually, they leave the verdant land behind. The ground hardens and as they climb higher the vegetation peters out completely. Soon the track meets a small steaming river.

'Come and feel this,' Tori calls out as he stops to scoop up a handful of water. 'It's warm and the higher we go the hotter it gets. We call this the Manga-a-te-Tipua, the enchanted stream. Great for the rheumatism!'

'Dad, can we stop now?' Moana complains. 'I'm feeling dizzy.'

'OK, let's have a breather, sit over here.' Tori directs them to an outcrop of rocks next to the stream and then produces bottles of cool water and some chocolate from his backpack. 'Don't drink the water in the river, kids, it's full of chemicals. Take your sneakers off and bathe your feet and while we're here, I'll tell you all a story about why we Maori have learnt to live with landslides.'

'Oh, not another one of your boring ancestor stories,' Hemi teases his father. Tori shakes his head at the boy in mock anger. 'Listen, young man, you can make fun of it if you like but they're your ancestors too, your heritage, and you should know your stories.'

Chastened, Hemi stays quiet but, not about to sit still, splashes up and down the stream, picking up stones and tossing them into the water. Moana sits as close to Frances as she dares, enjoying the scent and the difference of this exotic stranger.

Frances loves the way Tori includes his children in all their conversations, encouraging them one moment and gently chiding them at another. Sometimes he talks to them in Maori, other times in English.

'One of our ancestors, Te Heuheu Tukino, was the paramount chief of Taupo in the early 1800s. He was a giant of a man, with snowy-white hair and a tattooed face. He was well loved by both Maori and the first white travellers in this region, but he was also a fierce, victorious warrior known for his military planning and tactics, what we call whakatakoto parekura.'

Tori is warming up now, clearly enjoying his role as storyteller, drawing them in.

'He lived with his clan and several wives in a stockaded village at Te Rapa, not far from here. On a night before a battle he would gather his warriors and before addressing them he would recite a potent karakia.'

'What's that?' Frances asks.

'It's a prayer or a chant.'

Tori draws himself up and recites from the ancient incantation: 'Hira mai ai te whekite o te rangi'.

Moana and Hemi start giggling and are silenced with a glare from their father.

'It's my special prayer,' Tori tells Frances. 'I always try to remember to say it to myself in difficult times. It's supposed to ward off evil spirits and destructive powers of nature.

'But the story goes that just before the floods hit the hillside behind the village, the chief forgot to say the prayer to divert an impending disaster. The village was preparing a welcome for another visiting tribe when the floods hit. Part of the hillside that was pierced through by dozens of boiling springs suddenly gave way. A great mass of mud, clay, rocks and water thundered down into the village and Te Heuheu and most of his family were killed in a giant landslide.'

'So did anyone survive?' Frances asks.

'No one in the middle of the village did. Fifty-four of them died, including his wife. When they found her body she was holding the tribe's sacred greenstone mere — club — protecting it. The only members of his immediate family who survived were his brother and one son.'

Tori explains that the grief-stricken tribe wanted to bury their chief at the top of the mountain in a cave, believing the more important the person, the higher up they should be put to rest, but rival chiefs were against it, not wanting to strengthen the tribe's ownership of the land. 'There have been many wars over sovereignty of the land, not just with Pakeha but also between other tribes. And it still goes on today. So at first the old chief was buried elsewhere.

'Te Heuheu was a very sacred person when he was alive and once he died his power became even greater. So everything around him — his possessions, food — became forbidden to anyone of inferior rank. Even the lake was tapu because the landslide had swept into the water so they couldn't eat the fish. To remove the tapu and before the old chief could be exhumed, the tribe had to find others with equal status to perform some special ceremonies.'

'How could one man hold so much power over everyone?' Frances asks.

'When a chief dies it's like a mountain having its tip broken off. Our legends tell us that the stern anchor of the great Arawa canoe is firmly fixed on top of Tongariro and the prow anchor is equally firmly fixed on the east coast. We have the saying "Mai makeutu ki tongariro", which means the mountain is held fast, there for us for eternity. So to protect themselves from death or disaster after his death, the people brought in other chiefs and priests of the highest status from surrounding tribes. They performed ancient rites, including cooking special food in a sacred oven to remove the tapu.

'They were then able to exhume his bones and they took them and hid them in a lava cave on Tongariro not far from here. They rested on this mountain for sixty years and then they were removed again and buried closer to his home where he now rests in peace.'

'The caves sound amazing,' Frances says. 'Like a Maori version of the ancient Egyptian pyramids. Have you seen any of the lava burial places?'

'Yes, but they're secret places. I've seen them in these mountains and another on an island where there are many bodies of Maori princes and princesses lying in state in large lava caves. Frances,' Tori moves so close to her she can feel the warmth of his breath, 'our belief in tapu is a very serious and important part of our culture. Do you understand that?'

Frances nods slowly. 'I guess I do in principle but I don't really grasp it.'

'We see the world in a holistic way — everything in our lives, the spiritual, the intellectual and the physical, is bound with the life force of the environment, what we call the mauri, and the rest of the universe.

'In the old days, my people wouldn't even climb the sacred volcanoes because the chief was buried there and it was tapu. They were afraid to even look at the mountain for fear of breaking its tapu and courting death. Some wore wreaths of large leaves around their heads to cover their eyes so they could only look at the ground as they walked. These blinkers stopped them from accidentally looking at the volcanoes.

'The first Europeans who travelled here didn't care about such things and climbed the mountains. At first my people refused many of those who asked permission to climb. But the land wars between Maori and Pakeha and between tribes disrupted the traditional way of life and with the white man's laws and culture everything changed. And once the chief's body was moved away from the mountain, a condition my people put on before the area became a national park, the ban on climbing there was lifted. Now we climb the mountains from time to time for special ceremonies like today but the tapu remains and we're deeply respectful.'

Tori stands up, brushing the dust off his pants. 'That's enough storytelling for now. We'd better get moving — the others are waiting for us up the mountain.' He explains that six or seven elders started climbing to an area of sacred hot volcanic springs earlier in the morning.

'Unfortunately, not many of my people climb here these

days. A lot of the older people have very bad health problems like diabetes and kidney failure. Too much junk food, booze and smoking. And the young ones aren't that interested. That's why I bring my kids while they're young enough to want to come. It's important they learn their history.'

They walk for another half hour, lost in thoughts of the past. Moana sticks closely to Frances while Hemi leaps up and down the rocks like a restless puppy. The higher they climb, the hotter the stream becomes and the steamy sulphur envelops them. Suddenly, ahead on the track out of the volcanic haze, they hear a woman's voice, half chanting, half singing. The voice is strong and sure and the sound fills Frances with awe. Soon they are close enough to see her. Thickset build, with short curly black hair and wearing a dark blue tracksuit, she is standing erect. Her brown face is finely lined.

'That's my Aunty Tui I was telling you about,' Tori says quietly as they stop to listen.

'What's that song she's singing?'

'It's part of a lament written by Te Heuheu's brother Iwikau, who survived the landslide.'

Even Hemi is still as the woman finishes the chant.

As the steam blows away in a faint breeze, Frances sees three men and three women sitting on rocks near the singer, two of them dangling their feet in the hot stream. They look up without expression as Tori brings Frances to meet them then, almost as one, they stand and join Tui. Moving forward in a line, they each greet the stranger, shaking her hand and kissing her on both cheeks. They also embrace Tori and his children with warmth.

Unused to the instant familiarity, Frances feels a little uneasy, but returns their kisses and joins them when they return to the rocks.

'Although the springs are surrounded by the national park, our great chief Horonuku excluded them from the gift to New

Zealand. This is where they brought the body of his father to rest after the landslide and he was placed in one of the caves here. This is also sacred to us because hundreds of years ago when our high priest Ngatoroirangi came here looking for a homeland for our people after the great canoe crossing, he nearly lost his life in the freezing cold.

'The legend goes that he was crying out a prayer to the gods for warmth and light. He was answered with heat and hot water pouring out of the vents and craters of these mountains. He saw this as a sign that the people could make this their home, the mountains, the forests, lakes and desert below. So we have lived here ever since.'

As if to echo the past, a sudden jet of steam and hot water spurts out of a nearby vent. 'You can see our mana is still very strong here,' one of the elders calls out, making the others laugh.

While Tori chats to his family, Frances leads Hemi and Moana on a walk further up the mountain to take a closer look at the springs.

'Do you believe all that stuff about the gods bringing warmth here?' Moana asks Frances, searching her face closely.

'I don't disbelieve all those legends. The Native Americans have them too about the volcanoes in their traditional lands. They call Mount St Helens in America Loowit, the Lady of Smoke. Usually they have a basis in truth, a way to understand vulcanology and geology. But my world is more based on science,' she says, choosing her words carefully.

All around them, the sulphurous steam swirls up from holes in the rocks and the stream running down the slope. Shiny deposits of dark-grey sludge line some of the vents and every now and then there is the plopping sound of bursting bubbles of boiling mud.

'These springs begin as rain and snow with all the water

pouring through the holes in the ground until it finds the hot core of the volcano. Then it mixes with all the chemicals there like the sulphur and it boils up and hey presto, you have a geyser. Hey Hemi, keep away from the edge!' The boy is about to stretch his hand over to a steaming vent. 'That would burn your hand off. I'll show you my magic wand.'

Frances reaches into her pack and brings out a small bag. Opening it, she unwraps a thermometer, two bottles, some folding tongs and a thick glove. 'Here, let's see how hot it is.'

The three of them crouch down as Frances puts on the glove and attaches the tongs to the thermometer. She extends the device and sticks the thermometer into the vent for a minute. 'Abracadabra!' she says, watching their spellbound expressions. 'OK, let's take a look.'

The two children are wide-eyed as she retrieves the thermometer.

'Wow, it's over one hundred and twenty degrees — that's hot enough to burn you up.'

Taking the bottles, Frances fills them from the stream. 'May as well take some work home with me,' she says. 'I can test this back in the laboratory and let you know what's in it. Probably boron and ammonium sulphate and lots of other chemicals.'

'Where did you learn to do that?' Moana asks.

'The complicated stuff at university. But I had a very good science teacher at high school in England who taught me all about the way the surface of the earth is moving all the time. The parts of the world they call the oceanic and continental plates that fold layers and layers of rock, pumice and lava. Have you ever seen anyone make jam?'

'I have,' Hemi interrupts. 'My grandmother makes it. Plum jam and sometimes strawberry. I like that best.' He grins at her.

'Well, have you seen what happens when you boil up the fruit and the sugar together? As you stir the mixture and it gets hotter and hotter, little solid bubbles rise to the top. The more it cooks, the more hot pulp rises. Then, as it cools down you can see a skin forming on top.'

'Yeah, I remember that,' Moana says. 'I got into trouble once for poking it with a spoon and trying to peel it off.' She giggles shyly, her hand in front of her mouth.

'As that skin sets or coagulates, a new hot layer comes up beneath that and pushes the cooler layer aside and sometimes it forces it to slide under and melt. The skin keeps forming over and over again and each time the new layers push up, they make the old ones slide back under. And that's what happens to the lava and how it forms into layers of rock that keep moving.'

As Frances and the girl move away from the intense heat and sit together waiting for the samples to cool, Hemi runs back to join his father.

'Mum's gone away,' Moana tells Frances quietly, as though she has been guessing her unasked questions.

'Where to?'

'To Auckland. She comes and sees us sometimes but not very much.'

'Are you sad about that?'

'Yes, I miss her and I think Dad does too. But I love staying at my grandmother's place and Dad's always having us over. So it's not too bad. Are you married?'

'No.' Frances still feels odd thinking of herself as single after years of being committed to a relationship. Then she looks at Moana and adds, 'I almost was. But no, I'm not.'

Moana smiles at her but says nothing more.

When they rejoin the group, Tori beckons Frances over. 'Aunty Tui would like to talk to you. I've told her a little of your story.'

The two women kiss each other once more and marvel at their shared name.

'I have a tui which comes to sing to me every morning,' the older woman tells Frances. She mimics the sound three times over and gives a little laugh.

As Frances tells her about her mother being on the train at Tangiwai and the woman who took her into her house and helped her, Tui nods her head in recognition.

'That would be my Aunty Tui. She died last year just a few days before she turned eighty. She lived in the forestry camp for many years and then when her children were grown up, she and her husband moved to a town further north. He died many years ago now. She told me about the terrible train accident and all the people who were looking for their loved ones. We also lost one of our cousins, Rawiri. Aunty Tui was a grand old lady. Like another grandmother to me.'

They sit together quietly, each thinking of their lost ones.

'Are your parents still alive?' Tui asks.

'My father died a few years ago. My mother is still alive. She lives very quietly back in England. She never recovered from losing her baby.'

Tui looks directly into Frances' eyes. 'Of course she wouldn't, would she? Have you recovered, though?'

'It happened long before I was born. But I think I inherited the sadness.'

'That's not unusual. For us Maori, the dead are never far from our thoughts. But we draw strength from them. They don't want us to keep mourning. Perhaps it's time for you to let her go.'

It is the second time that someone has seemed to understand her loss for her sister yet challenged her grief. Frances feels both stirred up and relieved, as if she can start to let go of an uncomfortable emotion that has gripped her all her life.

'Did the accident affect the way you think of the mountains?' Frances asks.

'No,' Tui answers swiftly. 'We knew something bad would

happen there. It was predicted for many years. There was a lot of fear when we heard the Queen was coming from England. A white heron was sighted after the announcement and some of the old people saw this as a sign of great sorrow to come. They used to talk about it on the marae, in our meeting house.

'Tangiwai means weeping waters. Or it can also mean a place of deluging water. It has always been a place where you have to be careful. When the Pakeha built bridges there across the path of the volcano a long time ago, my ancestors knew there would be trouble. What are you expecting the volcano to do, stop being a volcano?'

'Are you frightened it will happen again?'

'We live with the mountains. We don't live in fear but we live in respect. It will happen again sometime. It always does.'

'Do you think we should try to stop it happening by doing some work at the Crater Lake?'

Tui guffaws. 'No, of course not. You can't stop a volcano. There's always a reason these things happen. Whether it's an eruption or a flood.'

Taking Frances' hand, she leads her back to the others before adding, 'There's always a meaning. It's not for you to interfere.'

'But don't you want warnings of when it might happen?'

'We'll know when it's going to happen.'

'How?'

Tui looks at her for a few seconds and then shakes her head slowly. 'We just know.'

CHAPTER TWENTY-TWO

❧

'Frances, a group of us are going to the pub tonight. I thought you might like to come.'

Sam's invitation takes her by surprise and before she can think of an excuse she has agreed to go. They have just completed a long day of data analysis in the laboratory and he seems to be trying hard to compensate for his previous behaviour.

'Watch yourself, Frances, Sam has some pretty disreputable friends,' Theo laughs.

'Why don't you come along and look after me then,' she suggests, hoping he will agree.

'I'd love to but . . . well, you know how it is. I don't like leaving Sue alone at night and she's not keen on the pub herself.'

'Talking of disreputable, did I see you having coffee with that Carmody guy who was at the meeting?' Frances asks, looking directly at Sam as they leave the office.

'Me? I don't think so,' he says uncertainly.

'I'm sure I saw him with you at a café in town the other week,' she persists.

'Oh, that could be right. Now I remember — I was having a coffee and he sat down to have a chat. Just a coincidence, that's all. Don't look so worried,' he adds when he sees her eyes widen.

'I'm not. Just thought it was odd, that's all.'

She accompanies Sam two blocks towards the pub in the main street. Loud rock music greets them as they push through into the biggest bar.

'Sam, over here!'

He takes Frances' hand and leads her through thronging groups of people who, from their loud conversations and singing, sound as though they have been drinking for some hours. Sitting on a group of bar stools around an elevated table covered in empty and half-full glasses of beer and wine are three men and two women in their late twenties and early thirties.

'Hi there, Sam. How're you going? Who's this then?'

Sam has his arm around Frances in a possessive way that makes her feel extremely uncomfortable. She slips away from him and offers her hand to the man who greeted them.

'Frances Nelson, I've recently arrived in Taupo.'

'I'm Aaron Priestley. We've heard all about you already from Sam.'

Sam grins sheepishly, then introduces her to the others.

'We've all known each other for years — since I arrived in Taupo,' Aaron says. 'We meet here far too often. Glad you could join us.' As he pulls a stool over for her he asks, 'How's the crater situation? Heard the Maoris are causing trouble as usual.'

Frances feels them all looking at her for her answer. 'It's a very divisive issue,' she says. 'Everything's being negotiated at the moment. I don't think it's straightforward at all. Everyone's entitled to have a say and it *is* a sacred area for the Maori. They feel their relationship to the land so deeply.'

The men at the table laugh at her response. 'Easy to tell

you're new around here. You'll learn, love, that no matter how many concessions we make, they'll just want more and more — more land, more money, more rights until there'll be nothing left for any of us. We'll be strangers in our own country,' Aaron says. 'And make no mistake, it's just as much our country. Drinks?' He moves to the bar and returns with a beer for Sam and a glass of white wine for Frances.

At first, she wishes she could leave but as the conversation moves on to other subjects, she starts to relax and enjoy their company. The two women are high-school teachers and tell her stories about their pupils and the town and some of the local gossip.

When one of them goes to the bar, her friend, Tania, leans over to Frances.

'Tess used to go out with your Sam before he was married,' she whispers. 'Then she discovered she preferred women and came out. He wasn't very impressed!'

'He's not my boyfriend. I don't know why you'd think that.'

'He certainly gives that impression. Sorry about that, I didn't mean to imply anything. It's just that he's talked a bit about you and we thought . . . sorry.'

'What happened to his wife?' Frances asks, thinking she has discovered the fount of all local gossip.

'Anna. She disappeared. One week she was with him, the next gone. Then we heard she'd run off with one of the timber workers from the next town. A Maori guy. Sam was really destroyed by that.'

'What's all the whispering about, girls?' Sam interrupts them.

'Just hearing a few local stories,' Frances looks at him apologetically, feeling caught out. 'Let me buy a round of drinks.'

As she places her order she sees a familiar reflection in the mirror behind the bar. Tori Maddison is sitting with an attractive Maori woman at a table near the door. They are drinking together and as she turns around she sees him lean over and kiss her on the cheek. Frances has the same gnawing feeling in her stomach she had when she saw Damon with the woman at the conference. Unsteadily, she returns to the table with the tray of drinks.

Frances feels foolish. She knows Tori owes her nothing. There is no relationship between them and she thinks how ridiculous she was to think that there could be: a woman with her background from the other side of the world and a man with a proud heritage he has no intention of compromising.

Sam moves closer and again puts his arm around her. This time she doesn't resist but leans into him and quickly drinks the entire glass of wine.

'Frances.' She turns to see Tori standing next to her. He is smiling but looks at her shyly.

'Hello,' she says in a voice that sounds strange even to her.

'Who invited you?' Sam sneers. 'This is a private party.' He has been drinking quickly and his face is flushed.

Tori backs away, his eyes narrowing, hard and hurting. He turns and walks quickly towards the door, beckoning the woman at the table to follow.

'Good riddance,' Sam says while the men join his laughter. The women glance and grimace at Frances, who pulls away from Sam's embrace.

'I've got to call the States tonight and we have an early start. Thanks for the drinks. Good to meet you all.'

Before Sam can react, she has crossed the bar and walked into the night. At first she strides quickly, heart thudding. Then she starts to run, the tears trickling down her face. The night air is as cold as a steel knife.

CHAPTER TWENTY-THREE

W hy the rush, Tori?' Mata has to run to try to catch her brother as he charges down the street. He doesn't answer so she streaks up to him and tries to link her arm in his. He shakes her away and she can see from the grim set of his face that he is extremely angry. When they reach his car she quickly jumps into the front seat as he starts the engine.

'What the hell is eating you?' Mata yells at him. 'Have I said something to upset you? I was only telling you about Cheryl because I think you need to know.'

Tori quickly pulls out into the traffic and accelerates hard. 'I'll drop you back at Mum's,' he says quietly.

Neither of them speak for a few minutes and then Tori bursts out laughing.

'What? Why are you laughing, you idiot?'

'I'm sorry, sis. It's nothing to do with you or Cheryl for that matter. Funny you said that though, because I don't think anyone else has upset me as much as her before tonight. I must be moving on, as the shrinks say.'

'I think you're bloody mad. Who then?'

'Those fucking scientists. Back there in the pub.'

'You mean Sam Hawks?'

'Yeah. And there's a new one. A woman. Thought she was different but I guess I was wrong.'

'Is she the one the kids were telling me about? Didn't you take her up the mountain?'

Tori is silent until Mata prods him hard in the ribs.

'Fancy her, do you? Normally you wouldn't give a damn what that arsehole Hawks says to you. What did she say?'

'Nothing really. It's just that she's obviously tied up with him. And you know he's mixing with Carmody so I have an awful feeling I might have been conned. You know we've got a fight on our hand with the bulldozer thing. I think Theo Rush has his heart in the right place but I have a feeling the power is shifting away from him.'

Mata looks across to her brother and reaches across to stroke his shoulder.

'Hey, Tori, you don't know that for sure. The kids liked her and they're good judges.'

Tori nods. 'Maybe. I can't tell.'

They quickly reach the outskirts of Taupo and the ute's headlights shine on a possum dashing across the highway.

'Missed,' Tori says under his breath.

They pass the dark forests on one side of the road and the moonlit lake on the other.

'So she's coming back? Cheryl.'

'I'm not sure, Tori. Just what I heard. She rang Mum the other day and said she was breaking up with that guy in Auckland. Says she's coming soon to see Moana and Hemi. Mum wasn't sure if she meant for a few days or for good.' Mata pauses to study her brother's face. 'Do you still want her back?'

'No. I mean I don't think so.' Tori can hear the emotion in his own voice.

He pulls up outside a line of small houses set back from the road.

'I'm moving on, remember?' He grins at his sister as she gets out of the car. 'I won't come in. Just want to get home. See you tomorrow and we can get back to the family business.'

He puts a favourite Dire Straits CD into the player and taps the steering wheel in time to the beat of 'Brothers in Arms' as he drives quickly towards his empty house. He feels rattled by Cheryl's imminent arrival, but the image that stays in his mind is of Frances and Sam.

CHAPTER TWENTY-FOUR

❧

T he usual,' Frances tells the waitress at the café she frequents most days.

'Sure, Frances. Won't be long.'

Sitting at an outside table, she flicks through the paper quickly then puts it aside, closes her eyes and feels the morning sun caress her face. Then, as she glances across the road by the lake she sees a familiar figure. Tori Maddison's bulky silhouette is unmistakable and he is heading her way, weaving deftly through the traffic. He hasn't seen her and at first she considers pulling up the collar of her jacket and hiding her face in her newspaper but instead she calls out to him.

'Tori, over here.'

He walks over without smiling, greets her briefly and begins to move away.

'Would you like to join me?' she says. 'My shout.'

He turns to face her, noticing how the sun catches her shining hair and eyes. 'I've a lot to do . . .'

'Please.' She surprises herself with her insistence.

He sits opposite her and orders a pot of tea.

'Tori, I just wanted to apologise for the other night. It was out of my control. I was upset myself and I left just after you. Sam takes things too far.'

At first he says nothing, then he points across to the lake. 'The fish are on the move. All heading upstream to breed. Only the strongest will survive,' he says.

'Is that what you think this is all about?' she asks. 'That it's the fighters among us who'll win?'

'Perhaps. I thought you might be different to the others. You say you're sorry but you looked pretty comfortable with that group.'

'You read too much into it. I met them for the first time that night. They're friends of Sam's and we just met them for a drink.'

'I'm sorry, Frances, I hadn't realised you and Sam . . .'

'We're not — we work together and that's it. Sam just had a bit too much to drink and was being overfriendly.'

He looks at her doubtfully.

'Anyway, I guess I hadn't realised you were involved with somebody yourself. Was that your wife?'

For the first time he laughs. 'My sister. My sister Mata. She was just up from Wellington for a few days. Family business.'

'I guess there's been misunderstanding on both sides.'

'Yes, I should have remembered the advice I was given by my grandmother when I was a little kid. She said, "When it comes to gossip, believe nothing that you hear and half what you see." I'll have to remember that in future.'

'We both will,' Frances says. 'I saw how important family is to you when we went up the mountain. And I envy you being able to go back generation after generation and have some connection to those people. I don't have much family.'

As he throws her a look of sympathy, she asks him about his wife. The question floors him, pain crossing his face. 'I didn't intend to be living alone,' he says at last. 'It wasn't what I wanted but it's what I accept.'

He pauses and stares at the tea he's swirling around in a large white cup. Eventually he turns to her with a question in his eyes.

'Oh . . . well, I'm on my own now too. And it wasn't what I planned either.'

'So we're a couple of dumpees?' he says and they laugh together easily.

He leans towards her. 'I'm glad I'm on my own otherwise I mightn't have given you a second glance,' he says. 'You remember we talked about the bund to save the fishing. I was wondering if you'd be interested in coming out on the river with me and some of my clients. Maybe you could catch one of those fish for yourself.'

CHAPTER TWENTY-FIVE

When the alarm clock wakes her, Frances can't believe it is already five in the morning. It feels like only minutes since her head hit the pillow. But she's looking forward to the day. If the lahar happens and the dam on the river's upper reaches isn't in place, the river and lake will be severely polluted and the trout hatchery destroyed. She wants to see the area for herself.

As she showers, her mind drifts back to Damon and their comfortable life together in Seattle. She still hasn't replied to his emails. A new one has come in every few days and there's a sort of pleading coming through his words now which gives her some pleasure. As the hot water pours over her body, she realises her anger has dissipated and her heartache eased. In fact, she hasn't felt that gnawing in her stomach for a while. She considers letting him know about her new life. In her own good time.

Although it's only a few months since her fresh start in New Zealand, she feels sometimes that, in her heart and mind, she's travelling on a fast-moving train across great distances.

When she hears a vehicle pull up outside she quickly finishes dressing, grabs her parka and bag. Expecting to see the tourists, she is surprised to find that Tori is alone.

'Hop in,' he calls. 'We'll get the others on the way.' His warm eyes and smile envelop her. She willingly returns his gaze.

'This should be a good payday, and we should have a good time as well. Win–win, eh? I've brought some gear for you too, Frances. Thought you might like to test your wits against some of our wily trout.'

The town is dark and still with little sign of life as they drive through the empty streets. Within ten minutes, they pull into the driveway of a luxury fishing lodge hidden among towering poplar trees. Dressed warmly in expensive outdoor clothing, the two men and a woman are already waiting outside, their breath punctuating the cool air.

'Morning all. I'm Tori Maddison and this is your carriage.'

'Thank you, sir.' One of the men doffs his cap and, seeing Frances in the front, ushers the others into the back of the vehicle. They have brought some of their favourite rods and he helps Tori load them into the rear of the four-wheel-drive next to a large picnic basket.

'We hear you're the hottest guide in town. You know where all the big trophy fish are?'

'I know where they've been,' Tori laughs. 'Can't guarantee they'll be still there though. We'll just have to wait and see.'

As they drive along a winding back road away from Lake Taupo where they glimpse fast-moving stretches of the Tongariro River between stands of trees, the newcomers talk excitedly about the day ahead.

The men, Paul and Tom, in their mid-fifties, are lifelong friends, bonded since student days by a mutual love of fishing that has survived the comings and goings of more temporary relationships. The woman, Christine, is newly married to Paul. It's the second pairing for both of them and when they gaze into each other's eyes they reveal a passion still alive with sexual promise. Tom lost his wife to breast cancer two years earlier so for now there's just the three of them. They have recently fished in Alaska and thrive in the tradition of fishermen the world over, swapping yarns about their best catches and the ones that invariably got away.

Tori loves the chat and they joke and taunt each other for the rest of the ride.

'Good, we're first here, always pays to be first,' Tori tells them as they pull off the road into a clearing carved out of the bush. 'It's just a few minutes' walk to the river.' They can hear the roar of the water as they push their way through damp bushes to the river's edge carrying their rods and waders.

Swift shallow water pours over large metal-grey stones, into deeper pools and around a bend at the spot Tori has chosen to start the day. A sunless dawn casts a misty pall over the river and a light rain starts to fall. Frances shivers in the early light, her hair still wet from the shower, and thinks longingly of her warm bed. But the high spirits of the others lift her and she joins in, drawing up the long rubber waders and pulling the hood of her jacket over her head.

Tori helps each of them to assemble their rods and select a lure. The Americans have listened to his advice and brought light gear and small flies and nymphs so they can stalk the fish up and down the river.

'Here, I've brought you one of my specials that Moana made,' Tori says as he ties a small dark-coloured nymph onto the rod he has brought for Frances. 'These are good for the river at this time of year. The fish think they're the real thing, tasty little grubs.'

He encourages her to walk out a couple of metres into the stream. Holding her waist from behind, he shows her how to cast the line in and out of the bubbling water. She practises a few times until he is satisfied. 'If you get lucky, hold it firmly and call out if you need help!'

Frances has never been interested in fishing before but she can see how the sport could seduce her. The river is so alive and she feels exhilarated as the water gushes around her legs and hips and she understands the joy of just being there. Catching a fish would be a bonus.

She flicks the line in and out, in and out. Suddenly, she glimpses a long shape in a calmer patch of water to her left. It is deep down and cruising towards her. Then it turns away as if to swim back upstream. Frances pitches the fly right over the shape. Her aim is accurate and the nymph hits the water and drifts on the surface. The trout rises to the top and she sees it open its mouth and take the hidden hook. Instinctively, Frances raises the rod and feels a strong pull as the trout breaks away to try and escape upstream.

'Tori, help! I've got one.' She feels her knees wobble and her stomach tighten as she is gripped by fear and excitement. Her feet feel unstable on the rocks below the water as the pull on the line increases.

'Just relax and try and keep steady.' He calms her by holding her arm. 'You're doing well. Hold on tight. There's going to be a fight.'

For the first time in her life, Frances feels the thrill of the hunter. The fish is trying to bore its way into the white water upstream and her pulse quickens as she winds the line in. She has to hang on with all her might. Her hood slips off her head and she feels light rain drizzling down her nose and her cheeks, heightening her pleasure. The line is slender and she worries it will snap. The fish leaps into the air and crashes back into the water, shattering the surface into tiny splashes like thousands of shards of broken glass.

The line holds fast and Tori whispers her encouragement, words that soothe her beating heart. He moves behind her in the stream, his strong arms holding hers, steadying her. Gradually she reels in the struggling fish. As it comes alongside, Tori takes the net from under his arm, bends over and captures the fish, making sure he keeps it in the water.

A large rainbow, about 45 centimetres long, twists in its woven prison, the sight filling Frances with a mixture of pity and admiration.

'Do you want to keep it or release it?' Tori asks.

'I think I'll let it go,' Frances says, not wanting to kill it on the spot.

'Now that's what I call beginner's luck,' he tells her flatteringly. 'We'd better at least take some evidence home.'

Tori beckons to Tom to bring the camera over, then turns to her. 'Take hold of it gently in your hands and keep it in the water,' he instructs her, 'and I'll show you how to release it safely.'

Like a child anxious to please, she reaches into the cold water and struggles to still the wild, slippery fish writhing between her palms.

She watches as Tori produces a pair of long-nosed pliers from his jacket pocket and, with a quick but careful twist, skilfully whisks the hook out of the trout's gills. Taking his camera from the American, who is peering at the fish in astonishment, he steps back into the stream. 'Hold it horizontally and point its nose upstream. Grip it firmly and smile. Show him who's boss.'

Frances laughs like a triumphant gladiator as Tori takes the photo and the other three cheer her on, envious of her victory.

'OK, get ready to release it. Ease your grip and let the fish feel you let it go.'

Frances feels a flush of relief fill her body as she lets go. The fish flicks its tail and shimmers away, swimming back up through the clear emerald-green water of the river.

'I can't believe you let it go,' Tom says as they return to the riverbank.

'It happens more and more now,' Tori says. 'A lot of fishermen are releasing at least part of their catches because they know that the ones you return to the river today will be the ones you may be able to catch tomorrow.'

'Or someone else!' Tom exclaims.

'In the old days when I was growing up here, men would take out massive amounts of fish — maybe a dozen a day if they were good. If that kept up, there would be nothing left. Now you're only allowed three a day each but many don't even worry about that.'

Feeling elated but drained, Frances tells Tori she is happy to leave the fishing to the others for a while. She watches as Tori helps to find Paul and Christine a promising place together, but then follows as he leads Tom along the now muddy bank, past weeping willows dipping their delicate leaves into the river, further upstream and around a bend.

Tori helps Tom tie on a new nymph, then beckons him to follow and signals Frances to stay where she is. Tom finds a spot near a pool, standing thigh deep in the water. He flicks the line with a sure confidence, his brow creased in concentration, his jaw determined.

Tori has returned to Frances when they all see one of the shapes move to the surface. The fish suddenly takes the nymph with tremendous speed and dives. It panics and looks to escape, boring upstream into the white water of the rapids. Tom slowly moves with it, but holding fast, ready for the contest.

He plays the fish as it tries to get away. It leaps out and tries again to escape, pushing into the white-capped current. Beads of sweat mingle with raindrops on Tom's tanned and smoothly shaved face. For twenty minutes, man and fish fight, one for glory, the other for life. The trout is tiring, coming out of the water. Tom hauls it into the shallows, wades over, his large feet dragging through the water, and flips it on its side. Marked with golden and speckled patterns, its body is big and shining. Fins quivering, its broad, perfectly shaped tail arches and splashes.

'I'm keeping this one,' Tom calls out and gives a thumbs-up sign to Tori, who goes to help with the final ritual.

The men net the fish and carry it, still bucking, to a small island of stone and shingle in the river. While Tori holds it fast on some rocks, Tom raps it hard on the head. One strike and it's dead. Frances feels sick, but Tom is laughing as he carries his trophy back to show the others. It's large enough to mount: Tori will hand it to a taxidermist to prepare for its final resting place above some distant hearth.

Paul and Christine have had no luck but share their friend's excitement as Tori and Tom carefully wrap the trout and pack it into an ice bin.

Christine pulls Frances aside. 'This is so good for Tom,' she whispers in her soft accent. 'He doesn't laugh much since his wife died.'

Now ravenous, they down coffee and sandwiches from the picnic basket. The rain has stopped and a few rays of sunshine warm them. Another four-wheel-drive pulls up but, spotting them, quickly leaves.

Tori guides the others to places he has fished for years, generously sharing his knowledge. Frances hears laughter upstream. Tom is having a lucky day and catches another two large trout. One he releases; the other he will take back to the chef at their lodge to prepare for their evening meal.

Leaving the others, Tori comes to sit with Frances, who is reading under a large willow. He looks dreamily along the stretch of river.

'One of my uncles was one of the first Maori to use a rod,' he tells her. 'Some very rich Englishmen used to come here and fish about eighty years ago and my uncle used to take them around the rivers. They gave the rod as a gift and then more and more Maori started to fish the Pakeha way.'

'How did you catch them before?'

'We tickled them to death,' he says, his face breaking into a grin as he sees Frances' incredulous expression. 'Just like this.' He reaches under her arms and tickles her and they roll about laughing as she tries unsuccessfully to break the strength of his arms to tickle him back.

A gust of wind interrupts their play, a shower of tiny leaves falling over them and blowing onto the clear waters.

'You wouldn't want to lose this, would you?' she asks, resting against his shoulder. 'You know if the lahar breaks through, you could lose this environment. All the research shows the path of the lahar could come right down the Tongariro River and into Taupo. The fish would die.'

He looks at her and sighs. 'Yeah, I'm trying to persuade the others we need to do something. It's not always easy. There's some jealousy too, I think. Some of them point to me and say I'm just acting for myself. I tell them they could do this too but they can't be bothered.'

As they hear the others approach, Tori gets to his feet. The cool air fills the warm void he has left behind. She watches him as he walks away, feeling a lightness of being that she has almost forgotten.

CHAPTER TWENTY-SIX

≈

As winter approaches, the days are noticeably shorter and the sun has barely risen when Frances arrives at the office. Theo has asked her to come in early as time is running out to finish testing the mountain's warning system in time for the skiing season.

He has beaten her there by half an hour and is sitting at his desk playing with some new equipment, a look of annoyance creeping across his face.

'Here's that gear we've been waiting for. It's supposed to help us detect any seepage in the tephra dam. When you're up there today you and Sam can try and make some more measurements so we can feed it back to the IT people for a computer modelling system.'

She notices he seemed tired and lacking his usual energy.

'Is everything OK?'

'Sure, just feeling the political pressure at the moment.' Looking up at her he adds, 'Not your worry. How are things with you? I'm sorry I've been a bit preoccupied and have probably neglected you. Are you settling in all right?'

Frances tells Theo about her visit to the sacred springs with Tori. 'I understand the Maori philosophy better now. They seem to have much more trust in the future than we do. It's hard to reconcile sometimes when I'm used to wanting control. I want to use science to prevent more disasters but I have to respect their point of view.'

Theo looks at her thoughtfully. 'Yes, I had to struggle with a lot of those conflicts too. I'm still getting leaned on to ignore Maori wishes and blast the dam, but I'm trying to keep them at bay. That's why it's so important to have the warning system working as well as possible.'

She is just about to mention seeing Sam with Carmody when Sam emerges from a back office, where he has been packing the gear for that day's trip up the mountain. Sam glances at her in a half-hearted greeting. Frances isn't relishing the hours ahead. Things have been a little tense between them and she wishes Theo was coming.

As a safety measure, they check the signals beaming back from the summit and two other spots on the slopes where they have placed the microphones, seismometers and barometers. Frances points to the steadily moving graph on the computer screen and the printout from the previous twelve hours.

'Look, there have been some small tremors around the mountain. But I don't think they're anything to worry about.' She checks the second monitor with the printout of the sound waves from deep inside the volcano. 'It's like listening to it belching,' she says. 'Sounds pretty steady.'

The temperature on the mountain is registering zero degrees with a wind factor of minus ten. They add snow jackets and trousers, hats, gloves and balaclavas to the pile of essential equipment.

By the time they reach the chopper pad alongside the lake, Luke Gallagher is ready for take-off. Double-checking that Sam and Frances are properly strapped in, he tests their headphones are operating so they can communicate through the intercom, talking to each of them in turn. After clearing their flight path over the radio with air-traffic control, he lifts the chopper slowly up, the wind-stream blowing up a splintered fan of water below them. Within minutes they are skirting over the lake towards the summit. Frances loves the thrill of low flying and the bird's-eye view of the shining water. She cranes over for a closer look when they fly over a mysterious island in the lake's centre. Tiny and heavily treed with dark, primeval-looking species, the island looks bleak and forbidding and Frances can see why the locals believe it is haunted by ghosts.

'Have you been to the island?' Frances asks Luke, taken aback by the reverberating sound of her own voice.

'No, don't want to either,' he says, raising an eyebrow at her.

'I have,' Sam tells them over the vibrations in the cabin. 'I went out there in a kayak but I wouldn't go back. Not after what I saw.'

'What was that?'

'There were two of us there — or should I say three. My friend and I went ashore and found a cave. Inside there was this dead Maori guy. He was sitting up wearing a feather cloak and looking straight at us. We nearly died of fright and got the hell out of there as quickly as we could.'

Luke laughs. 'Was he pointing a bone at you?'

'We didn't stick around long enough to find out. I just know I wouldn't go back.'

Tori had told Frances the island used to be a burial ground and only certain Maori elders were allowed to go there.

'Serves you right for trespassing,' she scolds Sam. 'How would you like it if strangers were going around looking at your dead relatives?'

Sam doesn't reply. He looks away from the others sulkily and

Frances regrets talking to him so sharply. She sighs: it's going to be a long day.

Soon they leave the water behind and are flying over the densely wooded areas leading to the mountains. The day is clear and the clouds high enough so they can land safely. Luke ascends rapidly, then slows as they approach the summit of Ruapehu, already dusted with the first snowfalls of winter.

'Hold on, everyone, we're going down. It looks pretty icy down there. We'll be on the ground soon.'

He lands expertly on a snow-covered plateau a short distance from the Crater Lake, lets the motor idle and then switches it off.

'Try to be back in ninety minutes,' he urges them as they unload their equipment from the storage hatch. 'The weather's unpredictable and we don't want to be caught up here.'

They'd brought along ice picks and crampons for their boots and this time, in deference to the cold, even Sam has traded his shorts for waterproof trousers.

A freezing wind bites Frances' face as she climbs through the snow towards the Dome Shelter, reminding her of the cold treks she has made up Mount St Helens. She muses that, for someone who prefers warm weather to cold, she has chosen the wrong job. But she pushes her body along, cursing the weight of the backpack, which makes the slipperiness of the icy rocks much harder to negotiate.

Fresh snow covers the shelter and they clear away some banked up against the door so they can check the equipment inside.

'It's all working perfectly,' Frances says with satisfaction as she tests the machinery. 'I'll check the pagers are working and then I'll lock up here and see you at the lake, Sam.'

She punches in the first of a list of ten numbers on her cellphone and sends the message. 'Testing reception from summit. Please respond.' She sends the same message to the other nine numbers, each part of the network of monitors for the early warning system. In spite of the sophisticated technology behind the system, it is the human link that will evacuate the area. This is the part that always makes Frances anxious, but her mobile registers the first reply and the others follow in quick succession. She breathes a sigh of relief as she locks the shelter and heads for the crater.

With the first falls of snow, the summit is quite different from the moonscape that greeted Frances on her first visit. Some lower craggy peaks still protrude brown through the whiteness and the rock periphery of the lake is exposed where the heat of the volcanic water has already melted it.

As she climbs down towards the lake she can see Sam trying to retrieve something from the steaming water with a probe. He suddenly reaches down and picks up some sort of white object, which he is obviously trying to hide.

'What have you found?' Frances confronts him.

Slowly and reluctantly, like a schoolboy caught out, Sam holds out one hand. It is empty. Then from behind his back he produces a skull.

'Gotcha!' he yells.

'My God, where do you think that's come from?' Frances recoils, shocked by the unexpected sight of the small, parchment-white relic of death. 'Who do you think it was?'

'How the hell would I know,' he says, clearly annoyed she has spotted his discovery. 'Could be a lost hiker or skier. Lots of people have gone missing up here over the years.'

'More likely to be Maori remains, don't you think? Isn't this supposed to be a burial place?'

'We could just pretend we never saw it,' Sam says matter-of-factly. 'I could just throw it back or tuck it under a rock. No one would ever know.'

'But of course you couldn't do that, could you, Sam? You know we'll have to take it back and report it.'

'How predictable you are.' He rounds on her. 'You realise this is going to complicate things up here. If you think the Maoris were difficult before, this will really up the ante.'

'I hardly think it's your prerogative to make those judgements.'

'No, you wouldn't, would you? But quite frankly I think you're losing your own judgement. You seemed to have forgotten you're a scientist, not a do-gooder for the Maori cause. Or maybe that Mr Maddison has got to you.' He goes to walk away, then turns swiftly and calls out, 'Here, catch!'

Sam tosses the skull in the air. Frances leaps forward to grab it before it hits the rocks, catches it and slips to the ground.

'What the fuck are you doing?' she yells at Sam. 'You're crazy!'

'Well, one of us is and I don't think it's me.' He picks up his pack and walks to the end of the lake where he starts taking water samples.

Frances is bursting with rage but she stays where she has landed and stares at the small skull nestled in her gloved hands. It looks so vulnerable. A man or a woman? Young or old? Who was left behind to mourn when this person died? How long has the skull rested at the top of the mountain? She touched skeletons during her university years but only in laboratories and felt little emotion about them. But to hold this now fills her with sadness. She traces her finger around the eye sockets and wonders whether the volcano had caused the death.

Standing up, she finds in her pack a pretty blue-and-white silk scarf Olivia gave her as a gift when she left Seattle. She carefully wraps the skull in it and places it in a plastic bag back inside the pack, making a mental note not to let her friend know what head the scarf ended up on.

As she turns and looks over the slopes towards Tangiwai she is filled with a new longing to know who found her sister and how they had felt. She knows she must contact Cedric again and see if she can discover more so she can lay some of her own ghosts to rest.

She sees that Sam has finished sampling the water and reluctantly joins him so they can take their survey measurements of the dam and probe it to provide new data for the computer model.

'Fortunately the snow hasn't built up too much around the dam. We can still measure it quite easily,' Sam says, refusing to meet her eye. 'Here, you take the reflector and I'll go across the other side with the survey gear.'

Frances was hoping he might apologise but she is learning that Sam Hawks never says sorry about anything.

'OK. Then I'll let Theo know about your find.'

Sam glares at her over his shoulder as he shuffles through the snow. Frances knows he's particularly narked because she could pull rank on him if she chose: her qualifications had put her above him in seniority.

The water level has risen another 15 centimetres and they insert new markers higher up the crater rim. When they finish and pack away their equipment, Frances dials Theo's cellphone.

'Hi, Frances, you're clear as a bell. How is it up there in the land of the gods today?'

'Funny you should say that, Theo. Maybe the gods are angry. Sam found a skull up here in the lake. I'm bringing it back.'

'Damn, that's not going to make life any easier,' he mutters. 'What's it look like?'

'I'm no expert but it looks pretty old. No idea where it has come from either. I've wrapped it carefully and have it in my backpack.'

'I'll have to alert the police. Not likely to be a crime but could be a missing person.'

Almost as an afterthought Frances adds, 'By the way, Theo, the water's a little higher today too.'

'You're full of good news, aren't you? See you when you get back.'

CHAPTER TWENTY-SEVEN

❧

The three of them have little to say as they flash down the Desert Road winding south from Taupo through the inhospitable Rangipo Desert. Sam is driving with Frances up front and Tori in the back seat. In spite of her objections, Theo has insisted Sam should be part of the visit to inspect the site recommended by the seismologists for the stopbank. 'We have to protect ourselves and it is important we have two people from our department there,' he told her.

Knowing Theo was busy with a media briefing about mountain safety for the ski season, Frances said nothing more. Since the dispute over the discovery of the skull, she felt there was little hope of friendship with Sam and the hostility between them was growing.

It is grey and overcast and the spindly sage-green vegetation looks menacing, poking up on both sides of the road like jagged weapons. Only the hardiest plants can grow here in the volcanic debris left over from the massive Taupo eruption which splintered once-mighty stands of ancient forests.

Sam accelerates the office's white four-wheel-drive to

overtake a slow-moving tourist caravan, one of dozens plying up and down the main road between Auckland and Wellington.

'Looks like we'll cop some rain today,' Tori remarks, pointing to the dark nimbus clouds settling on the eastern slopes of the volcanoes.

Twenty minutes later, they swerve off the main road onto a gravel track and Sam belts along the narrow access way climbing to the edge of the national park. A cloud of dust rises around them and small battalions of tiny sandflies suicide against the windscreen. Soon the track disappears and they bump their way over piles of pumice, rocks and tussock. As if to make a point, Sam screeches the brakes as he stops near a wooden post festooned with red reflectors.

'Since the '95 eruption, the point where a lahar could spill over has changed dramatically,' he says, retrieving his professional role and breaking the tension. As they walk to the top of a low-lying slope of Ruapehu, Sam points to a series of markers and templates already placed there.

'They show the size of the stopbank. You can see it will be very big, about three hundred metres long and three to four metres high, and if a lahar forces its way down the valley, it should stop it spilling into the Tongariro River system, where it would do a lot of damage.'

'It's a lot bloody bigger than I expected,' Tori says, kicking some loose stones. 'What will it be made of?'

'Gravel mainly, held together by cement. It has to be very strong because the force of a lahar is massive.'

'I think the iwi will have trouble with this. I can see the benefit to save the fishing and the flora and fauna, but a lot of the others don't agree with me. Does it have to be so large?'

'Well, it would if you want to save your own fishing,' Sam says, his voice laced with sarcasm.

Relieved Sam and Tori are at least being civil to each other,

Frances decides to stay out of the conversation. She shelters near the vehicle, instinctively keeping her distance as the two men pace around the remote outpost. A strong wind blows through her and she tries to block it out by zipping her jacket up to the neck. She watches them kicking pieces of ash and pumice out of their way as they immerse themselves in conversation. Soon they stop walking and are facing each other, still deep in discussion. The wind is whistling through her hair yet it picks up the crescendo in their voices.

'You arsehole!'

She thinks it is Tori's voice. She sees Sam strike him, his fist hitting Tori's head.

As she runs towards them a sudden roar of thunder booms directly overhead. A fork of lightning rips through the leaden sky. They are the swift overture for a heavy downpour.

'Stop,' Frances cries out, suddenly frightened by the raw-knuckled violence before her. But neither her pleas nor the cold drenching rain do anything to extinguish their red-hot anger.

'Please . . . please stop this!' Frances reaches the men, arms now locked around each other's shoulders like Roman wrestlers. She pulls at Tori and as he releases his grip and turns to her, Sam punches his chest.

'You bastard,' she screams at him.

He backs away. 'You bitch. Of course you would side with him!'

Sam, rain mingling with a trickle of rich crimson blood dribbling from his nose, retreats down the hill.

'I'm sorry, Frances,' Tori says as she surveys his face for damage. 'He threw the first punch. But I should have walked away.'

'I saw that. What did he say?'

'We were talking about bulldozing the Crater Lake again. He called me a fucking hypocrite for opposing it but supporting building the dam to protect the fishing. Then he started talking about you. I'm afraid it got very personal and I guess I lost it.'

'What a bloody mess,' she says. 'At least you don't look too bad. Probably a few bruises, though. Let's get out of this damn rain,' Frances says, taking his arm and leading him downhill.

Sam is in the vehicle, dabbing his face with a tissue. He starts the engine and accelerates as she runs over to open the passenger door.

'Don't even think about leaving us here!' she shouts.

He glares at her. 'Wouldn't dream of it,' he says, his words dripping venom.

Tori climbs heavily into the back. 'Are you OK?' He taps Sam on the shoulder.

Sam shrugs him off. 'Yeah, really great.'

Frances radios the office and is relieved to hear Theo's voice. Ignoring Sam's anxious glances, she tells him just that they are returning.

'You might be interested to know we've got the results of the skull you guys found,' she hears him say in reply. 'Tell you about it when you get back.'

As they exchange the bumpy track for the highway, Tori breaks the silence.

'What skull?' he asks.

'Ah, we still have secrets, do we?' Sam's voice is full of bitterness as he sneers at Frances and catches Tori's puzzled look in the rear-vision mirror.

She shakes her head and stays quiet, embarrassed and unsure of what to say. Tori respects the silence. For now, he will ask nothing more.

The Card Players

We were playing cards, the four of us — Mervyn, Charles, Rawiri and me. Three of us were old friends and we were heading north for a holiday. We'd bought some pies and chips at Taihape and we'd smuggled a few beers onto the train as you weren't supposed to drink. We invited the Maori chap who was sitting opposite us to join us. We needed a fourth for our game and he seemed like a good sort. A bit shy at first but he turned out to be quite a joker and by the way he shuffled the cards I could tell he was no novice. We were having a great old time over a game of euchre. I remember passing through Tangiwai Station quite slowly — I recall seeing the name but we didn't stop. We were in the carriage immediately behind the engine and a lot of people had already dozed off. But we weren't tired and wanted to play on. I was feeling good as I was winning. I had just scored another trick and was shuffling the deck.

Suddenly we were all thrown forward. Our carriage was hurtling off the bridge at a terrific speed and I was tumbling in the air. It was like falling down a steep hill and I was turning somersaults. We hit the river with a terrific jolt and the water started pouring in around us. Everyone was screaming. The water gushed through and the lights went out so I could hardly see anything.

The carriage landed on its side and I worked out where the windows were and called out to everyone to crawl through the broken windows. I climbed through one and cut my leg on a piece of glass. But before I could stop myself, I slipped and next thing I was caught up in the torrent and swept half a mile downstream. I kept being pushed under by the strong current and I could feel all my clothes being ripped off me. I swallowed lots of water and at one stage wondered if I would make it. I managed to find the strength to swim to the side and crawled ashore.

We were the lucky ones, my friends and I. We met on the river-bank back near where the bridge collapsed. But we couldn't find Rawiri. We looked everywhere that night but there was no sign of him. We felt bad, guilty even. Not that we knew him very well. It's just that when you sit down to play a hand of cards with a man, there's a bond.

The rest of us had come out of it relatively unscathed. Mervyn had bad burns on his feet and hands, though. When he got out of the carriage he had leapt onto the wrecked locomotive in front. Even though it was half in the water, it was still scorching hot from its own fire and seared into his flesh.

Some of the soldiers' wives came to help us. They wrapped us in grey blankets and we huddled together eating fruitcake and cups of tea laced with rum.

Other survivors were brought up to sit with us. There was one family who arrived looking like monsters from the deep. They were covered in engine oil and silt from head to foot. The parents and their son and daughter had been in the carriage behind us. They were all asleep when the train crashed and woke up in the water. They all squeezed out of a window onto the roof of the carriage which was upside down in the water. They said there was only about 9 inches of the roof sticking above the water and they had clung onto it, all holding their breath as a huge wave washed over them. They hung on for half an hour before being rescued.

We sat there for at least an hour. By then the place was crawling with people; soldiers and police, ordinary people from surrounding towns who had come to help. Then there were the other passengers and of course the bodies. They were piling people up by the river as they pulled them out. I kept going over to see if Rawiri was among them. But I never saw him.

I felt like I was caught up in a nightmare. We were all shivering with the cold. The river had been freezing and all of us were coughing from the silt that we had swallowed along with the water.

Soon a truck arrived to take us away. Mervyn had to go to the army hospital to have his burns treated. The rest of us stayed the night in the house of one of the forestry workers who lived in a camp nearby. Next day, we all went home to Wellington. None of us felt like going on holiday after that.

John Frederick, 21, passenger from Masterton

CHAPTER TWENTY-EIGHT

❧

'Come on, Frances, walk with me ahead of the men for the welcome.' Mata motions her forward onto the marae, located on a back street of a small settlement on the main highway. They walk through an elaborately carved gateway painted in traditional red and white onto a well-mown lawn that flows towards the meeting house. The day is crisp, and white cotton-wool clouds appear glued onto the still blue canvas of the sky.

'The women go in front but the men like to speak first,' Mata tells her as they walk slowly across towards the carved A-shaped building. 'They like to think they're in charge even though we women know they're not,' she says with an amused sidelong glance.

Younger than her brother by three years, Mata has offered to take Frances under her wing, promising to guide her through the rituals that will be demanded that day. She shares Tori's strong features — the smooth shiny brown skin, the clear dark eyes — but her cheekbones are even more pronounced with her black hair piled high on her head and secured with a white shark-bone comb. Her build is slimmer, emphasised by a well-cut purple jacket and skirt. A solicitor now working as a cultural adviser to a government department in Wellington, she travels home to help with iwi business when needed.

Theo trails closely behind, accompanied by a manager from their office. No stranger to the marae, he is comfortable with the ceremonies but anxious about what lies ahead.

'Good to keep the numbers up and Sam's not able to come, which I imagine you think is no bad thing,' he told Frances earlier as they were preparing for the meeting. 'I always feel like my head is on the chopping block when I go to the marae. The elders have a habit of putting you through the wringer and I think they enjoy seeing anyone from the government or a company squirm a little bit.'

As they both sifted through their papers for the meeting, Theo brought out a small square box from his desk drawer.

'Talking of heads, you know I'll have to disclose the discovery of the skull today?' he said. 'Our forensic people have confirmed it belonged to a young woman, pre-European, probably died in the early 1800s. Could be one of their forebears.'

'How do you think they will react?' Frances peered at the fragile relic, wondering again how the woman had died.

'I don't know, but it could delay what we want to do on the mountain.'

Foreseeing a conflict of interest, she hasn't mentioned the skull to Tori, resisting the temptation on several occasions. He hasn't mentioned it either but she suspects that he's waiting for her to raise the subject.

'By the way, do you like to sing?' Theo asked as they left the office, grinning at her puzzled look. 'Don't worry about it . . . you'll find out.'

She sighs and decides to give in to whatever the day will hold.

Wanting to make an impression, Frances has swapped her usual outdoor garb for an understated black designer suit she lashed out on before she left Seattle. It flatters her hips and flat stomach. She wears a powder-blue silk shirt to soften the 'I mean business' look she hopes will be effective when it's her turn to describe the early warning system.

A tall dignified-looking man of around 70 with tousled white hair brushed back off his long forehead is standing at the entrance to the meeting house, with Tori and several others mingling around him. Above the entrance is the carved wooden figure of a fierce warrior, two pieces of paua shell acting as his all-seeing eyes. As one of the women steps forward and starts chanting, her hands trembling in the air, Frances recognises her, and the poignant, powerful voice.

Mata whispers to her. 'Aunty Tui is one of our elders. She's singing the karanga. That's to call us in. Walk with me now. Stay close and I'll tell you what to do.'

When they are halfway across the lawn, Mata signals Frances to stop and bow her head.

'This is to show respect to the wharenui, the meeting house, and to the ancestors,' she whispers. 'And because you're new here you're considered to be waewae tau, or sacred, so you'll have to have this formal welcome before you are considered free of tapu.'

The elderly man comes forward and begins a new chant.

Frances feels the centuries shrink together as the sound punctures the air.

'That's Uncle Eruera. He's continuing the welcome. We can go to meet them now.'

As they move forward, he offers his hand. When Frances takes it, he leans down and presses his nose firmly against hers. It feels spongy and warm and intimate. She feels the beating of her heart and worries about the little box that Theo is bearing.

'Kia ora,' he says as he draws his face away, then presses her nose a second time.

'Kia ora,' she replies, then moves along a line of men and women that includes Aunty Tui and repeats the greetings. Tori is waiting for her at the end of the line. He shakes her hand, presses his nose on hers twice and follows with a quick kiss to both cheeks.

'You're doing well,' he says. 'Do you like the Maori kiss? It's called a hongi and goes back to the beginning of time. It symbolises the god of the forest, Tane, blowing the breath of life into the first human being.'

'I could get used to it — well maybe,' she replies doubtfully, resisting the urge to blow her nose, which feels strangely squashed.

When they move under a covered veranda at the entrance, Mata points at her polished black leather court shoes, telling her to remove them. She kicks them off, adding them to a line of others piled up outside the door.

Mata ushers them in and directs Frances to sit alongside her with the other women. The men sit together opposite.

The meeting house is cool and soft lights are reflected in the shiny wooden floor. It takes Frances a few seconds to adjust her eyes from the bright sunshine to the dark detail inside. The building has a steep ceiling. Around the walls there are finely detailed wooden carvings interspersed with woven patterned panels. On the rear wall is a line of photographs.

Frances senses the ghosts of the past and has to force herself to concentrate on what is happening in front of her. She's brought back to the present when she catches Tori's irritated eye as he tries unsuccessfully to wiggle his toe back inside a hole in his sock and she quickly checks that her own stockinged feet are intact.

Uncle Eruera is standing in the centre, speaking loudly in

Maori. He sounds angry, gesturing wildly as he makes point after point. His eyes are flashing as he paces up and down, tilting forward and thumping his walking stick. Seeing Frances flinch, Mata touches her arm.

'Don't worry, he always talks like that. It's all part of the tradition,' she says under her breath. 'He's welcoming you but challenging you, wanting to know your business, what brings you here. You'll have plenty of time to answer him soon.'

Frances feels her heart beating even more quickly, not relishing the moment she may have to take the floor herself.

Abruptly, the elderly man stops talking. He sits down and, eyes closed, bows his head. The air feels heavy as they sit waiting. Frances feels as though she's inside a strange church but does not know what part of the service will come next. Uncle Eruera suddenly looks up and nods at Mata.

Reacting to his cue, Mata walks to where he was standing. She closes her eyes for a few seconds. Then she starts to sing, her rich mezzo-soprano voice filling the room.

Kati au, ka hoki ki taku whenua tapu,
Ki te wai koropupu i heria mai nei
I Hawaiki ra ano e Ngatoroirangi,
Eona tuahine Te hoatu-u-Te-Pupu
E hu ra ki Tongariro, ka mahana i taku kiri.

As she listens, Frances glances towards Tori. He is looking at her. As Mata's voice soars around them, she feels a strange longing surge through her. The emotion ambushes her and leaves her confused. She looks away. As the last echo of the song fades, Mata stays standing. She bows her head, while the others sit in silence. Presently, she looks towards them.

'For the visitors here today, I will tell you about the song,' she says.

'It is a waiata aroha, a love song. It is about a young chieftainess called Puhi-wahine. She had been away from her home in Taupo from Hikurangi, the home of the Maori King Tawhiao. While she was there she fell in love with a young man in the village called Mahutu te Toko. But she was called back to her home and had to leave her lover. That is the song she sang as she wept for him.'

Mata returns to her seat. Then Uncle Eruera looks at Frances and nods. Mata taps her arm. 'He wants you to sing now,' she says quietly. Seeing the panic on her companion's face, she adds firmly, 'It's required.'

Frances catches a wry expression in Theo's eye. He is deliberately avoiding her gaze. She stands up, racking her brain for something, anything, to sing. Suddenly she recalls something and falls back on her schoolgirl French: 'Au clair de la lune, mon ami Pierrot'. Her voice is pure and clear but inside she feels like she's dying a thousand deaths. It's twenty years since she sang this in the school choir. She sings the words automatically, thankful they are etched in her memory, and returns to her seat. Both Theo and Tori nod approval. Her racing heart slows and she feels like Xena the Warrior Princess returning victorious from slaying a monster.

Tori stands up, looking as assured as the elder his people have been hoping he will become. He looks first at Uncle Eruera before calling on Theo to speak.

For thirty years, Theo has been visiting marae to talk to the iwi about the mountain and his work there. He has learnt a deep respect for them but knows nothing can ever be taken for granted. As he offers formal greetings, then starts to speak, Frances sees that his body is revealing all the anxieties of his sixty years.

'As we've discussed before, I'm extremely worried about the danger on the mountain. The Crater Lake is very full and it's only a matter of time before it overflows and we'll have another very large lahar that will cause a lot of destruction and possible deaths.

'There's a lot of pressure to bulldoze the dam that's blocking the outlet. While I respect your wishes, there are others who feel it's more important to do that work. I've come here today with Frances Nelson to explain what we think is the minimum that needs to happen.'

As Theo discusses the merits of building a stopbank on the lower slopes to protect the fisheries from volcanic destruction, those in the room listen impassively. No expression betrays what they are thinking and they turn down the request for questions.

Theo beckons Frances forward to join him. She holds up two photographs of the microphone system in place on the mountain.

'So far we've been receiving very strong sound signals that are telling us what's going on inside the mountain. That way, we hope if there's any dramatic change, we can predict whether there'll be an eruption or a lahar.'

Uncle Eruera leans over to the others near him and whispers to them. Then he stands and walks over to Frances.

'And what is the mountain saying to you?' he asks her kindly.

'Well, the soundwaves vary from day to day, sometimes from hour to hour. But they reveal if there's a tremor or a build-up of the gases.'

The old man smiles at her warmly for the first time. 'You're a very clever young woman,' he says gently. 'But I'll be surprised if you can outguess the mountain.'

As they both return to their seats, Theo takes the box he has brought and places it gently on a table placed nearby.

'Before we speak of other matters, I need to inform you that our scientists found some human remains, a skull, in the Crater Lake recently. We've had it analysed. It's of a young woman and could be two hundred years old. I've brought it here today to give to you so you can decide what needs to be done.'

Uncle Eruera sits up sharply and leans forward. Tori glances at Frances, then quickly looks away. Mata taps Frances on the arm.

'Did you know about this?' As Frances nods, she screws her face up in concern.

Uncle Eruera and Tori walk over to the box, remove the lid and gaze at the skull inside. They stay like this for several minutes, not speaking, but the change in mood is unmistakable. Eventually the older man breaks the silence.

'We are very disturbed by this. It is unexpected. It would have been better if you had left this at the crater and taken one or other of us there to remove it or bury it. This shows you why we feel so strongly about anyone tampering up there. It is best we end the meeting now.'

'I'm sorry if you feel offended.' Theo looks him directly in the eye. 'We've behaved with integrity and we were obliged to remove it to have forensic tests.'

The elder nods at him but says nothing.

'With respect,' Theo says, 'when can you tell us your response to the stopbank and the danger of the lahar?'

A cloud passes over the old man's face.

'To us the mountains are symbols of the authority of nature. We see them as our ancestors did hundreds of years ago — ageless, supreme. They are impervious to the relentless march of time.' He stands to leave. Then he pauses and says directly to Theo. 'Or to Pakeha deadlines. We will let you know when we have talked about it. When we are ready.'

CHAPTER TWENTY-NINE

⁂

A stiff breeze touches them as they leave the meeting house. Tori and Mata accompany the visitors to the whare kai, the dining hall next door, to share tea and biscuits, hospitality another essential part of the ritual to remove tapu.

Frances breaks the silence. 'I'm sorry that went so badly, Tori. I've wanted to tell you about the skull but it wasn't my right to do so.'

'I know it's not your fault. Those matters are more important to us than to others so we take it very seriously,' Tori says.

'What will you do about the skull?'

'The tribe will try and work out who the young woman was and bury her remains either in the family cemetery with a special ceremony if everyone agrees or in another burial area nearby if they don't. It's unlikely we'll ever really know because it's so long ago but it's important to her that she's laid to rest with full respect.'

Theo drinks his tea eagerly. 'A cup of tea never tasted so good!' he says, the worry evaporating from his face. 'I think I'll have a second.'

As they relax, Tori softly touches Frances' arm. 'Don't feel too badly about that. I know you did what you thought was best. It should be all right, although it will hold things up on the mountain.'

But Frances can see he is worried and begins to wish she had followed Sam's lead and left the skull where it was.

After morning tea, Mata offers to show the visitors more of the marae.

She leads them back inside the meeting house and takes them directly to the photographs on the rear wall. Different-sized coloured and black-and-white images of men and women and a few children stare back at them.

'They're all members of our family who have passed away,' Mata says. 'No matter how far our people wander, when they die, we all want to be back here where we belong.'

A shadow crosses Frances' face when she sees the photos of two very young children.

Tori sees her distress. 'I know what you're thinking,' he says. 'I'm sure your sister is at rest but maybe you need to find the place she died. We believe that the spirit, the wairua, can stay where a child dies. It can have its own spiritual force. Perhaps she's waiting for you to release her spirit, so all your family can be at peace.'

Frances is impressed by his deep faith. 'I've never thought about her like that before. It's not something we have ever discussed in our family.'

Mata takes her arm as they walk up a small rise to the family cemetery to the rear of the property. The damp green grass brushes their legs as they approach a small fenced area beyond which lie uneven rows of headstones. Hanging from the gate on a long piece of string, she notices a large Coca-Cola bottle filled with water.

Tori stops in front of a small monument fashioned in grey

granite and stands, waiting for Frances to catch up to him. 'This is the grave of my second cousin who was also on the train.'

Rawiri Jones
Beloved son of Hemi and Barbara
Taken by the disaster at Tangiwai
24 December 1953
Aged 22 years
'You live among us always'

'They didn't identify him for a long time and he was buried in Wellington. When they found out who he was, a lot of the family went there to bring his body back here.'

Frances stares at the words for a long time. 'He's the one my mother's friend Tui was looking for. Is that right?'

'It seems so.'

She bows her head and offers a prayer, thinking of the young man and her own sister going together to their deaths in a deluge of water.

'You have a much more personal way of dealing with your dead,' she says. 'We tend to brush death aside and move on with our lives. I haven't even seen where my sister is buried so I think that's why it is so much harder to accept. All my ancestors are buried at different places around England. I wouldn't know where to look. You can make your peace here whenever you want.'

'Yes, we Maori all know we have a home, no matter where we travel in the world. And when we die. Well you're probably looking at where I'll end up now.' He sees her wince. 'Don't worry,' he says laughingly, steering her out of the cemetery, 'I'm not intending to go to the next world for a long time yet.'

As they leave, Mata beckons Frances over, opens the bottle of water and pours some into her own hands, then passes it to

Frances. 'You must cleanse yourself after visiting the graves.'

Frances washes her hands and passes the bottle on to Tori, who grins at her. 'You'll get used to our funny ways.'

'I think I have a lot more to learn,' Frances replies.

As they drive back to the office Theo won't say what's on his mind until he swerves to miss a car that has crossed to the wrong side of the road.

'Damn,' he says. 'I knew that skull spelt trouble. We'll just have to hope it doesn't delay things for too long.'

Should she have been more honest about the skull in the first place? Frances feels like a fool, a very tired fool. Maybe she should have just left the skull there and taken the coward's way out.

As they speed back to Taupo, she hears Theo exhale deeply.

'By the way, kiddo, nice voice.' He starts to laugh.

Frances jabs his arm and shakes her head in mock exasperation, then can't stop herself from laughing too. 'Thanks for nothing. But I might have to expand my repertoire because it looks like that's not going to be the end of it.'

'You'd better believe it.'

The Messenger

Being Christmas Eve it was hard to get away from my friends who had gathered at the pub that night for a drink. But I'd told my parents that my wife Beryl and I would be with them by ten o'clock at the latest. So we were already running late when we saw a couple of cars stopped ahead of us on the road. As soon as I got out I heard it — an incredible roaring noise. You wouldn't read about it!

A chap came running towards me yelling that the road bridge had fallen into the river and there was a hell of a flood. Now, coming from a railway town it only took a second or two for me to realise the overnight express train was about to arrive and as I looked towards the line I could see the railway bridge was sagging in the middle. It looked ready to fall.

It was the strangest thing because while this incredible wave of water was washing down the river it was a beautiful night and I could clearly see Mount Ruapehu rising up in the distance behind. I grabbed my torch from the car and ran as fast as I could through the scrub towards the tracks a couple of hundred yards away.

I could hear the train coming even though the sound of the water was terrific. I saw the steam puffing from its engine into the sky before I saw the train. I was nearly there when it came around a bend. I flashed the torch and was yelling and jumping up and down to try and catch the driver's attention. I think he and the fireman might have seen me but the train was going too fast to stop in time, even if they tried to. I felt absolutely sick.

When the train raced onto the bridge there was nothing to hold it as the water had washed away the piers. It collapsed beneath the weight of the train and the engine nose-dived into the river and crashed into the bank on the other side.

The sound was deafening and I think the driver and the fireman would have died straightaway. The first carriage was dragged by the engine into the bank. I could see the faces of some of the passengers inside the next four carriages as they disappeared into the darkness of the river. I'll never forget it as long as I live.

The last two carriages somersaulted as they crashed into the water. They had broken free of the rest of the train. The sixth carriage was dangling at a sharp angle over the edge, half of it still on the track attached to the rest of the train. The lights were still on and I could see passengers inside, some of them moving but others looked like they were still asleep.

I leapt onto the track and climbed into the van at the back of the train where I found the guard, unaware of what had just happened.

'Half your train's in the river!' I told him.

'Where the hell have you come from?' he said.

He didn't seem to believe me at first. I kept saying, 'It is, it is!'

I must have persuaded him because he came with me through the other carriages where there was a lot of confusion with passengers trying to work out what was going on.

'Move to the back of the train,' we told everyone. 'Just move slowly and don't take anything with you. There's been an accident.'

When we reached the end of the carriage, we were looking out straight into the river. We were urging the passengers to walk back but suddenly there was a huge bang and we knew the back coupling had broken. Next thing I felt myself falling. The whole lot: us, me, the guard and all the passengers all went into the river.

Everyone was screaming. It was bloody pandemonium. We hit the river and started floating. People calmed down a bit and just hung on until we tipped over and just stopped.

Strangely the water level had dropped all of a sudden. One minute flood, the next, just the normal river.

We were able to get nearly everyone out and wade to the bank. I'm sorry to say we lost one young girl in the carriage — about 14 years old I reckon. Her head was trapped beneath the seat and even though the water level wasn't that high, she drowned before we realised she was there.

By this time, there were loads of people arriving to help. Everywhere were survivors soaking wet, plastered with mud and oil, *shaking and crying. Lots of them had bad injuries and many had lost all their clothes, ripped off by the flood.*

But I knew there was worse news to come. There was no way many of those poor souls in the first carriages stood a chance of escaping.

Percy Allen, 29, electrician from Taihape

CHAPTER THIRTY

Winter has now set in and the sky is overcast but, after several days of intermittent rain, it is dry. Now that Frances is familiar with the roads, the three-hour drive back along the lake and past the mountains goes quickly. She's on her way to Cedric's to meet some of the Tangiwai group. When he rang he also gave her Beverley's number. Full of apprehension Frances dialled and, to her surprise, the small, quiet voice on the phone agreed to a visit. Thick cloud obscures the volcanoes as she passes dozens of cars with skis on their roof racks. She double-checks her bag, ensuring her mobile phone and pager are both functioning should the warning system activate an alarm.

The small road to Cedric's farm double-backs off the highway near Tangiwai. The bitumen lasts only a couple of hundred metres before giving way to rough gravel that makes her car bump and vibrate.

Soon she sees the gate with its name, The Poplars, and turns in, crossing a cattle grid and following a winding track upwards to the wooden farmhouse, perched in isolation on a small rise away from the river. Two other cars are parked outside on the rich green grass alongside an old tractor with barely discernible red paint.

As she pulls up, she sees Cedric waving her to park in a flat, empty space. He greets her with an affectionate kiss, as though they are old friends and, taking her arm, leads her inside. They pass through a kitchen owing its heritage to the sixties with orange-painted cupboards and bench top, cork floors and lacy café curtains. Seated on a floral couch and armchair in front of an open fire in the small lounge room are three others.

'This is my wife, Pauline,' Cedric says. 'And these old buggers are Percy Allen and Trevor Atley.'

'Not too much of the old from you, Cedric,' Percy says as they all rise to shake her hand.

Once strangers, they became forever linked by the tragedy that connected their lives all those decades ago. They were all young when they met beside the river, rescuing the desperate survivors from the train wreck and retrieving the bodies of those who perished in the river. Now in their seventies and eighties, they share their memories like the survivors of a terrible war who have seen sights they can never erase from their nightmares.

Frances feels like an interloper but Pauline entreats her to join them, hastily offering a cup of tea from a large china teapot and freshly made scones.

'You know a lot of people believe the bridge was condemned and should have been rebuilt?' Percy says suddenly, directing his question at Frances. 'They say the volcano wasn't to blame. They used to go on and on about it to me.'

Frances sees an expression of bitterness in his faded eyes, a weariness in his lined face. 'No, I never heard that,' she says, her voice rising in surprise.

'Percy was there when the engine and first carriages went off the bridge. He climbed into the front carriage that was still on the tracks and ended up in the river himself. He saved lots of people.' Cedric turns to the friend he has seen through decades of suffering and self-doubt. 'You were a right hero, weren't you, Percy?'

'I just did what anyone else would have done. Nothing more.'

He sighs and sips his tea, staring at the tiny dancing flames as Pauline pokes at the fire and adds another piece of wood. It displaces a half-burnt log beneath and a shower of sparks crackles and hits the mesh fireguard.

Frances waits for Percy to continue, sensing his reluctance to say more.

'Tell her the talk about the cover-up at the inquiry,' Pauline prompts him. 'Go on, love, it's ancient history now anyway,' she says, giving his arm a little squeeze of affection.

He pauses a moment longer and runs his hand through his thin mane of white hair.

'They did paint me as a hero — it's true,' he says at last, 'but then the finger-pointing started. There was lots of talk going around that the bridge wasn't safe. It was damaged by a smaller lahar in the twenties and one of the piers in the middle was shaky. A lot of chaps on the railways told me later it was supposed to have been replaced and that if it had been it would never have collapsed.'

'Then a fire destroyed all the maintenance records just as the investigation was starting,' Cedric says. 'It did look bloody suspicious. Of course the inquiry cleared anyone of blame, except the volcano, that is. Trouble is, a lot of people took it out on poor old Percy here.'

'Why did they do that?' Frances asks.

Percy stares into the fire and shakes his head slowly. 'You tell her, Cedric,' he says.

'Well, they started saying Percy was being used by the government, that they were exaggerating the hero stuff to take attention away from the bridge. And it was called an accident and no one was paid any compensation. Nothing.'

'Yeah, I went from hero to villain in three months,' Percy says. 'I was like a pariah. You'd have thought it was all my fault. Sometimes I used to wish I'd never been there, never seen the train.'

'There, there,' says Pauline, putting her arm around him, 'that's not what all those people you saved thought. If it wasn't for you a lot of them would have drowned.'

'I've seen that happen a lot,' Frances says. 'Every time there's a natural disaster, whether it's a volcano, a bushfire, a flood or whatever, there's always a search for a scapegoat. I think it's just human nature, looking for someone to blame. It makes some people feel better. It's easier for them to make sense of it if they cast blame, especially when people have died.

'But I can tell you when Mount St Helens blew up in Washington, it was the same thing. Everything was washed away, all the bridges except one went. They couldn't withstand the pressure of the mudslide. Maybe we'll never know for sure about the Tangiwai bridge but the force of that water was so enormous, I think it would have gone anyway.'

Percy looks at Frances closely for the first time. 'Were you there?' he asks. 'At Mount St Helens?'

'Not when it happened, but I worked on the volcano years afterwards. I could see where the mudslides went. The landslide was much bigger than here but the effect was the same. A huge lahar full of melted snow and rocks and ash swept down the valleys and took everything with it. I don't really believe one shaky pier in the middle of one bridge would have made all that much difference.'

As Pauline pours more tea, they begin to talk about it all

happening again and ask Frances if she believes they're in danger from another lahar from Ruapehu.

'Yes, I have to be frank, I think you are. That's why I've come here to work, to help make sure everyone is evacuated if that happens.'

'Is it true the Maori are stopping work that could prevent it?'

'That's hard to say,' Frances says. 'They don't want bulldozers at the crater, that's for sure. But I'm not convinced that would fix the problem anyway. The forces in the volcano are such that an eruption could destroy any engineering work in seconds.'

'And you still feel like that, even though your own family lost so much?' Cedric asks her.

The doubt that plagues Frances surfaces once more. 'I do struggle with it, I have to be honest with you. It's hard to accept you can't control the forces of nature when we're so used to trying to control everything else in our lives.'

'I learned long ago you can't do that. I learned it far too young really. I was only eighteen.' Until now, the third man has not spoken a word. As he turns to Frances, she can see a gentleness in his still blue eyes that hints at deep sadness.

'Tangiwai taught me that,' he continues. 'None of those poor souls could do anything about what happened to them.'

'Trevor was there just after the crash. I told him you wanted to find out more about the rescue,' Cedric tells her.

'Yeah, well I don't usually go on about it. After it happened I just tried to put it to the back of my mind. But I'll help you if I can.'

'It's important to me to try and piece together where exactly things happened, where you found the bodies. Would you come back with me back to bridge?'

'Sure. There's still plenty of light left in the day. We can go now.'

Frances feels as though she is leaving old friends. Pauline and Cedric both kiss her goodbye, but Percy stays in his seat and just nods at her, lost again in his own memories of that bleakest of nights.

The Rescuer

I had been at the pictures with some of my friends in Taihape. It was Christmas Eve and we were all in good spirits with a few days off ahead of us and had come into town for the night. Most of us worked on farms, me with my father. We were waiting outside the Returned Servicemen's Club for my father, because being under twenty-one, we weren't allowed in. We weren't allowed to drink.

A friend of my father's pulled up beside us driving one of those old grey Mack trucks they had then. He was extremely excited.

'Come on, the express train's crashed at Tangiwai, it's in the river,' he told us. 'We've got to help.'

We were pretty shocked and jumped on the back of the truck and headed over. It took only ten minutes to get there. The road bridge was down too and there were quite a lot of people already there. Someone had gone to the forestry camp nearby and set off the fire alarm.

It was dark and at first we couldn't see much. A few minutes after we arrived, some army people turned up and erected some strong floodlights that pointed out over the river.

My God, what an awesome sight! It was catastrophic. The carriages were everywhere, ripped to bits. I could smell all this sulphur. And I could see people swimming, hanging on to one of the carriages and others climbing out of the water. We waded out into the water. It was still moving fast. But almost immediately we could tell the depth was dropping.

There were still passengers trying to get off the train. The poor things were so confused. Many of them had no idea of what had happened and they were crying out for their friends and relations. The carriages were broken up really badly and full of mud with luggage everywhere. One of the army men told us to spread out down the riverbanks as lots of people had been swept away.

About a hundred yards down I saw this man so heavily covered in oil from the train's fuel tender and silt from the river he couldn't speak or see. He was just sitting there on the bank like a zombie. By now *there were some ambulances around and some army trucks. I helped people onto them to be taken to the hospital at the Waiouru Army Camp 10 miles away. There had been lots of Christmas parties in the district that night so there were more people around than usual.*

I helped bring in lots of bodies to the camp. We laid them in rows on the dance floor of the army hall. Lots of them had no clothes on. It was pretty hard for us to deal with that. There was one man — all he was wearing was this bright striped tie, the only thing that wasn't ripped off him. We were told to look out for anything that might help identify people. We had to look for wallets, jewellery, watches, clothing and papers, anything to help with the job.

There were lots of children killed too and we put them in a room where there had been a Christmas party. I'll never forget it. There was a screen there and behind it where the band used to play were piles of sodden clothing and kids' toys, a yellow rubber ball, some rag dolls and so on.

But there was worse to come. My friends and I were there for days after. Most of the passengers died in the torrent and were washed miles away. Next day we found the steel underframe of Car A one and a half miles downstream from the railway bridge. We had to search the riverbanks and the farms, digging around in the sand. We found things, things I don't want to see again. Pieces of bodies, some had lost heads, arms, legs. We had to take everything back in bags to the trucks. They were trying to match them up to the bodies in the morgue. And the worst thing of all . . .

It was on the third day and I had been combing up and down a bend on the river about half a mile downstream. By that time we were getting used to noticing the smallest things. I saw something unusual, something sticking out of a sandbank a few feet back from the water. There were little fingers. I dug around and knew it was a child. I kept digging and uncovered a little girl's body.

Trevor Atley, 18, a rescuer at Tangiwai

CHAPTER THIRTY-ONE

❧

Frances feels the same sense of dread when she pulls into the car park near the Tangiwai bridge. Following in his red utility truck, Trevor parks alongside her. The smell of sulphur is much stronger this time and a gusty wind blows it into her face. Boosted by autumn and winter rains, the river is flowing more strongly too. The greyness of the day oppresses her spirit as they walk towards the memorial.

'You might think it's odd, but I haven't been to this spot before,' Trevor says as he scans the words on the stone as if looking for a solution to some lifelong puzzle. 'I was working on the other side of the river after the train crash.'

His mobile phone rings and she hears him giving some instructions on how to operate a generator.

'I've just hired a young fellow at my farm,' he explains. 'I need more help these days. But he's having trouble working out how everything works.'

The rushing water draws them over to the river and they gaze into the foaming current. The bridge rises up in front of them.

'Over there.' Trevor points downstream to a large tree on

top of the riverbank. 'That's where we found one man. He was only young and when we saw him draped over the top branches we thought he was dead. But he was knocked unconscious and apart from a few scratches, he was unharmed. Nearly everyone else in his carriage died, all washed away.'

They linger for a while, then carefully pick their way through loose dirt and grass, down the bank to the water's edge.

'Can you remember who you found? Cedric may have told you: my parents were on the train with my baby sister. She was drowned. Do you remember a child?'

Trevor stops and his eyes meet hers. He looks as though his past has rushed forward to collide with the present.

She sees his recognition and although she feels very afraid, she is desperate for him to talk to her.

'No . . . no, he didn't say anything about a child,' he says at last. 'But I do remember. That is, I did find a little girl.'

Until now, she has barely heard the noise of the flowing river. Now it is deafening her, as if it is crashing over her bones, flooding her being.

'When I found her, I had to stop searching for others after that. It was too much. I couldn't go on.'

She watches a tear course its way down his weathered face, until he raises his arm and wipes it quickly away with his shirt sleeve.

Questions burst into her mind but she pushes them aside, knowing she must wait for him to talk in his own time.

'Walk with me,' he says eventually, gesturing a way they can navigate downstream, walking beside the river, tip-toeing around large cold iron-grey rocks. 'You might get your feet wet, though.'

They walk for several hundred metres until they reach a point where they can go no further. There is no room between the river and the bank and they leap onto large rocks protruding from the water. Frances slips on the green slime of a half-submerged rock, her shoe fills with icy water and the cold travels through her body like a frozen spear. Trevor reaches out to steady her. Although he is around 70, a lifetime of farm work has given him the fitness and agility of someone decades younger.

The river narrows and they make their way back to where the bank is wide enough again to walk comfortably. A few minutes on and Trevor stops and sits on a rocky ledge.

'Just here,' he says. 'It's a long time ago but I'm pretty sure it's here.'

Rising out of the middle of the river is a small island of sand and rocks, studded here and there with willow trees.

Frances sits beside him and calls on all her strength to wait just a little longer for a truth she has been searching for all her life.

'It's still as bleak as ever,' he offers, seeing the questions in her eyes. 'It had been raining all day and late in the afternoon I was looking around this area. The water had dropped right back and I waded over to the island. That's when I saw it.' He stops as though trying to remember some forgotten detail. 'It was a tiny hand. I knew straightaway I had found a child.'

He is finding it hard to speak the unspeakable, fumbling with words, fighting back tears that he has always suppressed.

'I dug around until I had uncovered the body. It was a little girl. All her clothes had been washed away and she was covered in silt. But she was still holding a teddy bear. While she was in the river she must have used all her might to hang on to it. And she wore a bracelet. It was covered with black silt but it had stayed on.'

Frances reaches into the pocket of her jeans and pulls out the bracelet she took with her everywhere.

'You found my sister.'

Lying in the palm of her hand, its dull golden links and tiny heart give off a subdued glow, like a long-lost treasure unearthed in an archaeological dig. She presses it into Trevor's thick, lined hand.

He turns it over, examines the locket and sees engraved on it the faded initials 'VN'. He traces a finger over the letters, then encloses the chain in his fist.

Frances reaches out to him and they embrace, neither now trying to stop their tears. They stay like that for a long time.

The insistent call of a native hawk hovering overhead brings them back. Frances knows the time has come. She quickly removes her shoes, one already soaked through, and rolls her jeans up to her knees.

Carefully, she wades across the river, the water chilling her and the hard stones piercing the soles of her feet. She steps onto the islet, wet black sand creeping between her toes. She feels she has been here before. Slowly she walks to the highest point, sinks to her knees and stays perfectly still, just listening. A sudden warmth spreads through her body and she knows that Valerie's spirit is here, in this desolate place. As a light rain starts to fall, she bows her head and silently prays for her sister and her parents. The drops of rain running down her face, she picks up some of the damp sand and sifts it through her fingers. Then, taking a handful, she stands and gently throws it bit by bit into the part of the river where the water is flowing swiftest.

'Thank you,' she calls over to Trevor, who has not moved. She picks her way back across and returns to him, taking his hands in hers. 'No one in my family has ever had the chance to say thank you. Without you we may never have known what happened to Valerie. It was devastating for my parents but at least they saw her and had some certainty. Thank you.'

Trevor grips her hands, his face close to hers. 'I'm so sorry. Sorry for your family. I've never talked about this before. I've kept it to myself until today. I'm so glad you came.'

'I went back to the river to help again. It was three days after the crash when I found her . . . when I found your sister. I dug her out and carried her back, pretty much the way we came here today. I don't know how I did it. But I guess we all find the strength when it's needed.'

He is silent now, his sorrow spent. They sit there together as the water rushes on past them. Trevor suddenly shivers and pulls himself up, then bends down and helps Frances to her feet.

'Here, you'd better hang on to this. It belongs to you,' he says, handing her back the golden chain.

The hawk still hovers above, quiet and watchful. Then, on a sudden gust of wind, it banks steeply like an old biplane and disappears.

The Forensic Pathologist

I examined the first forty bodies that arrived in Wellington from the Tangiwai Railway accident on 28 December 1953, and then another seven that arrived over the next couple of days. Of the forty-seven bodies, twenty-five were female and twenty-two male.

Many of them had been exposed to the elements and submerged in water so there was some urgency to complete the examinations to help with identification as soon as possible. I wasn't able to do full postmortem examinations but from the external appearances, which were carefully noted, certain conclusions could be drawn.

In many of the bodies there were advanced postmortem changes which rendered recognition of features virtually impossible and, in some, injuries to the face and skull added to this difficulty. Despite the use of a refrigerated room to store the bodies, postmortem changes progressed with some rapidity.

In most cases there was evidence of injuries before death from fractures of the jaw and bony injuries of the face and skull indicated the deceased had been thrown violently forward at the moment of the accident. This was supported by the presence of severe fractures of the forearm in several people. It was clear a few had been killed instantaneously while others had received fatal injuries including loss of limbs.

In many cases external appearances suggested death by drowning; there was pallor of the trunk and limbs and suffusion of the eyeballs.

I was very struck by the extent to which silt had penetrated the soft tissues of the bodies, even underlying areas where the skin was quite intact. This was particularly noticeable in the tissues of the face and head where collections of this material could be found in the depths of the scalp between the muscle and the bone of the skull.

This phenomenon occurs in bodies in contact with sand over a period, but its occurrence to such a marked degree in the present instance could be accounted for only by the bodies being exposed to a current of water containing a great amount of solid material in a finely suspended state. I believe the pressure from the silt was why so many of the bodies had been stripped of their clothing. I am satisfied from what I saw that some of the victims were killed by the force of the crash and that those who escaped injuries of this sort were killed by asphyxia from silt or by drowning.

With the help of relations, twenty-six bodies were identified beyond doubt. We were able to confirm the identities of a number of people from other countries with no next of kin but with some identification still on them. For instance, there was a woman from Grafton in New South Wales in Australia. I cabled her dental records to a pathologist there and we confirmed her identity. There was also a couple from Holland and we were able to confirm their identity through fingerprints.

There were twenty-one bodies remaining in the mortuary. I have carefully documented all distinguishing features, including tattoos on a couple of the younger men, and have removed some pieces of jewellery so that identification may be possible in the future. On the morning of Thursday, 31 December 1953, the bodies were removed to the Karori Cemetery for burial. The coffins were placed side by side in an 18-metre grave.

Footnote: The following April, the bodies were exhumed and my colleagues and I were able to identify the bodies following descriptions of missing persons and their personal effects.

Dr Gordon Douglas, 51, forensic pathologist

CHAPTER THIRTY-TWO

⚮

The land folds into itself as Frances approaches Taumarunui in search of Beverley. Steep green hills engraved with the circles from endlessly marching sheep crowd each side of the winding highway. The road straightens and she flashes past small farming settlements, following a wild river edged with limestone cliffs and on into a valley towards the town.

Wide tree-lined streets intersect each other on the flat floor of the valley. Fresh from dropping its load of fertiliser on a distant farm, a top-dressing plane buzzes out of the hills that rise up and surround the town. On one side of Hakiaha Street, the thoroughfare into town, a small triangular red and white carved Maori ceremonial building stands defiantly in the shadow of a large new police station. The one long main street is lined with shops on one side and the railway line and station on the other.

Frances, stopping to buy some flowers for Beverley, is struck by the number of utilities and trucks parked along the street and people chatting on the pavement.

'It's farmers' day,' a dark-eyed young woman with curly

black hair and three studs in her ear tells Frances as she wraps a bunch of crimson carnations with a delicate white plant she says is baby's breath. 'I've been flat out. They're all stocking up and lots of the women come in same day each week to buy a bunch of flowers. Even a few of the men make it in here sometimes.'

Outside small groups of teenagers loll about the shops, buying takeaway food, playing pinball and video games, on the lookout for some excitement to break the monotony of small-town life. Three young Maori boys wearing beanies hover together outside a DVD hire shop, laughing and ribbing each other.

Within minutes Frances is pulling up outside a neat white-painted weatherboard house with a small veranda and a closely clipped lawn, similar to many others in the tidy street. Rose bushes still in hibernation and lavender plants line the tiled path to the house. She rings the bell which tolls like a miniature Big Ben. Seconds later the door opens.

'Hello, you must be Frances. I'm Beverley.' She has the softest voice Frances has ever heard. 'Thank you so much,' she says as she takes the flowers. 'Do come in.'

Inside the house nothing is out of place. A newspaper has been folded evenly into quarters and tucked neatly on a shelf beneath a glass coffee table. An elaborate glass clock sits dead centre on a wooden mantelpiece above a scrupulously scrubbed fireplace in which an electric heater is throwing out a volley of warm air. On either side of the clock sit two elegant white porcelain cats on hand-crocheted doilies, eternally keeping an eye on the time.

An immaculate floral-patterned wool carpet covers the floors and a well-upholstered cream lounge suite with tapestry-covered cushions looks barely used, except for one worn spot in the middle of the sofa. Frances starts as a large orange cat springs from nowhere and sits right there.

Beverley squeezes next to her pet, which meows in protest. Frances sits in one of the two armchairs and the women regard each other for the first time. Frances notices how unlined Beverley is for a woman of her age, her pale face and hazel eyes framed by perfectly groomed silver hair tinted a slight mauve.

'Tea?' Beverley breaks the silence. 'Best to start with a hot cup of tea, don't you think? And I'll find a vase for the beautiful carnations.'

'That's kind of you, thank you.'

Frances searches the room for clues about her host but is disappointed. There are no photographs and nothing that would betray much at all about Beverley Corbett, except for the small electric organ on one side of the room, its lid closed. Frances walks over to look at a small pile of sheet music on top. It is nearly all church music and some Bach and Beethoven. The exception is a small songbook called 'Greatest Love Songs Ever Written'.

Beverley rattles in with a tray holding a teapot, crockery and a plate of fresh jam tarts.

'Hope you're hungry,' she says as she carefully sets the tray down. 'I just made these. I bought the raspberry jam from the church fête last week.' She returns with a tall crystal vase full of the flowers and places them next to the clock.

As they drink their tea, Frances relays greetings from Cedric and Pauline.

'They were so good to me,' Beverley says. 'They helped me then and they helped me through the years. Such good people.'

Frances reaches into her bag and brings out a black-and-white photograph of her parents and Valerie. Her father is wearing a suit and tie and his jet-black hair is slicked back in the fashion of the fifties. Her mother is wearing a tailored woollen jacket and a felt hat with a protruding feather. In her arms is Valerie, in a sleeveless lacy dress, the tiny chain bracelet on her chubby wrist.

'They look lovely,' Beverley sighs.

'Can you tell me about that day on the train?' Frances asks. 'My parents may have been in your carriage. They had that little girl with them, my sister. She was just a toddler.'

Even as she says the words, Frances feels her throat catch.

Beverley thinks for a moment or two. 'It's such a long time ago now . . .' Her words trail away. She nibbles on one of the tarts, and her cat, which has been ignoring them both until now, is suddenly alert and watchful. Beverley breaks off a piece of the tart and puts it in the cat's eager mouth.

Beverley's eyes mist over and for a minute she seems lost in her own memories. 'Oh yes,' she says, remembering Frances, 'I do recall seeing quite a few families on the train. It's a terribly long time ago now. But I knew you would ask me. Cedric said you would. So I've been thinking about it again. It's very painful, but I can remember hearing children laughing and crying. I do remember one little girl, a pretty little thing, running up and down. She came up to all of us. Not shy. Maybe that was her. I can't say.'

'Do you remember anything else about her? Maybe you saw her parents, my parents?'

'No, I'm sorry. I can't. As I say, I really only had eyes for my David. We had only recently announced our engagement and we, and we . . .'

'I'm sorry, Beverley. I can only imagine how terrible it must have been. I didn't mean to upset you.'

'It's all right. You must think I'm a foolish old woman still blubbing after all these years.'

'No, not at all. I wasn't there. I didn't know my sister — I was born a long time after she died — but I still grieve for her.'

'The trouble is they never found David. I still see him in my dreams, floating out there somewhere. I was in his arms one moment and then . . . he was gone forever.'

'Do you remember much about the crash?'

'Nothing — I was asleep. I woke up under the water. Drowning. But when I was pulled out I could hear people screaming who were trapped in other carriages. I can never get those screams from my ears. I'm lucky to be alive. Nearly everyone else in my carriage died. I still don't know why I was spared.'

'That's what my mother used to say. She'd say, "I was the one who should have died, not my baby." My father didn't say anything at all. He'd just sit there staring at the newspaper.'

'That must have been hard for you when you were young.'

'It was but we all have to deal with what's served up. I just got used to my parents being quiet and solitary. It's all I knew growing up. Maybe you noticed them at the army camp. Do you remember much about that?'

'Unfortunately, I do. It's not the sort of thing you can ever forget. I went there every day for a week afterwards hoping to find David. I never did. But I helped identify three of our friends and I saw so many bodies, so many bodies. I'm sorry, Frances, I don't remember seeing your parents.'

As Beverley reaches into her pocket for a lace-edged white handkerchief the cat leaps off the couch. Frances goes to the older woman and strokes her arm.

'I'm sorry if all this has upset you. Have you ever been back to Tangiwai?'

'Never. And not likely to. What's the point? He's gone.' Beverley's eyes are red and her sad mouth struggles for control. 'I never saw his face again. And now, now I can't even remember what he looked like. I try to remember the sound of his voice.

But it's gone. Just as though he never existed. For years, I waited and hoped he might walk through my door but . . .'

Frances hugs her. 'Maybe you should go back,' she says. 'Perhaps I could take you.'

'Perhaps,' Beverley says presently. 'I don't usually like to travel. I'll have to think about it.'

CHAPTER THIRTY-THREE

❧

Thick snow blankets the mountain and a bitingly cold wind gnaws at the three scientists as they unload their gear from the four-wheel-drive in the car park below Whakapapa Village. None of them is looking forward to visiting the summit but Theo has insisted that he needs both Sam and Frances to complete the surveying for the computer modelling project.

Carrying cross-country skis and backpacks, they mingle with hundreds of skiers and snowboarders, trudging up through the snow to the first chairlift. With their orange ski overalls, jackets and orange safety helmets, they stand out among the more fashionably attired visitors. Attaching their skis, they by-pass the queue to the lift. Sam shares a chair with a skier. Frances and Theo take the next one and are quickly are whisked up the first set of slopes.

Even with her strongest sunglasses, the reflected glare off the snow makes Frances squint. Bitterly cold air currents blow across the mountain, forcing her to put on the balaclava she stuffed into her snow jacket. She is thankful she remembered to wear thermal underwear.

'You're a tough old thing, Theo, you don't seem to feel the cold so much,' she says, leaning close to his ear so he can hear her.

'I guess I'm used to it after all these years. And I can't stand having my face covered. Makes me feel like I'm suffocating.' He pauses before saying, 'Did anyone ever tell you you look like a burglar?'

Frances grins. 'Hey Theo, if ever Sue gets sick of you . . .'

They switch to a second chairlift but a few minutes later it stops, suspending them over a deep ravine. 'Damn, I hate it when this happens,' Theo says. 'Hang on to all the gear — we'll never find anything if it drops down there.'

Frances squeezes his arm. 'Don't worry, I know the drill.'

The minutes crawl slowly by as they dangle in the air like insects caught in a spider's web. Although it is freezing, Frances absorbs the warm strength of Theo and deliberately draws close to him so their arms are touching. He makes her feel like his favourite child and it's a sensation she craves, one that her own father denied her.

The chairlift jerks. 'Don't know why we stopped,' Theo says. 'But glad it wasn't for too much longer. We've got a lot of work to do.'

Frances enjoys observing the experienced skiers below her, skilfully manoeuvring around moguls, zigzagging rapidly down the slopes. She sees a few teenage boys on snowboards bombing out of control down a steep incline. Moments later, two of them crash into a snowbank and then stagger to their feet, laughing and unharmed. A ski patroller rushes to check they're OK, then admonishes them for their recklessness.

The highest T-bar is operating so they're spared some of the climbing of the summer ascents. As they're pulled steeply up, Frances feels the bar drag uncomfortably on her bottom. She clings tightly to her gear until they eventually arrive together at

Knoll Ridge. She follows Theo to the lift operator's hut where they stow their skis.

It's another brisk half-hour climb to the summit. On this clear day, the view is spectacular and they can see a fourth volcano, Mount Taranaki, on the western horizon. Like Ngauruhoe, belching out steam a short distance from them, it is perfectly cone-shaped and seems much closer than 130 kilometres away.

When they reach the summit, Frances hears Theo's pager go and then his mobile phone rings. 'Yes, yes, OK, thanks for ringing. We'll be careful.'

He tells them that the laboratory has picked up an unusual seismic signal. 'They say it's screw-shaped, maybe a tornillo. We'd better keep an extra lookout. Let's get a move on and be ready to leave quickly if we have to. Oh, and make sure you all keep your safety helmets on.'

An uneasy sense of *déjà vu* makes Frances nervous. She recalls a day in the crater with Olivia at Mount St Helens when they received a similar warning from the university laboratory. Nothing eventuated but that did not ease her anxiety now.

'Theo, are you sure we shouldn't leave now?'

'The chances of anything happening immediately are a thousand to one,' Sam interrupts. 'It might surprise you but we do know what we're doing.' He crunches on through the snow towards the crater.

'You don't have to come if you're not sure,' Theo reassures her. 'I'm sorry Sam's so brusque. You know how he is. But we'll be out of here before you know it.'

Frances nods her agreement. If it were her decision, she knows she would leave immediately, never taking the changing mood of a volcano for granted. Against her better judgement, she continues climbing.

From where they stand the muddy grey water of the lake looks like a giant dirty puddle plopped in the centre of a cone of virgin-white snow. They rely on the crampons on their climbing boots to grip the snow and ice and use their ice axes to help traverse the crater. A freezing westerly cuts through Frances' balaclava.

She catches up to Sam, who is assembling the electronic distance meter so they can begin their surveying of the tephra dam. Today, it will take both of them to measure any growth in the dam, which looks like a giant sandbank.

'The snow's going to make our measurements a bit un-reliable,' Sam says to her. 'Let's get going. You take the reflector over there,' he says, pointing Frances towards the opposite side of the lake.

They have an uneasy truce but Frances is grateful that when it comes to the science, it's business as usual. The two of them move around the crater quickly. Each time he positions the meter in the snow, he clicks the laser beam on, aiming it towards Frances, who is holding the reflector. He presses a small button on the meter each time, capturing the distance.

Theo is below them, closer to the lake, taking new photos to compare with some shot on their last inspection.

'Holy hell, look at that!' he shouts.

A large bubble is rising from the surface of the lake, up and up like some strange alien clawing its way out of the volcano's throat. The three of them stand transfixed, too in awe to move. The dome-shaped object makes no sound and from where they are they can't detect whether it is all water or rock. Then, just as quickly, it disappears, sinking back into the muddy depths of the crater.

'OK, let's pull out, quickly, just in case,' Theo says.

As they move to the top of the ridge and look back, they see the bubbling again, only this time the object is bigger. Suddenly the top of it opens up and there is a violent explosion as water and rocks are hurled high into the sky.

'Run for it,' Sam shouts. The mountain is shaking and they can hear rushing water. As they run, the rocks splash back into the lake but then the ground around them starts to move and there is an enormous bang as the volcano leaps into life like an angry imprisoned beast suddenly released from its cage.

Frances and Sam reach the top of another ridge and can see Theo further down trying to follow them. As they watch him they see spirals of liquid and debris catapult out of the lake like an upside-down waterfall.

'Hit the ground!' Sam shouts.

Frances stabs her ice axe hard into the ice, flings herself face down into the frozen slipperiness, tightens her helmet, pulls her pack over her head and holds onto the axe for dear life. She hears the hissing first, then feels water pelting her body. It's hot and starts to sting as it saturates her clothing and the acid seeps through to her skin. The ice around her melts and she can feel her ice axe coming loose. As she starts to slide, she digs her boots into the snow and, mustering all her strength, rams the axe into a thick ridge of ice.

Glancing up, she sees black rooster tails of water blasting into the sky, punching into giant steam clouds above. She glimpses a flash of orange a couple of metres away and thinks it is Sam. She shouts out his name but there's so much noise around her she can barely hear her own voice.

As she pulls the pack over her head again she hears a voice faintly calling her name on her tiny radio. She thinks it is Theo but she can't risk reaching for it from her pocket.

Seconds later she feels another assault. Black sticky ash rains down on her. Every time she takes a breath she chokes, the blackness penetrating her nose and her mouth, right through the balaclava. She can smell and taste gas and feels sick knowing it is poisonous hydrogen sulphide.

'Sam, help me!' she shouts as hard as she can.

She hears sounds like the whooshing of a stormy ocean, then whistling noises as huge rocks pummel the side of the mountain. The axe is loosened again and the ice scrapes her face as she slides a little further down until her left foot catches on a ledge. She brings her right foot up and pushes in. Steady now, she looks back up. Rocks are falling around her like bombs and flaming fragments of shrapnel fly through the air, hissing as they burn holes in the ice where they strike.

She glimpses Sam on another ledge. He raises his head towards her and gives a thumbs up. More rocks are falling and he buries his head once more. Frances struggles to breathe. The gas assaults her lungs and makes her want to throw up. Its sickly fumes are infiltrating her body and for a moment she wonders if this will be the end of her. But then an icy saviour, a freezing blast of air, roars at her. She gasps and swallows. The cold wind penetrates her mouth and her throat and seems to blow right through her, washing away the nausea and purging her mind. She claws her way back up the slope to the ledge nearest to Sam. Using the last of her depleted strength, she pulls herself up onto it. From here she can see the Crater Lake and she is met by a sight that both stirs and terrifies her. Huge rocks are whizzing over the water, colliding and crashing into each other. They churn through the water like dodgems in a fun-fair in hell.

Halfway up the ridge she can see an unmoving orange figure. Frances retrieves her radio. 'Theo!' she shouts again and again. He is not responding. His legs are spread-eagled in grotesque angles in the snow. As she inches forward she hears another whizzing sound and a shocking pain spirals through her shoulder as if she has been smashed by a baseball bat. The last thing she remembers before a silent blackness descends is that she does not want to die.

CHAPTER THIRTY-FOUR

Tori is mooring his boat in the town marina when he sees it. At first he thinks it is a large flock of birds migrating, travelling high in the distant sky towards Taupo. It billows and curls on air currents, rising and falling this way and that like a dragon dancer unsure of which way to go. As it comes closer he sees it is much denser than at first glance. It comes more in a wave now, winging on the southerly breeze, parts of it dispersing here and there. Tori hurriedly finishes securing the rope, sensing a peculiarity in the early afternoon light. He shades his eyes to focus on the formation and quickly sees that it is not birds at all. It is a great black cloud of volcanic ash.

He can hear his heart thudding in his ears — Frances! She was heading up the mountain that day. He grabs his jacket and starts to run, pulling out his mobile phone as he goes and punching in Frances' number. She doesn't answer and the phone switches to her voicemail. He jumps into his vehicle, still listening as he screeches away from the boat ramp into town. He finds the Office of Seismology and bursts through the door, searching, hoping for signs of her.

A dozen or so people are rushing around with phones and files and no one bothers to look at the wild-eyed man wearing a fishing jacket who is trying to get someone's attention. He puts his arm out to stop a young woman carrying a briefcase who is about to leave the building. 'I'm looking for Frances Nelson. Do you know where she is?'

'She's with the others on Ruapehu. There's been an eruption and we're trying to get them off the mountain.'

'Is she OK? Do you know what happened?'

'Sorry, that's all I can tell you.' She runs out the door.

The crackling of a two-way radio is constant in the background and Tori follows the sound into a room to the side. A curly-headed middle-aged man who would look at home in a university lecture theatre glances up as Tori taps on the door.

'Sorry to disturb you, I'm a friend of Frances Nelson. I'm trying to find out what's going on up the mountain.'

'Come in, I'm Ben Walker from the volcano watch group,' he says, beckoning over his shoulder. 'I'm just getting information now. The army is trying to land a chopper up there to move her and the two others from the summit. Sam Hawks radioed for help.'

'Do you know if she's OK?'

'Not yet. I'm sorry. We're all waiting to hear. The trouble is there might be another eruption and a lahar so we're all switching on to high alert.'

'Can I stay and listen?'

'Sure.'

Reports from civil-defence marshals, park rangers, ski patrollers and other seismologists in the area start to filter in over the radio.

Black ash has fallen on the slopes of Mount Ruapehu. Everyone has been told to evacuate except for a skeleton emergency team. Thousands of skiers and workers have rushed to their cars, causing a traffic jam as they all try to drive down the only road at the same time. The ski lodges are ordering everybody to leave at once and, further down the mountain, the Chateau is telling guests to prepare for evacuation in the event of a major eruption.

'They're trying to establish a central data bank so we can locate people known to be on the mountain. We're already worried about a missing group of soldiers who were snow-caving on the upper reaches,' Ben tells him.

Waiting in the tiny radio room, Tori leans back in a swivel chair, closes his eyes and focuses on sending his spirit high up to meet Frances. As if in a dream, he feels himself walking in slow motion, up and up and up, over craggy ridges and snow-covered valleys, drifting over icy crystal peaks until the volcano starts to engulf him in steam, gas and ash and an incredible heat. He is sinking into the snow, shocked to find it hot rather than cold. And he's calling out to her. He sees the ghosts, the atua, the guardians of the sacred mountains, warning him to go no higher, pushing him back down the mountain, away from the crater. He cries out to Frances again and again. But he hears no reply. He feels himself sliding and sinking, further and further away. Through the steam and mist he sees the face of his grandfather trying to tell him something and he remembers.

'Hira mai ai te whekite o te rangi.' The words of the powerful prayer rise up from within him. 'Hira mai ai te whekite o te rangi.'

'What's that?'

Tori opens his eyes, to hear himself uttering the ancient incantation over and over.

'Just a bit of prayer,' he says to Ben, looking slightly abashed. 'Didn't realise I was making such a racket.'

'We've found them, we've found the scientists!' They're interrupted by a man's voice crackling over the radio. It's breaking up but they can make out some of the transmission from the helicopter.

'Injuries. I repeat injuries. At least one serious. Evacuating to hospital ASAP,' the voice says.

'Sounds as if prayers might be in order,' Ben says, turning back to Tori and shrugging when he sees he has already gone.

A mixture of hope and fear pulsates through Tori as he runs from the building. Outside a swirling eddy is spreading the ash, spoiling Taupo's usually pristine air. As he drives towards the marae, fragments of black ash rain onto the windscreen. He can see it settling onto suburban lawns and open paddocks like some biblical pestilence. He sprays the windscreen with water and turns on the wipers but it turns into a muddy haze and soon he is struggling to see the road ahead.

He knows where he will find Aunty Tui. As he approaches the meeting house, he sees her sitting cross-legged on the floor of the veranda, puffing on a small bone pipe and humming as she blows out the smoke. She greets him briefly with her eyes.

'Tangiwai, Tangiwai,' she utters quietly, removing the pipe. 'The deluge is coming.'

'Frances . . . she's up there, is she . . .?'

'Aue,' Tui shakes her head. 'I can't say. I don't know. There's a reason for everything. We must wait and see.'

He bends to kiss Tui on the forehead. 'Pray your hardest, Aunty. Pray for all of us.'

'Ae, Tori, ae. I will.'

CHAPTER THIRTY-FIVE

'Frances, Frances, can you hear me?'
      She can hear her name but can't open her eyes. An agonising pain is ricocheting through her body. The woman is calling her again. It's a voice she doesn't know. She feels hands moving over her, lifting one arm first. When they lift the other, she screams. As she starts to come to she can see the outline of two figures leaning over her.

'Wriggle your toes. Can you do that?'

Frances flexes her feet. She feels she wants to vomit. 'Yes, I can,' she says.

'OK, OK, take it easy, you'll be all right,' the woman says. 'You've been hurt and we have to get you out of here quickly. Just stay still.'

Frances begins to remember the eruption and realises she is still on the mountain. She feels herself being lifted and then lowered again.

'Good, you're on the stretcher now and we're going to put you in the chopper. We're just putting you on oxygen. You've swallowed a lot of gas. Just breathe normally through your nose.'

She tries to focus but her vision is blurry. She feels the mask cupping her face and breathes in deeply. As the two people carry her she can see the helicopter ahead with the rotor blades still running. It's much bigger than the one Luke Gallagher normally flies but she can hear his voice. Her whole body aches as they load her inside the chopper but she feels slightly reassured as Luke throws her a smile. 'Don't worry, love, we'll get you out of here soon.'

'Are you all right, Frances?' Sam is sitting on the other side of the chopper but he removes his oxygen mask and comes forward to help pull the stretcher inside. Surprised by this unusual show of concern for her safety, she smiles at him gratefully.

'I don't know. I think so,' she says. 'Just a lot of pain and I think I've broken something.'

The oxygen curls through her lungs and she breathes it in hungrily. A third paramedic hands her some tablets and a paper cup of water. 'Here, take these, they'll help with the pain.' As she swallows them, she suddenly remembers and grabs Sam by the wrist. 'Theo, where's Theo?'

'They've gone to bring him back. He's further down,' Sam says.

'What happened? I remember hanging on during the eruption but then I must have passed out.'

'You did. Think you caught a rock. I was a bit luckier — just a lot of bumps and bruises. I called for help and the chopper came fifteen minutes later. It couldn't land any sooner. We've just had a close call. Wasn't our time to go.'

Frances' mind is racing. 'Are they evacuating? What's happening?'

'I don't know. I think so. The alert has gone out. They're worried there could be further eruptions. There's nothing we can do.'

She hears the paramedics returning. 'He's bad,' she hears

one say as they bring Theo in on another stretcher.

He is lying unconscious, barely recognisable. Caked in dried blood and ash, his face around the oxygen mask is like an ugly red and black patchwork. There are holes burnt through the arms and legs of his jacket and trouser. They pull back one sleeve, insert a needle into his left wrist and attach a drip.

'OK, we're getting out of here. Strap yourselves and the patients in,' Luke yells. 'This ash will rot the chopper if we don't get out of here fast and I don't want to stick around for another eruption.'

As they rise up, Frances can see the remnants of a dark cauliflower cloud above them. The chopper darts sideways to avoid it, then quickly flies away towards the town.

Glancing over to Theo, she softly calls his name. He doesn't reply and she's not even sure if he's breathing. Barely able to keep her eyes open, she can still taste the gas that has left her throat raw. For the first time in years, she suddenly wants her mother and father, and she starts to cry. Then she remembers that her mother is continents away and her father is dead. Her mind spins. She thinks of Tori and, sensing his presence, suddenly no longer feels so alone. The vibrations in the helicopter are deafening, but soon they fade to the level of the soft flapping wings of a moth until she doesn't hear them at all as she drifts into a deep sleep.

CHAPTER THIRTY-SIX

❧

Tori hurls a bucket of water to clear the windscreen then drives like a man possessed towards the hospital. By the time he arrives, the ash is covering all the buildings and cars in the streets and people are rushing inside to escape the blackness as it tries to infiltrate eyes, noses and throats.

The accident and emergency desk is crowded with the sick and their carers, vying for attention. The ash is affecting the weak-lunged and a trail of parents have started to arrive with crying and coughing children in tow. The hospital has already nicknamed the ailment 'Ruapehu throat'. Her brow furrowed in frustration, the sister in charge is trying to prioritise the wave of cases when Tori calls out to catch her attention. Looking annoyed, she nevertheless beckons him forward.

'I'm waiting for a friend, one of the scientists, who is being evacuated from Ruapehu. Is there any news?'

Her brow relaxes, she checks her watch and then looks more kindly at him. 'I'm sorry. We're all just waiting for them to arrive.'

As he sits flicking through old magazines, he feels nauseous.

The waiting room is hot and the cacophony of the sick and the smell of cleaning fluid oppress him. He returns outside. Ash is still falling but more lightly now, like the tail end of a black snowstorm. The car park is carpeted in ash and he can see the footsteps of those arriving at the hospital emblazoned on the concrete like a cruel parody of the Walk of Fame on Hollywood Boulevard. The ash sticks to the soles of their shoes and turns the polished cream-tiled floor inside to a dull, dirty grey.

As he hears the chopper approaching and sees an ambulance pull away from the hospital to meet it, he starts to run. He doesn't know where he's going but he follows the sound of the siren to the rear of the building. Finding the strength of the desperate, he effortlessly scales a brick wall and a wire fence and keeps running across a paddock. He stands waving furiously as the draught of the descending chopper blows his hair asunder and distorts his expression.

Luke Gallagher recognises him and waves back. As soon as the chopper touches down, the ambulance backs in as closely as it can. The door opens immediately and the paramedics unload the first stretcher.

Tori sees Theo lying motionless, his usually vibrant tanned face oddly pale. Streaks of dirt and blood remain in the creases of his brow and neck where they have escaped the attention of the paramedics. He is quickly put into the ambulance where a waiting doctor immediately starts to examine him.

Frances' usually shiny honey-coloured hair is matted and sticking to her head, her eyes are closed and her face is drawn, but he can see the oxygen mask moving slightly as Frances breathes in and out. He waits by the ambulance and as they bring the stretcher over he reaches out to touch her hand, a gentle squeeze. He feels the warmth of her but nothing more.

As he is watching her being loaded into the ambulance, Tori feels someone's eyes burning into him. He sees Sam walking from the chopper, escorted to the ambulance by a paramedic. The two men exchange glances but say nothing.

Siren blaring, the ambulance rushes to the hospital entrance. The helicopter, needed back at the mountain, takes off again, Luke waving as he leaves. She is alive and Tori knows, wants to believe, she will survive. A tear rolls down his cheek. He sinks to his knees, a great wave of relief and gratitude rolling through him.

When he returns to casualty, he sees Shona, tear-stained and distressed, with his children.

'I went to find you and Aunty said you would be here,' she says, grabbing hold of his arm. 'I've heard Frances is injured. Is she OK?'

'I think so, she's here now being looked after. Are you all right?'

'Tori, it's Bill. He's missing. He's up there on the mountain.'

'What was he doing? How do you know?'

'I had a call from one of his mates at the army camp in Waiouru. He went up there on a survival training course with others and they think they were snow-caving up the top. They can't contact them. I've tried ringing his mobile but there's no answer.'

'Stay here with us, Shona. At the moment there's nothing you can do except wait for news.'

'No, I'm going to drive up to Ruapehu as far as I can. I have to be closer to him. He might need me.'

Kissing her on both cheeks, he sees mirrored in her eyes the same fear he carries inside. 'I'd probably do the same thing. Keep in touch and, if I can, I'll come up too.'

He watches as the automatic doors close behind her and then turns to give Moana and Hemi big bear hugs.

'Is Frances going to die?' Hemi asks, and Moana hangs on his reply.

'Of course not,' he says, hoping he's not revealing that he shares his son's fears. 'Let's just wait a while and we may be able to see her.'

Moana links her arm in her father's and rests her head on his shoulder as they sit together like a couple of kids nervously waiting for a vaccination injection.

Hemi fidgets and wriggles, scanning the sick and injured curiously until he starts to look bored. 'Dad, I'm hungry,' he says.

Tori slips him a ten dollar note and points him in the direction of the café. 'Yeah, off you go. A man still has to eat, even in an emergency.'

A neatly groomed woman with short grey hair is trying to win the sister's attention.

'I'm here to see Theo Rush,' Tori hears her say, and he goes over to introduce himself.

'Are you Mrs Rush? I'm a friend of Frances Nelson, who just came in with Theo from the mountain.'

He can see the strain and fear in her eyes as she turns to him.

'Yes, I'm Sue,' she says, shaking his hand. 'Have you heard anything?'

'We're all just waiting,' he demurs. 'Join us if you like.'

Her face is pleasant and, for a woman nudging 60, fresh and clear. But she wears a look of resignation that reveals more than mere words ever could. As she greets Tori's children she simply says, 'Theo was always prepared for this.'

They sit together, each imagining what their future might be without the ones they love. Tori watches the hands of the large white clock on the waiting-room wall moving with infinitesimal slowness. With each tiny movement, his self-doubt increases. Maybe he is fooling himself when he thinks Frances will recover.

How could he bear to lose her now, when they are just beginning? It's only a few months since they met, yet he feels fundamentally changed, finds it hard to remember his life before she came into it. He was happy then, wasn't he? Sure, he was missing his wife, but he had the kids, plenty of fish, lots of money . . . Now he thinks of Frances all the time. Nothing else seems as important.

He focuses again on the clock and is surprised to see that less than half an hour has passed.

'Mr Maddison, Mrs Rush? I'm Doctor Vicky Adams.' A striking-looking woman with red hair pulled into a smooth pony-tail comes towards them. Clipboard in hand and stethoscope slung casually around her neck, she summons them into the treatment area.

'Kids, stay here, don't go anywhere,' Tori calls over his shoulder as the swing doors close behind him. As he follows her, he notices that, beneath her white hospital coat, the doctor is wearing blue jeans and red sling-back shoes.

'Please wait here, Mr Maddison,' she says, pointing to a wooden bench. 'Frances is going to be OK. She inhaled a lot of toxic fumes, which really knocked her around and has made her very tired, and she's hurt her shoulder. She's in X-ray now but they'll be bringing her back down soon so you can see her then.'

Then she draws Sue aside and in hushed tones talks to her about Theo. Tori can't make out the words but as she taps the clipboard to emphasise what she is saying he sees Sue's face fall and her eyes look down as she lets out a deep sigh. The doctor leads her away and they disappear behind another swing door.

His mind spins with a mixture of relief and concern. Frances will be OK. The words make him want to leap into the air with joy. OK is such a nothing little word, yet now it equals fantastic, beautiful, incredible, miraculous. He feels guilty being so happy when Sue has clearly had serious news about Theo's condition. He finds a nurse and checks whether he can bring Moana and Hemi through as well. When he returns with them, the nurse ushers them into the casualty treatment area and points towards a closed curtain.

Tori gently slides the curtain back and peeps through. Frances is lying on the bed, one arm in a sling, an oxygen mask on her face. As she hears him enter, she looks up and her eyes light up instantly with pleasure. With her freshly washed hair and dressed in a white hospital robe, she looks much younger, child-like.

As he goes to her side she lifts the mask and he leans over to kiss her lips for the first time. They part reluctantly, laughing and crying all at once until she flinches in pain when she bumps her arm.

'God, that hurts. They don't think it's broken but the tissue is damaged and I'm going to have some huge bruises. I think I was hit by a flying rock.'

'Don't move. No more kissing. We don't want you to die of passion,' he jokes.

Moana and Hemi come closer and, ignoring the warning, Moana leans over to kiss Frances on the cheek. She hands her an early flowering daffodil she found in her grandmother's garden. Its centre is the colour of egg yolk and the petals around it pale lemon. Frances smiles at her as she smells the sweet freshness.

'I've got something for you too,' Hemi says. From behind his back he produces a lollipop which he plants next to her where its bright red and yellow wrapping shines against the whiteness of the sheets.

'I've got something good to tell you, Frances,' he says.

'What's that?' she encourages the boy.

'Mum's here,' he says with a big smile.

'Oh shut up, you idiot,' Moana interrupts and the smile dies on his lips.

Frances opens her mouth in surprise to say something then quickly closes it again. Her eyes are seeking answers as she turns to Tori.

'Don't worry. She's staying with the kids at my mother's house. She's just here for a week. Then she'll go back to Auckland.'

'She says she wants to stay and you won't let her!' Hemi suddenly snaps before running out of the ward.

'Moana, please follow him and make sure he doesn't leave the hospital.'

Tori shakes his head and drags a chair over so he can sit close to Frances. Taking her hand, he raises it to his lips and holds it against his cheek.

'I'm sorry, Frances, the boy is upset.' He struggles for the words then meets her gaze. 'What he says is true. She did ask to come back. To come back to me. To be honest, if you hadn't come into my life I might have let her. It's not always easy with the kids. But you've changed everything. You're the only woman I want in my life. You have to believe that.'

A terrible doubt trickles through Frances' mind. She has lived with deception before and not recognised it. But Tori is looking so worried and upset that she dismisses her qualms. She brings his hand to her lips, silently signalling her trust through her eyes.

The sliding of the curtain interrupts them and Dr Adams appears with X-rays in hand.

'You're extraordinarily lucky your shoulder and arm aren't broken. They're badly strained and bruised. You're going to be sore for a couple of weeks but otherwise I'd expect them to mend well. We'd like to keep you here for another two days — you've inhaled a lot of nasty gas.'

'What about Theo, Doctor? Will he be OK?'

'I'm afraid he's in a critical condition, Frances. He's in intensive care and we're preparing him for surgery.'

'What happened to him?'

'I can't say too much more. His wife Sue has asked to visit you so she may want to tell you more. She'll probably come and see you soon.'

Her face pale, Frances starts to quiver and Tori holds her hand more tightly.

'It could have just as easily been me. It's just that Sam and I managed to crawl over the crater's lip. He must have been hit by more of those hot rocks. God, I hope he'll pull through.'

'The good news, Frances,' the doctor adds, 'is that Sam Hawks escaped injury almost completely — just a few scratches and he's already gone home. Now I think you need to rest. We're moving you to a room in another ward in about ten minutes.'

CHAPTER THIRTY-SEVEN

❧

As soon as Tori turns his phone back on, it beeps to tell him there are three messages. They're all from Shona. She is heading for the Chateau and asks if he can meet her there.

He delivers the children back to his mother's house and after hugging her, leaves quickly to avoid confronting Cheryl, who is due back any minute from the supermarket. For the first time, her return to Taupo has not distressed him. He feels little emotion towards her at all and his only concern is that her unexpected change of heart might disrupt the family harmony.

She arrived, without notice as usual, two days earlier. When Tori dropped by late in the day to see his mother, she was waiting for him. He noticed immediately something was different. Her eyes engaged him for the first time since their parting, and her thick long hair had been layered, highlighting her attractive face. She asked him to go for a walk with her, something she had not done for years.

Sensing trouble, Tori felt guarded but agreed to go.

'I'm really missing the kids,' Cheryl began. She then took

his hand. 'I'm missing you too, Tori. I've been a fool. I want to come back.'

Tori's mind raced. He squeezed her hand, then let it drop as he struggled for the words that could express his feelings.

'Cheryl . . . you left me. You didn't give me any say in that decision. I've had to make my own way with the kids without you. Now . . .'

Cheryl tried to take his hand again but this time he resisted. 'No. It won't work. Not now. It's been too long. If you want to come back to Taupo I can't stop you, but it will never work between us now. It's too late.'

He could see her face change and harden. 'It's that slut from the volcano centre, isn't it? The American. Hemi told me all about her.'

'This isn't about anyone else, Cheryl. This is about us. And us is no more. You made sure of that.'

He turned back to the house with his stomach churning. He knew he was doing the right thing but he wasn't sure if he was being truthful. If Frances hadn't been around, maybe . . .

He sees Cheryl's car arriving just as he is leaving. He waves but does not stop. The ash has stopped falling but he can see traces of it on the roadside and drifts of it floating on the edge of the lake. As he drives, he rings Uncle Eruera, his sister Mata and other elders in the iwi to let them know about Frances and Bill. As Bill belongs to their tribe, they will want to follow the progress of the search and prepare themselves to come if needed.

He yawns deeply as fatigue creeps up on him. Realising he hasn't eaten since breakfast, he pulls over for some takeaway food. The shop is crowded with locals he recognises and skiers on their way home to more distant towns and cities.

As he orders fish and chips and coffee a voice behind him says, 'The trout aren't going to like that ash, Tori. It's made a helluva mess.'

He turns to see Smithy, whose face is sweaty, dots of the ash sticking to his nose and in his hair.

'You're looking a bit messy yourself, eh, Smithy. What have you been doing?'

'Checking all the marinas and around the lake generally. We've been worried about water contamination and the ash can wreck all the machinery as well. Gets right into things. It'll wreck all the paintwork on the cars too.'

'Yeah, it's ruined all my washing that was hanging on the line,' a woman next to them says. 'All the sheets are streaked with black and the clothes are stained.'

Tori's food arrives. 'Got to run, Smithy. My cousin Bill is lost up the mountain.'

'Sorry to hear that, mate.' Smithy claps a hand on Tori's shoulder as he leaves.

Tori devours the food hungrily as he continues driving, the warm, golden, batter-covered fish and crisp chips immediately satisfying his empty stomach. The coffee gives him an instant lift. A stream of cars is still travelling north but there is very little traffic heading for the mountain and eventually he almost has the road to himself.

Dark rain clouds fuse with smoke and ash to hide the volcanoes. The beauty of the landscape seems to have evaporated and the wild tussock foothills are forbidding. He recalls the stories of the haunted, gale-swept desert that frightened him as a child, sitting on his grandfather's knee in the gloom of evening. 'Travel with caution and be respectful in the high country lest you be borne down by sleet and ice or smoke and ash from the mountain,' the old man would tell the wide-eyed boy. 'You mustn't do anything to offend the tapu of the holy mountain.'

When he reaches the turn-off to the volcano, Tori sees a roadblock and a policeman waves him to the side of the road. 'You can only go as far as the Chateau. The army has plenty of people up there looking and we don't want any more civilians to worry about.'

Shona is sitting in the hotel lounge waiting for him. Despite the season, her midriff is still very much in evidence between low-cut black jeans and a tight-fitting red sweater. He resists the temptation to tell her that her stiletto boots might not suit the local climbing conditions. Thinking how happy her appearance would make Bill if he were here, Tori gives her a hug and tries to reassure her. 'He's a tough old warrior. If anyone can survive, he will.'

Beckoning a waiter, Tori orders two brandies. The rich auburn liquor warms and steadies them.

'Stay here,' he tells Shona, 'and I'll try to find out what's happening.'

In the volcano observation centre alongside the hotel, Tori asks the two seismologists and an emergency rescue worker for news, explaining that he is Bill Harp's cousin.

'Nothing happening,' one of them says, looking up from a bank of scientific equipment and radio receivers. 'The volcano has gone dead. At least for now. But we'll be here all night, just in case. I'm afraid the soldiers haven't been found. There are a couple of dozen army people up there digging around and a few sniffer dogs. The trouble is the ash from the eruption covered the top of the mountain where we believe they'd dug in yesterday. They were supposed to be out this morning but then the eruption happened. The rescuers couldn't start as early as they wanted because we were too worried there could be a big explosion.'

'I'm here with Bill's girlfriend. Should we just wait until we hear something?'

'They're packing up now. It's getting too dark. They'll start again at dawn. We're in radio contact with the rescuers. You'll just have to keep checking with us here.'

Tori finds Shona curled up on a sofa asleep, looking like a

lost child. Leaning over her, he gently taps her arm until she wakes.

'Is he going to die?' she asks him immediately, clutching his hand.

Tori struggles to disguise his fear. 'I don't know. There's always hope. But it's nearly dark and they've stopped the search until daybreak. I'm going to have a look around myself.'

'I'll come too.' Shona jumps up and nearly falls over. They both look at her boots and laugh.

'Just stay here, sister,' he says kindly. 'Maybe a few prayers . . .'

The light is fading fast and he avoids the few soldiers he sees, knowing they will stop him. He drives slowly up towards the top car park at the foot of the snowfields, thankful he has put chains on his tyres. It is deserted and dark when he arrives. Snow has already covered the tracks of the rescue vehicles. He takes his torch and, pulling up his parka hood, heads towards the track he knows will take him in the direction of the search.

For a few minutes, he climbs steadily, forgetting the cold. But the torch is of little use and he's finding it harder to make out the contours of the rocks. Suddenly a huge rumble makes him lose his step. He trips and crashes onto his side. Ignoring a searing pain in his knee, he stumbles to his feet. As heavy drops of rain drip down his face he realises the noise was thunder, not an eruption. As he looks up, he sees a bolt of lightning flashing down the mountain, illuminating the bluish-white slopes. He shudders as he recalls this omen of death from his people's legends.

He tries to move forward but the heavy rain drives him back. He slips and falls again, crying out as the pain in his knee intensifies. Lightning skirts around him and he knows he is no match for the might of the mountain. His leg aching, he turns back with a heavy heart.

Shaking and drenched, Tori shelters in the hotel foyer, not yet able to face Shona. He finds the bathroom and as he washes his hands and face he regards his frightened face in the mirror. For a moment he thinks he sees Bill's features mingled with his own. He gasps and the mirage fades until he is looking deep into his own eyes again. He breathes deeply — in, out, in, out, regaining control.

He finds Shona asleep again and gently strokes her shoulder, but this time she doesn't move so he knows he must leave her alone in her vigil. He will return home to collect his people and prepare for the time when the mountain decides to deliver Bill back to them.

CHAPTER THIRTY-EIGHT

❧

Frances wakes as the last minutes of daylight dissolve into night. For a moment she forgets where she is until reminded by a dull ache in her shoulder breaking through a barrier of painkillers.

'Frances . . .' Startled, she turns to see Sue sitting in the grey visitor's chair alongside her bed, her soft features invaded by anxiety.

'Is Theo . . . how is he?'

'Not good . . .' Her voice fades away, then rallies. 'Are you feeling OK?'

'I'm fine. Lucky escape, I guess. I'm so sorry about Theo. I lost sight of him. It was crazy up there. Everything just seemed to explode around us. There were hot rocks flying everywhere. I can remember trying to see where Theo was but I couldn't move. And then . . . then I can't remember anything until the helicopter came.'

Sue is kneading her hands as she listens, trying to visualise those last moments for herself. 'I know you couldn't do anything. Theo's always been philosophical about the volcano. I suppose

I always thought it might come to this. Yet I hoped we would be away from here before it did. I think another year and he'd have given it away. And now . . .'

'You haven't given up on him that easily?' Frances smiles, trying to penetrate Sue's despair.

'No. It's just that he's in such a bad state. He's still in a coma. His skull is cracked and he has broken bones in both legs and quite severe burns on his legs and arms.'

Ignoring her own pain, Frances leans forward to take Sue's hand as she starts to cry.

'The worst thing is . . . I'm sorry—' She reaches down to her handbag on the floor, removes a handkerchief, dabs her eyes and blows her nose. 'The worst thing is they don't know yet whether he has brain damage. Even if he pulls through physically he could be affected for the rest of his life.'

'I'm truly sorry, Sue. We all know we do a dangerous job and something can go wrong at any time, but none of us really believes it will happen to us.'

'I know. Theo loves those mountains.' As Sue stands to leave she gives a resigned shrug of her shoulders. 'Sometimes I think he loves them more than me.'

'No, you're wrong,' Frances says. 'Whenever I've been up the mountain with him, he always talks about you. You're his rock, really.'

As Sue leaves the room, a nurse enters, carrying a large box. 'You're popular,' the nurse says, placing the box, which Frances can now see is full of red roses, on the bedside cabinet. She hands her a pile of emails and phone messages.

As Frances flicks through them she is astonished at the speed of communication in the vulcanology world. 'Glad that mountain was no contest for you, Frankie! Hurry and get well. I want to go climbing with you again soon. xxx Ollie.' There are other greetings from her colleagues in Seattle, old friends in the

Philippines and from other scientists around New Zealand. Her mother, contacted by the hospital, has asked her to phone.

She opens the small envelope attached to the flowers: 'My darling, Thank God you're safe. I love you and I want you to come back home. Damon.' Taken by surprise, she doesn't know whether to laugh or cry. So often she had longed for such warmth from Damon yet the words sound hollow, as though they are coming from a complete stranger. She struggles to conjure his image in her mind. His face, once the epicentre of her desire, has faded from her mind and heart. Nor can she recall with any clarity the pain that used to leave her drained and distraught.

She picks up the bedside phone to call her mother.

CHAPTER THIRTY-NINE

❧

We'll all go together. We'll just wait up the mountain until they bring him down. It's what we must do.' Uncle Eruera lifts the rear door of his old navy-blue Holden station wagon and watches as Tui and Tori load into the back a pile of large fern fronds still wet with the cool morning dew. 'I've rung Bill's mother, and his sisters are trying to find his father. They'll all be getting up there as quickly as they can.'

Mata comes out of their mother's house carrying two large plastic bags. 'I've got sheets and blankets, just in case,' she says, putting them alongside the ferns.

'Mum and Cheryl will mind the kids. I'll drive Mata in my car and we'll see you up there,' Tori tells Uncle Eruera.

As they reach the turn-off to the mountain, Mata looks surprised as Tori drives in the opposite direction.

'Just a very quick detour via the hospital,' he tells her, mocking pain as she jabs his rib teasingly.

It's too early for visitors but he persuades the sister to let him see Frances. She is sleeping peacefully, a faint smile on her lips, so he decides not to disturb her. As he turns to leave, a flash of red catches his eye: sunlight is piercing through the ruby roses. He tiptoes over and reads the card.

He has taken too much for granted. Of course she has someone else. Why did he ever think otherwise? Yet she seemed sometimes to care about him as much as he did about her. You're a fool, Tori says to himself, you can't will her to be in love with you. He thinks again about Cheryl, waiting for him, wanting him again, together with their children. It would be so easy . . .

As they approach the intersection to the road to the Chateau, Tori phones Shona.

'I haven't heard anything, they're still looking,' she tells him. 'The soldiers have been up there since dawn.'

When they arrive he can see Uncle Eruera's car already parked outside the hotel and the old man is leaning out the window talking to Shona and an older woman. As Tori pulls up he vaguely recognises her as Bill's mother, although he hasn't seen her for many years. He waves a short greeting and beckons Shona to come with Mata and him to the volcano observation centre.

Their faces grim, the seismologists he met the day before mutter their hellos. While one returns to the task of monitoring the seismometers, the other indicates their presence to a third man, an army sergeant, who is talking on the phone. His face flushed and lined with exhaustion, he tells them to sit down.

'I'm sorry,' he falters. 'We found them fifteen minutes ago. One of our field doctors has just phoned us. I'm afraid they're all dead.'

Shona sinks to the floor moaning. Tori and Mata each take an arm, pull her up and hold her very tightly. She clings to them.

'No, no, not Bill! It's not fair. He was so beautiful. It's not fair.'

She continues crying out Bill's name in a litany without hope as they lead her outside. Tori whispers to Uncle Eruera and Tui and they gather around Bill's mother and sisters, closing into a tight circle of grief.

Tori, automatically assuming the responsibility of the elder, approaches the sergeant with a look that says he won't take no for an answer. 'Our family wants to take Bill's body away. It's important for us.'

'I understand, but we'll have to wait until our doctors have completed their examinations and released him. The police are already up there so they'll have to be involved too. They'll be able to do that up there in the ambulance. So I don't foresee any major difficulties as long as the family sign a form saying they'll take responsibility.'

'We need to go up there to help bring him down,' Tori says. 'Can we get through? This mountain is our spiritual homeland. We must say special prayers as close to where he died as we can. This must happen as quickly as possible.'

'It's at your risk. I can provide an escort to take you up to Whakapapa. There's only a few emergency workers up there because of the fear of more eruptions. They will be bringing the bodies down there to the ambulance on skidoos.'

The tiny cavalcade winds up the mountain road, the women quietly weeping, the men's faces set in sad resignation. Mata and Bill's mother wrap their arms around each other in the back seat while Shona rests her head against the door, tears washing a line of mascara down her cheeks. They trail behind an army truck, two young soldiers in the front, lamenting the loss of their mates.

At the top of the road, an ambulance is parked. Its rear door is open, light flashing on its roof and two paramedics and the army doctor waiting alongside. A police jeep is parked next to it. Presently, they hear the sound of the skidoos, the straining of the small engines desecrating the alpine stillness as one by one the ski patrollers arrive with their tragic cargo.

As the paramedics help the patrollers remove the stretchers bearing the bodies, Tori steps forward. 'Please, can you leave them there for a few minutes, on the ground. We need to pay our respects to our dead right now.'

The paramedics place the ghostly forms, wrapped in sheets and covered in plastic, in a line on the side of the road. Tori can tell from the bulky shape which is Bill. He gently pulls back the makeshift shroud to reveal his face.

Shona falls on her knees, ignoring the cold hard gravel that cuts through into her skin. 'He looks like he's just sleeping,' she says, stroking his frozen cheek. 'He's so handsome.'

Bill's mother joins her on the ground. Her shoulders hunched over her lost son, she starts to weep. 'Aaeee, why him? Why my son? It should have been me! I wish it was me!'

The mourners gather and Uncle Eruera starts to chant an ancient karakia to release the spirit of the three men into the care of their ancestors.

A freezing eddy swirls around them and Tori thinks he can hear creaking and groaning coming from the heart of the volcano beneath them. He glances up to the summit where gusting wind blends little pockets of sodden ash with new deposits of snow. He trembles as he remembers the lightning streaking down the mountain the night before, warning of imminent death.

'We pray for the souls of all these men. May they rest in peace for eternity. It is done,' Uncle Eruera says and steps aside.

The doctor motions at the paramedics to place the other two bodies into the ambulance. 'I understand you want to take your cousin's body home with you,' he says to Tori. 'I examined him up the mountain and can officially pronounce him dead. I just need to fill out the death certificate now. And you'll need to sign a release. The police have agreed,' he says, handing Tori a form. Quietly, he tells him, 'They were all asphyxiated. There was no air getting through to the snow cave.'

Bill's mother opens the back of the car and with great tenderness the men lift Bill's body carefully onto the bed of ferns. She hands Tori a plastic bag of Bill's clothing she has brought from home. 'He always liked these,' she says. 'It's what we would like him to wear.'

'Uncle and I will take Bill to the undertaker to be prepared,' he tells her. 'Don't worry, we will wait there with him until he is ready. He will never be left alone and we will bring him home for the tangi.'

The light is fading and it is well into evening when the two men return to the marae with the coffin. When they pull up, four younger men step forward to carry the casket into the wharenui. Already about thirty other family members are milling around, waiting. Hemi and some young cousins are chasing each other around the buildings, shrieking with laughter.

'Taihoa e tama. Stop that, Hemi,' Tori gently chastens his son. 'All of you kids quieten down a bit. Follow me.'

Women who have been preparing food in the brightly lit hall for the three-day tangi that lies ahead, hurry out to join the men who are forming a procession behind the coffin. Inside, they pass rows of mattresses covered in fresh linen and blankets lined up on the polished wooden floor in readiness for the many relatives who will be travelling from towns and cities throughout New Zealand for the funeral. They place Bill's coffin at the end of the room on the floor and Uncle Eruera moves forward to remove the lid.

The young boys nudge each other and edge forward. Awestruck, they take in the still features of the man they remember for his boisterousness. He is dressed in a black corduroy shirt, open at the neck, a newish pair of blue denim jeans and polished black leather shoes. Around his neck is the silver chain and greenstone pendant of Tangaroa, the great god of the sea, that he always wore. His short black hair is glistening, his brown face glowing in the soft light.

'You are home,' his mother whispers as she leans forward to touch his hand. Her tears course down deeply etched gullies on her face as she feels the coldness of her son. 'We will stay with you, my darling boy.'

Throughout the evening, cousins, sisters, brothers, aunties and uncles take it in turn to make impromptu speeches about Bill, commemorating his death and celebrating his life. Occasionally, they burst into song, tunes that Bill loved or others of a more sacred nature. The children sit quietly on their beds playing board games.

Every hour or so new arrivals are announced and the elders file out to the entrance to perform the traditional welcome. Sometimes it is a carload of people; occasionally, just a lone figure who has journeyed for hours. Each must be welcomed. The visitors doze on and off. Bill's mother, father and sisters barely leave his side except to visit the dining room.

At two in the morning when the wind has dropped, the lake is gently lapping and the night is at its stillest, a small bus arrives at the entrance of the marae. Eight adults and half a dozen sleepy children spill out onto the lawn. Uncle Eruera walks out to greet the relatives who have driven six hours from the north of the island for the tangi.

Most of the mattresses in the wharenui are now occupied and the room is full of the living, twisting and turning in a half-sleep while the body of the one they have come to honour lies forever motionless.

Hemi can't sleep. He searches for his sister among the rows of mattresses until he sees Moana's glossy long hair pouring out from under a sheet.

'Moana, I'm scared,' he whispers, shaking her. 'The kehua might get me!'

She lifts the sheet and he crawls in beside her. 'There's no ghost here,' she says quietly.

He clings to his sister, gratefully inhaling her warmth, but he doesn't quite believe her. He can see the coffin at the end of the meeting house beneath the rows of photos of people he knows were, and still are, part of his family. Above him the carved likenesses of his ancestors and the great spirit gods seem to be staring right at him and he shivers.

'Will Bill be OK?' he says in a small voice. But his sister doesn't answer so he nestles closer to her, closes his eyes and breathes in time with her until his fears fade into sleep.

CHAPTER FORTY

❧

On the third and final day of the tangi, Tori drives to the hospital early. Frances is already waiting for him out the front of the building, the crisp breeze from the lake blowing her soft hair. Her arm still supported by a sling, she climbs into the front seat awkwardly.

'So good to get out of there and breathe some fresh air.'

Her face is pale and her eyes greener than he remembers. They lean towards each other and kiss softly.

'So good to see you.' She kisses him again.

'Are you sure?' he searches her face, afraid to mention the flowers.

'As sure as I have ever been,' she says, and for now he has to be satisfied with the answer.

'I'm sorry this will be a sad day to be going home. Do you mind if we go straight to the marae? Bill's funeral starts soon.'

'Of course — I want to be there. How is Shona?'

'She's bearing up. She's been coming and going to the marae. Not being Maori, she hasn't stayed all the time but Bill's close family never leave his side. Today will be very tough for them.'

When they arrive, the size of the crowd of people filling the grounds takes her aback.

'You can see he has lots of relations,' he smiles at her. 'Also quite a few soldiers are here from Waiouru. It will be a big send-off.'

An elderly priest dressed in a funereal black suit with a purple scapular around his neck is shaking hands with people.

'That's Father Ryan. Been coming here for years for our funerals.'

Standing inside the ceremonial gate, Aunty Tui and Moana catch sight of them and wave them over. Aunty Tui kisses Frances' cheek warmly, gently patting her injured arm. Tori hugs Moana. Shyly, the girl waits for Frances to make the first move, then rushes to hug her when Frances smiles.

'Careful! It's still very sore!' Frances is touched by Moana's affection.

She hears the now familiar voice of Uncle Eruera calling out the ritual welcome to her and other small groups of mourners who are arriving at the same time. Moving forward with the group, she presses her nose on his and a line of others leading to the meeting house.

'You're getting good at the hongi,' Tori whispers to her as she wrinkles her nose at him. 'Do you want to see Bill before they close the coffin? There's time.'

'I suppose so.' She hesitates. 'Yes, I do.'

The coffin has been brought outside onto the veranda of the meeting house. The shiny mahogany and ornate silver handles contrast strangely with the muted wood of the building. Like sentries, Bill's family keep watch. Dressed in black with a scarf covering her head, his mother sits alongside while his sisters hover close by.

Frances stands back, not sure she is ready to confront death so closely. Sensing her nervousness, Tori squeezes her hand tightly and ushers her close to the body. She glances in at Bill's face, barely recognising the figure who so recently was bursting with life. Feeling a little like an intruder, she nods a greeting to the family.

'Frances!' She turns to see Shona, her eyes heavily made up but still red from crying. Her long blonde hair cascades over her shoulders, contrasting with the dark Maori women around her. They embrace warmly.

'I'm sorry I haven't been to see you,' Shona apologises. 'It's just . . .'

'Don't. No need. I'm just so glad I was able to get here today. I'm so sorry about Bill.'

Death has not interfered with Shona's fashion sense. She wears a tightly fitting black jacket with a low-cut white bustier beneath, a silver and paua-shell pendant Bill gave her for her birthday, a short skirt and high, black patent leather stiletto shoes.

Tori touches Frances' arm. 'I have to leave you for a while. I'm part of the rituals. I'll catch you later.'

Shona links arms with her and they drift away from Tori back onto the lawn. Frances, dressed in black pants with a tailored pink shirt and smart leather pumps, murmurs to her friend, 'You always have the knack of making me feel dowdy.'

'Bill wouldn't have wanted me to drop my standards,' Shona replies lightly. 'Though I don't think all the family are that impressed.' She nods her head towards an unfamiliar group of women who are looking at them. 'By the way, in case you haven't noticed, the one giving you dagger looks is Tori's ex-wife, Cheryl.'

Frances sees a tall, curvaceous woman with thick curly black hair glaring at her. Her dark flashing eyes and the set of her full mouth instantly remind her of Moana.

'I think I'll just keep out of her way,' she whispers.

From the veranda, a loud voice speaking in Maori makes them turn back. The people around them are pressing forward.

'It's all about to start,' Shona says. 'Come towards the front.'

Standing next to the coffin, a white-haired man in a hound's-tooth sports jacket and neatly pressed trousers is talking loudly and gesturing wildly.

'That's Bill's father. I hadn't met him before,' Shona says. 'He lives a long way from here and just arrived yesterday. I felt a bit strange meeting him. He's making the first oration.'

The two women stand side by side, both feeling like outsiders.

'I hope you're not feeling too tired. This will go for at least an hour. It's like a long storybook about Bill's life and calls on the ancestors to care for him in the afterlife.'

Frances squeezes Shona's hand. 'Thanks, I'm fine. But you're the one I should be worrying about. You must have been through hell.'

An air of casualness mingles with the solemnity of the occasion. Children wander in and out of the lines of adults, the smaller ones chasing each other. Some in brightly coloured T-shirts and shorts, others in tracksuits, they run barefoot wherever they please.

A group of bulky Maori men, some with heavily tattooed arms and faces, files to the front and begins a vigorous haka: 'Ka mate, ka mate, . . .'

Frances sees Tori in the middle of the second row. He is taller than many of the others and his handsome features also make him stand out. She notices, too, that his firm chest and stomach contrast with some of the pot bellies flopping around him. She is mesmerised by his sheer physical presence, and by the power and intensity of the chanting.

'It's their final farewell to Bill, their fellow warrior.' Frances hears Shona's voice breaking and sees she has started to cry. She puts her arm around her friend, flinching when her injured shoulder hurts with the movement.

'I'm sorry,' Shona says. 'I really don't want to lose it in front of everyone here, but I've seen Bill do the haka lots of times with those guys. I can't stand it that he's no longer here.'

As the men leap into the air with a final full-throated cry, then retreat to the side of the crowd, Mata leads out a group of women, with Moana trailing self-consciously at the end of the line.

'There's the bitch,' Shona says, regaining her sense of humour when she spots Cheryl in the front row.

Frances can't stop herself commenting. 'She's very beautiful, don't you think?'

'Maybe in a superficial, tarty sort of way. Bad eye make-up and no class. Nothing for you to worry about.'

Frances suppresses a smile, but she can't take her eyes off Cheryl and wonders how seriously she is trying to draw Tori back into their relationship.

Mata's melodic voice suddenly pierces the silence that has descended on the marae.

E tangi ana koe, Hine e hine,
Kua ngenge ana koe, Hine e hine.
Kati to pouri ra, noho i te aroha,
Te ngakau o te matua, Hine e Hine.

The other women join her, their voices rising in sweet harmony. As they draw out the final note, the mourners bow their heads as one.

Looking relieved, Moana walks over to Frances' side and surprises her by taking hold of her hand.

'You were wonderful,' Frances says. 'Where's your father?'

'Umm, don't know. Maybe with Mum,' she says, looking away shyly.

Frances can't stop herself turning around. She sees them standing together a few metres away. Cheryl has her arm through Tori's and as she watches she sees him stroke her hand. Frances quickly looks away. She feels nauseous. If it wasn't for Shona and Moana still holding on to her hands, she would try to escape.

'Look, Frances, they're starting,' the girl tells her.

As two elders secure the lid of the coffin, the priest steps forward: 'Let us say Te Inoi a te Ariki, the Lord's Prayer.' Then he walks towards the coffin and sprinkles it with holy water. Taking the brass-chained incense holder, he waves it over the coffin, releasing the pungent aroma of burning frankincense and myrrh.

Frances lets herself be swept along with the crowd as they follow the priest and the pallbearers, who include Tori, up the hill towards the little family cemetery. Frances can see the open grave ahead, freshly dug that morning by the men at the marae. Bill was a heavy man and his friends struggle as they bear him on this final journey. At last they reach the grave and gently lower the coffin next to it. As the priest sprinkles more holy water, Tori steps away from the others and begins to speak, his voice deep and clear. 'Haera ra, Bill.' As Frances listens to his farewell he catches her eye and his face softens.

As the men start to lower the coffin into the grave, Shona stands beside Frances, weeping softly. Suddenly, they hear a woman scream and Bill's mother lunges forward. She leans down into the dark chasm, wailing and banging her fists into the earth. Her daughters hold her tightly but do not pull her back, allowing her to continue her loud lament. As her voice fades, they ease her up onto her feet. She is covered with mud — her grey curly hair, her face, her black suit — but she makes no attempt to remove it. Her daughters hold her close and this time prevent her from falling down again.

As the men start to pile the dirt onto the coffin, Frances feels heavy drops of rain hitting her face.

'There's going to be a downpour,' Tori says as he appears at her side. 'It's a good omen but we're all going to get very wet.'

She looks into his eyes and he smiles at her.

'Sorry I had to leave you to look after yourself. But I had to concentrate on the ceremony.'

Frances nods but says nothing.

'Everything OK?' he asks.

'Sure.' Before she has time to say more, Cheryl sidles up to Tori, holding out her arm.

'Tori, coming with me?' she asks.

'Ah, Cheryl . . . this is my friend Frances. I'm looking after her for the rest of the afternoon so I'll catch up with you another time,' he says as he takes Frances' arm.

Cheryl's face contorts in a look of disgust but she says nothing and walks off down the hill.

Frances says nothing but Tori presses her. 'Are you sure you're OK?'

'Of course. It's just that I feel uncomfortable with your wife around and it looked as though you might have patched everything up with her.'

Tori laughs for the first time that day. 'Hey girl, you have nothing to worry about there. She's history with me but she's still family and the mother of my children so there are certain things I have to do.'

'Like holding her hand?'

'Only like a brother,' he says, 'but I'm flattered that you're jealous.' After a short pause he adds, 'At least I don't go sending her red roses.'

'Oh those,' Frances says. 'They were from my ex — and

that's what he'll always be.' She begins to relax, happy to be at his side again.

As they reach the dining hall she sees family members carrying large trays of steaming food, roasted meats and root vegetables inside to long tables.

'Hope you're hungry, Frances. You're going to try the food from your first hangi. All that food's been cooking since early this morning in the underground oven.'

'I'm not sure I am hungry. It seems a little too soon after the funeral to eat.'

Tori rests his arms on her shoulders and tilts her face up towards him. 'Now we leave all the darkness and the sadness at the grave. We walk out into the sunlight and we celebrate Bill's life.'

'You put so much importance on the funeral, don't you,' she says. 'We tend to brush it aside and avoid confronting it. Rushing away from work for just a couple of hours, if that. Certainly not three days.'

'Death is part of life. That's what we believe. We know we'll all die and we'll live again in the afterlife. Bill still walks among us. We've buried him but he'll continue to share our lives. He has just gone before us.'

CHAPTER FORTY-ONE

❧

A sense of strangeness runs through Frances on her first day back at the office. So much has changed since the eruption. Theo's desk is tidier than she has seen it, abandoned, lifeless. She runs her finger along its edge as she skirts past it to her own workplace, still littered with tiny reminders of her life: a framed photo of Olivia and her in the crater of Mount St Helens, another of her holding the trout she had caught with Tori in the river, her battered reference book on the Pacific Ring of Fire and her favourite porcelain mug, its whiteness broken up by pretty alpine daisies.

She has visited Theo daily, trying to stifle her tears as she avoided looking at the empty space on the bed where his left leg should have rested. Too badly shattered to save, it was amputated from the knee down.

Theo's mind had been saved, though. For the first week after the operation they had all but held their breaths, waiting. One morning she was standing by his bed gazing at his scarred arm. Once covered with thick blond hair, it now looked like a bald newborn bird. Suddenly he opened his eyes and gave her such a look she had to step back. It was an unexpected gaze of recognition, of intimate familiarity. He laughed at her. 'You look like you've seen a ghost!'

They were all worried about how he would react to his injuries, especially the loss of his leg, but he seemed so pleased to be alive. He told Frances he couldn't wait to leave the hospital so he and Sue could start to live their lives all over again.

'Doesn't look like I'll be climbing for a while.' He dismissed her concerned expression. 'I can still feel my toes, you know, even though they're gone. I fully intend to be back on the other foot as soon as I can.'

She walks over to the seismometer. One of the relieving scientists from Wellington is looking at the printouts from overnight. The zigzag graphs are small with no signs of unusual activity. As she looks over his shoulder, Sam comes up behind her.

'Good to have you back. We've missed you.' He looks genuinely happy to see her and as Frances turns he reaches out to embrace her, pulling her close. She hugs him back but pulls away when he shows no sign of letting go.

'You're looking wonderful, Frances. How are you feeling?'

'Better,' she smiles at him. 'And glad to be alive.'

'You can see it's still quiet up the mountain. Nothing much has happened since we were up there. A few tremors but that's it,' Sam tells her.

'Are we still on high alert?'

'No. We've dropped back from level five to level two. But we're still watching it round the clock. I think we have things under control up there at last. Everyone in the region knows the drill if the alarm goes to evacuate. But I hope it won't come to that.'

'What do you mean?' Frances asks him.

'Ah, it's just that the level of the Crater Lake is now steady. It has stopped rising.'

'Are the skifields open?'

'Yeah, most of them. The ash wrecked them but the fresh snow has covered that. But the numbers are right down. Lots of people are too scared to return just yet. Anyway, the spring melt is already beginning.'

'I'm worried about the equipment on the summit. Has anyone been up there to check it?' Something about Sam's demeanour is bothering Frances.

'I went up last week with a couple of the ski patrollers. It's remarkably intact underneath the Dome Shelter, though the hut was a bit of a wreck. We're having that repaired. But the microphones are still doing their job.'

'Good. I was hoping not to climb up there just yet.'

'I don't think you should. Leave it to me.'

Frances sifts through a pile of mail on her desk, noticing a blue envelope addressed to her in Damon's familiar handwriting. She flicks it open. A get well card with a caricature of a skier with bandaged limbs makes her smile. 'Glad to hear from Olivia you're on the mend. Did you get the flowers? More importantly, did you get my message? What do you think? Missing you. Love, Damon.'

She selects a tea bag from the small staff kitchen cupboard — English Breakfast, the flavour her parents used to like. As she pours the boiling water over it she knows what she must say to him.

Since leaving the hospital, she has thought a lot of her old life in Seattle, the happy years when Damon and her were so close. When they first started making love, they couldn't get enough of each other. Once, they spent two entire days in bed, just getting up now and then to shower and grab snacks and drinks from the fridge. The intensity of their passion left them breathless and limp, their apartment sweetly disordered. Sometimes he would phone her at the lab and suggest a lunchtime rendezvous. They would race home and devour each other. It all seemed so long ago, like trying to hang on to the details of a dream that was evaporating quickly as wakefulness takes hold.

Returning to her desk, she sips the tea, its warmth permeating her and giving her strength. She logs on to the Internet and sends Damon her answer, then sits back, feeling satisfied.

Among the many emails in her inbox, her eye is drawn to two older ones from head office in Wellington, written when she was still in hospital. She opens the one titled 'Re: Sam Hawks Appointment' and reads 'Sam Hawks has been appointed interim manager of the Taupo office. All staff will be under his authority. The position will be advertised in the near future.'

Her heart misses a beat as she opens another titled 'Remedial Work at Crater Lake':

The Minister of Public Works has given her approval for the use of bulldozers on the summit of Mount Ruapehu at Crater Lake. The decision to allow the machinery to break up the tephra dam was taken after consideration of all competing interests. The Minister accepted the recommendation of the acting manager of Taupo's Office of Seismology, Sam Hawks, to proceed immediately. She believes that while the intervention may not be acceptable to everyone, it is in the wider interests of public safety.

'Sam!' Frances cries out. 'Sam!' she shouts out again, turning to look for him.

'The boss has gone back up the mountain for the day,' one of the scientists says as he walks over to her carrying a printout. 'They've got more bulldozing to do and he wants to make sure it's done properly. Anything wrong?'

Frances grabs her phone and quickly punches in Sam's number. She's surprised to hear his cellphone ringing on the desk opposite hers where he has left it behind.

CHAPTER FORTY-TWO

✎

D id you know about the bulldozers?' Tori sounds unusually aggressive when he rings her just minutes later.

'I've only just found out myself.' Frances is annoyed by his accusatory tone. 'The Minister gave her approval while I was away. I came into work today for the first time. Sam's behind this and he's taken advantage of Theo's and my absence. I haven't even had a chance to talk to him about it. He didn't tell me and he's cleared out.'

'Well, we're furious about this desecration. It's been kept very secret. I hope you'll be able to do something immediately to get those machines off the mountain. I hear there's already been some working in the Crater Lake and the dozers are still up there.'

'Tori, I don't know if I can do anything . . .'

'I thought you were senior to Sam, Frances. We're counting on you. I've got to go now. There's a meeting at the marae about this. I'll call you later.'

He rings off abruptly before Frances can reply. She sits, angrily tapping her fingers on the desk.

'How dare he?' She feels equally cross with Sam and Tori and tries to separate her reasons. Tori has attacked her unfairly — at least that's what it feels like. She has forgotten that arrogance she detected the first time they met. Now he's expecting her to do the impossible.

I must be stupid to think that we could ever bridge the gap between our lives, she thinks. She feels used, as if Tori is taking advantage of their friendship to further the ends of his iwi. As for Sam . . . Once again she wonders if he might be right after all. Maybe she has been unreasonable about this, unfair to him. The last thing she wanted to see was more deaths on the mountain. Wasn't that why she became a scientist after all? She has come here to help solve the problems, not walk away from the difficult decisions.

Tori didn't even bother to ask how she was feeling. She has seen him only a few times since Bill's funeral. He has seemed preoccupied and although he was affectionate, she wonders if he is having second thoughts about reconciling with his wife. He denied it when she asked so she has left the subject alone.

Just when she has begun to believe she could belong to this country, a sense of isolation strands her once more. She clicks open her email to Damon: 'Thank you so much for the flowers. They were beautiful. My injuries were relatively minor and I have now recovered. In regard to renewing our relationship, pity you trashed it. Let's leave it there in the dustbin of finished love affairs. Frances.'

For a moment she thinks she has been a bit abrupt. 'God, get a grip on yourself,' she mutters. 'One thing I'm certain about is that I don't want to go back to him.'

She walks swiftly out of the office, heading for the one person she can turn to for advice.

Bathed in sunshine, Theo is sitting in a wheelchair on the veranda of his home, which looks out over the lake. He is wearing a hand-knitted moss-green jumper and has a pile of newspapers on his lap.

'Frances, great to see you. Come and sit down.' His voice is warm and although his tan has faded, his face has regained a healthy pinkness.

As she leans over to kiss his cheek, she grimaces when she sees the trouser leg tucked around his knee.

He catches her expression. 'What's up? Everything OK?'

'Look, I just wanted to see if you are all right. You don't need to know about work.'

'I don't need to know, Frances, but I'm sure as hell still interested. You don't invest thirty years of your life in something like that and . . . I was going to say, walk away, but I guess in my case it's limp away.' He laughs loudly until a bout of coughing stops him.

Frances pats him on the shoulder and notices for the first time how the accident has altered his whole appearance. Once, he appeared young for his age; today he looks every day of his sixty years.

'Sorry, Frances,' he says, reaching for her hand. 'I guess keeping a sense of humour about all this helps me get through it. Now what's this all about?'

'While I've been away, Sam's been very busy. He's in your job for the time being and he's managed to persuade the Minister to allow bulldozers up on the summit. They've already done some work and I understand there are two bulldozers up there now and guess whose name is now mud with the Maori?'

Theo sighs deeply. 'I had heard and I suppose I'm not surprised really,' he says after a while. 'When times are good and there are no bad headlines to worry about, the politicians stay out of things. But after the eruption, it was probably only a matter of time before they gave in to the likes of Sam. There are a lot of powerful interests backing intervention at the summit.'

'What can I do about it? I feel so helpless, Theo. The early warning system is working well but they see that as too passive. In this climate, they don't want to take what they see as risks with public safety, and cultural sensitivities seem to have gone out of the window. We told the Maori we wouldn't intervene and now I feel responsible. What should I do?'

Theo sees the deep lines creasing her forehead and the sadness shadowing her eyes.

'Hey, listen, girl. The one thing is not to take this personally. You're not responsible. I've been around the track a few times, long enough to know when the wind changes there's not a lot you can do about it. Suddenly, political correctness sounds like a dirty word to the politicians so they feel they can ride roughshod over Maori feelings.

'You know I've always been against intervention. I think it's idiotic to take bulldozers up there. But I'm afraid I don't think I can be of much help. I did what I could but the tide has turned. I'm already yesterday's man.'

Frances smiles at him. 'I don't think so. But I understand what you're saying.'

They sit together until Theo breaks the silence. 'How's that Tori going, by the way? Great guy. How are you two getting on together?'

'How did you know?' Frances asks, surprised.

'For one thing, you always had that slightly startled look when he was around.' Theo laughs. 'And now you're blushing.'

She grins.

'And I guess I have to confess that Sue dobbed you in. She said Tori was waiting at the hospital when we were brought in and he was in a real state. Obviously more than just an acquaintance.'

'Yeah, well we have seen a bit of each other. But Theo, I don't know what I'm getting myself into. There's always a conflict of interest with my job. He's just had a go at me about the bulldozers. As if I drove the bloody things up there myself.'

'Forget about all that. What do you feel about him, Frances? In the end that's what's important in life — the people and how we treat them. Heaven knows how I would have survived without Sue.'

'I like him a lot but we come from different worlds. I just doubt him at the moment and I suppose I doubt myself.'

'Let me tell you something, Frances. I haven't been completely straight with you. I had another visitor earlier today — Tori.'

She raises her eyebrows in surprise.

'I've known him for many years. We trust each other. He also came to ask my advice about the intervention, but he also told me about his feelings for you. He's not toying with you, Frances. He's a deep thinker and he's serious but he's also weighing things up.'

'And his wife?'

'He talked about her too. But from what I was hearing, he's just keeping the peace on the homefront. You're the one he's interested in. Maybe you have to let him know a little more about your feelings. I think he's waiting for a signal.'

'Maybe you're right, Theo,' she replies, getting up. 'I'd better get back to the coalface. Thanks for hearing me out. I wanted to explode at Sam when I found out — probably lucky he wasn't in the office. I'll have to deal with that now. And thanks for letting me know about Tori.'

She sees his face in her mind as she drives back to the office. Theo's right, she thinks, maybe I have to be more honest with Tori, let go a little. Maybe I have to start trusting again.

CHAPTER FORTY-THREE

Sam chuckles to himself as he walks across the helipad and greets Luke Gallagher, who has just finished refuelling the chopper. For once, he feels satisfied. He's in control of the mountain and has finally outsmarted the do-gooders.

'Ready to go, Luke?' he says with a new air of authority. 'I need to get back up to the summit to supervise those bulldozers.'

'Sure thing. I just need another couple of minutes to get the chopper ready and then we can go. But you can hop in.'

Luke springs the chopper to life and Sam puts his headphones on. As the pilot checks the fuel levels and the flight path, he says to Sam, 'Surprised you haven't had any flak about the bulldozing. How did you keep that quiet?'

Just as Sam is about to answer, Luke notices a car pull up. Four Maori men, Tori Maddison among them, jump out and start running towards them.

'I take back what I just said, Sam. I think the word's out!'

'Stop! Come back, you bastard!' Tori is yelling and waving his arms.

'I think that's our cue to get out of here. Let's go,' Sam says.

As the chopper lifts, Tori, Uncle Eruera and two others from the iwi stand watching it rise, their hair blowing furiously in the downdraught, their faces set in angry resignation.

Luke gives them a sheepish wave. He's surprised to see Sam do the same, until he notices he has two fingers in the air.

As the chopper descends towards the summit, Sam can see the contractors are already waiting with their bulldozers, two smaller machines that could be partly dismantled and dropped in by chopper. Even Sam acknowledged that driving a big dozer up the mountain would cause too much damage.

It has cost plenty to secure the drivers' services, to provide them with accommodation further down the mountain and to transport the machinery there.

'We need danger bonuses,' one contractor told him. 'You'll have to pay us four times our normal rate because of the altitude, the cold and the fact that we won't be able to show our faces around town for a while or some of those Maori blokes will punch our lights out.'

Sam agreed without much negotiation. He needed them and felt confident that with public fears about safety running at an all-time high, the department wouldn't be quibbling about an extra few thousand dollars.

'You sure this is going to work?' Luke asks as he lowers the chopper.

'Absolutely. It's going to take a bit longer with the small dozers but I'd stake my reputation on the fact that if we can dig a trench behind the dam wall so we can drain the water out, we'll all be much better off.'

'Yeah, well you're right about one thing — it's your reputation.' Luke glances at him wryly. 'Hope you've made the right call, Sam. Certainly not what the boss, I mean, not what Theo wanted.'

'Theo was too long in the job and he lost the plot. He was

sucked in by the Maoris and didn't think he had any control over the volcano.'

'Well, he was right about that! Poor bastard. I'm going to drop you off just near that ridge. I'll be back in three hours to pick you up.'

A strong cold wind buffets Sam as he strides along the ridge towards the bulldozers and he pulls his woollen hat further over his forehead. One of the men working on the mountain beckons him over.

'The water level's shot up a bit in the last couple of days,' he says. 'Look at that marker on the edge of the crater. That was right out of the water. Now it's nearly in it.'

Sam walks over to look at it more closely. He circles the rim of the crater, carefully noting the other markers and sees the water has crept closer to them too.

'OK,' he calls out, 'let's get on with it. Bring the dozers over towards the edge of the dam and we'll continue digging the trench at the northern edge.'

He doesn't show it, but Sam is puzzled by what is happening in the Crater Lake. A week earlier he thought the pressure of the water would surely be relieved as the dozers managed to clear away some of the tephra that was building up and blocking the outlet. He's hoping another week will be enough to create the trench that will let the water continue to drain out.

The roaring of the bulldozers and the howling of the wind blend together in a cacophony that blocks out all other sounds, so it is the pungent smell of sulphur that first grabs Sam's attention. Stepping back and listening hard, he thinks he can hear the sound of alarms ringing out below the summit. Instinctively he reaches into his pocket for his mobile phone, but it's not there.

Then he sees rocks tumbling off the crater's edge into the water and a yellowish column of smoke rises up before him.

'Run!' he yells.

The two drivers abandon the bulldozers and, with the two assistants, clamber up the ridge. Sam is ahead of them.

'Run! Run for your lives!' he shouts again, but a hellish boom drowns him out as the earth beneath them explodes.

CHAPTER FORTY-FOUR

❧

Frances hears it first. Two of the seismographs start to emit a small alarm as they detect an increase of vibrations inside the volcano. Then, simultaneously, the mobile phones connected to the alarm network start ringing. Frances has hers in her hand. On the next desk Sam's also begins to ring.

'My God, the volcano's going off again,' she calls to the other scientists in the next office. 'The early warning system has been activated. And the seismographs are going berserk. Let's get going.'

Frances calls Luke Gallagher. 'Sam, where is he?' she barks, her voice urgent.

'On the summit. I'm back in Taupo and I'm going back for him in an hour or so.'

'It's too late. The warning system's gone off. I'm sure the mountain's going to erupt or the crater's burst. We won't be able to land there. I'll be at the pad in five minutes.'

She throws extra batteries for her mobile phone into her backpack and rushes outside, banging into Tori as she does so. 'Let's go,' she says, grabbing his arm and pulling him along the street to her car. 'The mountain might be erupting again and Sam's up there with some workers. It's going crazy up there!'

Sam comes to and tries to lift himself up. He's lying face down on a bed of black ash that is burning into him. Blood from cuts to his forehead drips down his face. He can't feel his legs and there is so much gas that he can barely breathe. The ground around him is shaking violently and he remembers where he is.

Ahead of him one of the bulldozer drivers and the two labourers are lying on rocks that are glowing with heat and steam. Their limbs are placed in peculiarly odd postures and Sam realises they're dead. He can see the bulldozers turned on their sides, like a pair of huge praying mantises.

He tries to call out but can't summon up his voice. Time seems to be standing still until he hears a roaring noise from the crater behind him. Although he feels desperately afraid, he can't muster the strength to turn around.

'Help,' he whispers, slightly comforted by his own raspy voice. 'Please help me.'

At last he feels his feet and then his legs, but they're burning and wet. He closes his eyes and succumbs to the mountain. As he exhales for the last time, a wave of water rises behind him. As it washes up over the rim of the crater, it picks Sam's body up and hurls it down the side of Ruapehu.

CHAPTER FORTY-FIVE

❧

The pale afternoon light dances on the rippling waters of Lake Taupo as Frances, Tori and Luke fly swiftly towards the trio of volcanoes on the horizon. Ruapehu is puffing plumes of black smoke spattered with what, from this distance, look like giant angry fireflies.

'Sam . . .' Frances begins. 'If he'd taken his phone, maybe he could have got out.' From the back seat Tori places his hand on her shoulder.

'I don't think we can hold out any hope,' Luke says. 'They would have been right there when the volcano erupted. But I'll try to get as close as I can.'

She thinks of Theo, now home with Sue, and wishes he was here, with his calming confidence. She resists an urge to ring him about Sam. That will have to wait.

'We can't get too close to that smoke,' Luke warns them. 'The last thing we need is any ash getting on the chopper. It's like concrete — if any flies into the engine it will wreck it in a couple of hours. But we should be able to get near enough to see the big picture.'

They fly over the summits of Tongariro and Ngauruhoe, for now silent witnesses to their noisy neighbour. The smoke is dissipating to the east and Luke steers the helicopter to the western side of the volcano.

Below them they can see lights shining from the Chateau and lodges dotted around the foothills. Higher up, they see a handful of people running from lodges sitting above the snowline. A line of cars is heading down the mountain: the warning system is working.

Up here, Frances feels vulnerable and afraid. As they fly closer, she and Tori scan the crater with binoculars. There is no sign of Sam or the contractors.

'Look, there!' Tori yells suddenly. The silhouettes of the two bulldozers lying outside the rim of the crater appear briefly but disappear just as quickly as white fountains of steam arc out above the summit.

'Luke, let's get out of here fast!' Frances' voice is urgent. 'It looks like it's going to blow.'

The pilot banks away sharply and flies them back above the Chateau where they can circle and observe in safety.

Frances is talking on the phone to the scientists in the observation centre below when Tori shouts, 'My God, look at that!'

Jets of black ash are roaring out of the crater above them, followed by huge clouds of steam. Together they fill the sky, blocking out the sun. The helicopter shakes and quivers as a large explosion echoes down the mountain. Luke banks the chopper quickly and flies further away. 'No point aggravating the beast,' he says.

Although they're now several kilometres from the summit, the mountain's furious fireworks continue before their eyes. Wave after wave of ash, rocks, water and flames shoot into the air. Like birth contractions, the loud explosions become more frequent as the volcano expels debris from its very core.

Suddenly the explosions stop and the smoke rises high above them, blowing away on north-easterly winds. Then they see them: like twin black serpents sliding down the white pristine slopes, two mudflows are speeding down into the valley.

'Can we get closer now, Luke?'

With a slight nod, Luke takes them back above Ruapehu, carefully avoiding clouds of ash. The lahars have run right through the skifields. Three large metal pylons lie like felled trees in one valley, a string of chairlifts they used to support flung around like unwanted scrap metal in a wrecker's yard. There's no sign of life on the slopes.

'Let's check the western side. That's what worries me the most,' Frances says.

They circle around until they can see the edge of the crater.

'Fuck, look at that,' Tori yells.

A torrential mudslide is oozing out of the crater, pouring over the rim then crashing down the mountain. The bulldozers can no longer be seen.

Frances starts to tremble and lets out a sob.

'He wouldn't have had a chance, love,' Luke says. 'Do you think the bulldozing helped cause this?'

'No . . . I don't think so. It might have weakened the rock beneath the crater rim, but nothing would have stopped this. And it looks as though the rest of the tephra dam has been blasted by the eruption.' She turns to Tori. 'Aunty Tui was right — all the bulldozing in the world couldn't have stopped this lahar.'

A wave of dirty water full of blocks of ice and rocks gathers momentum as it races down through the Whangaehu Valley. They hover above as it rushes into the river, turning it into a wild, dangerous torrent.

'I just hope and pray everyone has heard the warning,' Frances says.

She reaches for her phone and calls Cedric. There is no reply.

'Damn,' she curses. 'I hope they're not anywhere near the river. It's headed straight for Tangiwai again. It will be there in less than two hours.'

She rings back to base to check the early warning system has been fully activated.

'Yes,' the operator tells her. 'As far as we can tell, everyone has been contacted. There won't be any trains or other traffic crossing the bridges. There certainly won't be another Tangiwai disaster.'

Still, Frances feels uneasy about Cedric.

The ash has darkened the sky, throwing a deathlike pall over the mountains and the valleys below. They all start shivering.

'No wonder we're cold,' Luke says. 'Look at the gauge, the temperature has plummeted. It's dropped about ten degrees. We have to refuel soon. Shall we return to base?'

'No, let's pick up fuel down at the Chateau. I think we should stay around longer,' Frances says. 'And I'd like to fly over Tangiwai if we could.'

On the ground, she tries Cedric again. This time he answers.

'Don't worry, I was telephoned hours ago. I was just out checking the animals were OK. We've pulled them back from the riverbanks. Looks like we're better prepared this time.'

'Thank God,' she says.

Back in the air, they see lines of cars along the main roads where people are taking photos of the mountain. There are several ambulances parked around the Chateau waiting for the dead and injured. They ascend rapidly and circle the crater once more.

The constant eruptions have all but emptied the lake, its contents spewed down the mountain. Steaming fumaroles now exposed on the scarred rocky walls of the vent are puffing out clouds of gas. Bright yellow patches of sulphur stain the edges, stretching up to the rim that has been blasted out of shape.

'They wouldn't have had a chance against that,' Tori says.

The icy high slopes have escaped the lahars but are pockmarked by red-hot rocks that have rained down on them. A deep coating of ash covers the summit and nearly buries the Dome Shelter.

'Let's head down the valley,' Frances says.

They fly westwards, following the muddy trail of the lahar. Near where the bund was going to be built, a dirty tributary has forced its way down towards the Tongariro River. The normally blue-green transparent waters are grey and muddy and they watch as the heavy silt-laden current flows towards Lake Taupo. Flying swiftly, they catch the lahar as it powers further and further west towards Tangiwai. They pass it, soon reaching the Tangiwai bridge where they hover. Frances cannot help but think how different things would have been fifty years ago, if there had been guardian angels like them, keeping a watch over the mountain's pulse.

As they circle the area they see cars banked up, kept well back from the expected path of the lahar. Along the railway line they see a goods train stopped, waiting.

'It's worked, Frances, the system's worked,' Tori says.

'Yes. I wish Theo was here to see it.'

Although it's noisy in the helicopter, they can hear the rumbling of the muddy torrent as it heads towards the bridge. The wave smashes through a small road bridge, scooping up the debris in its jaws and expelling it across the surrounding farmland. A giant electricity pylon that has been swept off its foundations is lying in a paddock.

From the air the torrent looks like a dirty black tongue, licking up everything in its path. Now it is closing in on the Tangiwai railway bridge. Frances watches helplessly as it hits. At first, the current surfs under the bridge. Then the height of the wave submerges the railway line and, just as it has done dozens of other times over the centuries, gushes on, flooding around the bends of the river.

The flow is already weakening, the river dropping. The helicopter doubles back. The bridge seems to be largely intact. Although its overhead frame has been smashed and bent, from the air it's difficult to see if there is damage beneath.

'They'll have to get the engineers to go over that with a fine-tooth comb before any trains cross it,' says Luke.

Frances remembers the doubts of those who saw the bridge wrecked in 1953, those who thought a weakened pylon was to blame for all those deaths. No one will ever really know the answer to that. She also recalls Tui's sardonic question that day they first met in the steamy mists on the mountain. 'What are you expecting the volcano to do, stop being a volcano?'

CHAPTER FORTY-SIX

⸎

Holding her hand firmly, Tori leads Frances along a narrow winding track through the forest and on towards a hidden part of Lake Taupo. The night air is warm and still. A half-moon shines through the trees, flashing silvery glimpses of the lake and throwing a soft light onto the two figures as they move soundlessly together.

They tread carefully to avoid tripping on rocks and tree roots protruding from the path. On either side, thick vine-covered trunks rise to the sky. From time to time, they hear the nocturnal call of the morepork from a hidden eyrie high in the branches silhouetted against the night sky.

He carries a basket in his other hand, she the warm rug and towels he handed her as they left his car.

'Just another few minutes,' he murmurs.

She starts when she hears rustling close to the track.

Taking a torch from the basket, he puts his finger to his mouth to silence her. 'I don't think we're alone,' he whispers and, seeing her alarm, adds, 'Nothing to worry about, just follow me.'

Tori creeps a metre or two off the track, trying not to make a sound. Frances is hard on his heels. He shines the torch just ahead and the beam hits a ball of brown feathers with a very long curved beak pecking through the forest litter.

'That's a kiwi,' he says, enjoying her surprised look. 'They're hard to find but there's usually a few around here if you know where to look.'

For a few seconds, the bird keeps shuffling through a pile of leaves until it appears to catch something in its beak and scurries away, safe in the darkness.

Stepping lightly, they continue on the path until she can hear trickling water and her nostrils are filled with the faint smell of sulphur.

'Very close now,' Tori says, caressing the palm of her hand with his thumb.

The trees thin and they meet a small swiftly flowing stream. Tiny wafts of steam rise from the water and they follow it to a clearing where it feeds into a large natural pool surrounded by ferns and ponga trees.

Tori bows extravagantly in front of her. 'Welcome to your own private baths, madam. This is the hot pool my family have swum in for generations. No admission fee and togs are optional.'

Frances smiles, feeling safe and easy in his company. As she bends to test the temperature of the water, Tori spreads the rug on a smooth mossy patch alongside. He takes four large candles from the basket and, one by one, lights them and sets them by the pool so that their soft flames cast golden honey streaks of sparkling light across the water.

Frances removes her shoes and dips her foot into the water. 'It feels like a lovely hot bath.'

Tori hands her a small bottle of cool water from the basket and she drinks deeply.

She turns to see him sitting on the ground, staring at her, his deep brown eyes tempting her, pulling her to him. She knows that, more than anything, she wants to be with this man. She goes to him and he pulls her down. Taking her hand, he lightly kisses the inside of her wrist, then traces a line there with his tongue.

Their lips meet and their quick hands search each other, faces and bodies, as though they have been lost and finally reunited after a long, forced separation. But Tori slows them. Half lover, half protector, he encourages her to sit, strokes her face, smooths her hair. She responds with dozens of tiny butterfly kisses on his forehead, down to his nose, his chin and around his neck.

'Do you want to go into the water?' Tori asks softly. 'I promise you we won't be disturbed.'

She smiles her agreement and they shed their clothes.

As she stands naked in the forest, Frances' skin shines like polished alabaster in the moonlight. Tori's gaze travels from her eyes, which can no longer hide her desire, to the white hollow of her neck, down to the fullness of her breasts, the gentle contours of her stomach to the soft downy furrow between her legs.

Her eyes, in turn, are drawn to his high cheekbones, his sculptured shoulders and thick muscular body. His firm brown skin glistens.

He reaches out, pulls her close to him and kisses her deeply. As her body clings to his, she feels him harden against her.

'You look spectacular,' he says. 'Remember when Mata sang the waiata aroha, the love song about the young chieftainess? That's what you are to me — a princess of the forest, my puhi-wahine. And you should never have to wear clothes again.' She laughs at him and spins around. 'Or maybe just a few feathers here and there for when you go to town.'

He takes her hand and helps her into the pool. They wade into the middle where the warm water surges around their bare bodies up to their necks. Frances feels so alive: her skin is tingling and as she runs her hand down from her breasts to her thighs, her skin feels like silk. She can feel large rocks on the bottom of the pool and when she totters on one, Tori grabs her hand to steady her.

'It's OK, it's perfectly safe. Follow me.'

They swim to the far side and Tori guides her to a long, submerged stone ledge where they can sit comfortably, their heads supported by an edging of smooth logs.

'Stay there, I'll be back in a moment.'

She watches his body glide back through the candlelit water. As he walks out, small streams of water glow as they trickle down his firm strong buttocks. He wades back, triumphantly holding aloft a bottle and two plastic long-stemmed glasses.

As the warm water from the earth's core cradles their bodies, their mouths are cooled by the crispness of the white wine. Presently he puts both the glasses on the side of the pool and reaches for her. Frances leans her head back into the water until her breasts are floating, her erect nipples breaking the surface. He slides beneath her and runs his fingers down and down between her legs. He feels the soft velvet slipperiness of her and gently strokes her. As she moans, he rubs her harder until she cries out and a ripple of pleasure shudders through her body.

She rolls over onto him. Their tongues explore each other's mouths and she guides him into her. Their bodies move together, slowly at first, then more quickly and harder, riding a wave of ecstasy.

He stays inside her for a long time. 'I love you,' he whispers in her ear at last.

'And I love you,' she whispers back, gently kissing his neck. 'Now that I've found you, I never want to lose you. I don't want to be like that poor princess, singing a weepy love song about losing her lover.'

He squeezes her tightly. 'There's no risk of that. There have been too many broken hearts. I'll always be here for you.'

They half sit, half lie together on the ledge, a tangle of limbs, enveloped by the warm waters like twins in the amniotic sac of their mother's womb.

CHAPTER FORTY-SEVEN

❧

'They've blossomed just in time for Christmas,' says Tori as he and Frances drive south from Taupo towards Taumarunui.

The red flowers of the pohutukawa trees dotted along the road cry out for attention among the muted grey-green foliage of the gnarled branches that host them. The blue waters of the lake lap onto stony beaches, propelled by little gusts of wind and the wakes of small fishing boats.

'Water looks good,' Frances remarks.

'We're lucky. All the mud and silt has disappeared. Fishing's almost back to normal, although it's a bit early to tell how much of the hatchery was damaged upriver. Could have been a lot worse.'

The road is full of traffic with thousands of cars heading north and south for Christmas. Long, winding lines of cars towing caravans and boats, packed with restless children bound for beach holidays and family reunions, slow the journey.

'Do you think Beverley will be able to go through with this?' Tori asks.

'I think so. We've talked about it a lot — for months now.

I told her we'd be there by early evening. We don't want to have to rush.'

'No rush? You're starting to sound relaxed, a bit like me.' Tori laughs.

When they turn off the main road at Turangi and drive west, the traffic thins and Tori accelerates. Out of the ski season, few people are heading up the mountains, though after the eruption business had plummeted anyway. The three volcanoes rise dramatically before them, traces of late snow dusting their peaks, which glow a deep pink in the setting sun. The trails of the lahars and ash falls on Ruapehu have been swallowed by the mountain, fading into rocky ravines.

The traffic increases again when they take the turn-off north to Taumarunui. The thick summer foliage of the trees glistens in the last of an amber sunset as they pull into town.

'Just need to pick something up from the florist,' Frances says, indicating the way ahead. 'They said they'd be open late tonight.'

'Not more of those red roses?' he asks with a grin.

She moves closer to him and nuzzles into his neck, scattering it with kisses.

Customers buying last-minute flowers for Christmas cram the tiny shop. Bouquets still awaiting delivery to the fortunate ones whose families and loved ones have remembered them are squashed next to a line of aluminium buckets crammed with brilliantly coloured roses, carnations, lilies and gerberas.

Flushed and weary from a dawn start, the young florist, who has increased the number of earrings in each lobe to five, recognises Frances and disappears behind a curtain.

'Here it is, the only wreath on order today,' she says, returning with a large white box she passes over the counter. 'See if you like it.'

Nestled inside is a circle of flowers, the blood-red wispy

flowers of the pohutukawa tree entwined with delicate, impossibly white bunches of baby roses.

'It's beautiful. Just right. Thank you.'

'There's a card there for you to write on.'

'Yes, we'll need that.'

As they stop outside the house Frances glimpses a lace curtain in the front room pulled back and dropped again. Beverley walks outside, looking tired but happy to see them.

Dressed to travel in neatly pressed navy-blue trousers topped with a Liberty print blouse, she fiddles with a brooch securing it at her neck — a delicate gold circle, decorated with a pair of blue enamel lovebirds. She tells them it was an engagement gift, her only memento from her long-lost fiancé. 'It's been packed away for years. I thought today was as good a day as any to give it an airing.'

As the two women embrace, Tori stands and waits to be introduced, shuffling a little shyly.

Frances turns to him, pulling him towards them. 'This is Tori. He'll drive us to the station.'

Linked by their affection for Frances, Beverley and Tori simply smile at one another.

'Perhaps a little something before we go?' Beverley asks, not waiting for a reply as she walks inside.

The table is set for a Christmas Eve tea: fine-china plates, silver cutlery and three small stemmed crystal glasses sit atop a starched white cloth.

'Sherry?' Beverley is already filling the glasses with the sweet golden liquid from a decanter. As they toast one another, she returns to her kitchen, re-emerging with a plate of sandwiches and another of rich dark fruitcake. 'The ham's freshly cut and the bread baked today. Hope you like hot mustard. And have some cake. I baked it myself. It's been soaking in brandy for two months.'

As the old lady passes the plate towards them, Frances can see her hand quivering.

'Are you feeling OK? About the journey, I mean.'

Beverley throws her a smile. 'Yes and no. I wouldn't be doing this without you, Frances. You know that. But you've become like a daughter to me and I trust your instincts on this.'

'Time to go,' Tori says, awkwardly stacking the pile of delicate plates. 'Don't want to miss the train.'

CHAPTER FORTY-EIGHT

❧

As they drive towards Taihape, Frances glances anxiously at Beverley in the back seat. Although this drive will take a mere two hours, it has taken her more than fifty years to summon the courage to return to the town where she will board the train and complete the journey.

Half an hour before the overnight Northerner is due, the station platform is already busy with passengers arriving. The three of them sit together on a long wooden bench, not talking, just waiting. As the minutes pass slowly, more people gather at the station. Then the train — clean, modern and utilitarian — pulls in.

'Not the same as those wonderful old steam trains,' Beverley says, her eyes misty with memories. While bleary-eyed passengers jump off the train to grab a hurried drink and late-night snack, Frances hands the white box to Beverley.

She glances inside and her eyes meet Frances'.

'I've written on the card. I hope you approve.'

Beverley flicks over the tiny cardboard card embossed with a silver edging:

'You know what to do. We'll be waiting for you. Be brave,' Frances says, hugging her friend. Beverley nods and walks tentatively to the train. Glancing over her shoulder she tells them she'll take a taxi home at the end of her trip.

'I intend to finish this journey alone. Thank you so much, Frances. Bless you.' She climbs into the brightly lit carriage, locates her well-upholstered seat facing forwards, to Tangiwai, and sits there comfortably. She feels oddly elated, surprised by an unaccustomed lightness of being. Frances walks over to the edge of the platform and places her hand against the window. Beverley puts her hand up to meet it and they smile their secrets at each other.

Tori is waiting in the car, no sign of impatience on his face. It is Frances who reminds him of the need to hurry. 'We have to beat the train to Tangiwai. Let's get going.'

Just as it was all those decades ago, the night is clear and fine. In the main street, stragglers from Christmas parties are meandering from restaurants to pubs. Some have dropped loved ones at the station to take the same train, never doubting they will be delivered safely to their destinations.

They are quickly devoured in darkness as they leave the lights of town and drive along the winding road towards Waiouru. As they pass through the small town, both of them think of Bill, who so loved his life in the army and the challenge of knocking callow youths into military shape.

The traffic has dwindled. Most travellers have stopped for the night, seeking refuge in motley roadside motels. Still Tori and Frances drive on and on through the darkness, their headlights illuminating ghostly trees and unidentifiable shapes along the roadway.

They spot the sign marking the township of Tangiwai.

'Just a little bit further, Tori, and we're there. You'll have to slow down soon and take a right turn. It's easy to miss.'

Frances leans forward in her seat, and he can see her clenched knuckles reflected in the windscreen.

'Take it easy.' Tori reassures her by reaching out to touch her hand. 'It will be all right. You've waited a long time for this.'

'Here! Turn now.'

The tyres crunch on the gravel as they arrive in the deserted car park where a full moon illuminates the memorial.

'Look, Tori, look at the mountain.'

Before them, Ruapehu rises majestically, a dark silhouette with its snowy cap barely visible.

'Poor Sam,' Frances says. 'He was stupid to get involved with Carmody but I think he really believed in what he was doing.'

'I know. I didn't wish him any harm. But we've all learnt that the mountain isn't selective about its victims. Let's head down to the river,' Tori says. 'The train will be here in five or so minutes.'

They edge their way down the uneven track towards the bank, Tori shining his torch ahead of them.

'Wait, wait for me,' Frances says. He reaches back into the darkness, finding her hand and holding it tightly.

They can hear the rushing of the water before they see the river. In the darkness it sounds so much louder.

'Poof, the sulphur is really heavy tonight,' she complains.

The chemical vapours surround them, mingling with a dampness already rising in the night air.

It sounds eerie and distant at first, the rumbling echo of the train heading towards the Tangiwai bridge. Seconds pass and the noise rises. They see a beam piercing the darkness as the headlights of the train disturb the night. Then the sound softens.

'It's slowing down, Tori, just as we hoped.'

The locomotive almost comes to a stop as it approaches the bridge above them. Tori points the torch upwards, flashing it on and off three times. A tiny light in the second carriage of the train responds — once, twice, three times.

The window by the light is open. As the train drives onto the bridge they see a hand waving the torch out of the window. Then, in a single throw, the wreath is tossed in the air and starts to fall, down, down, down, until it hits the quickly moving current beneath the bridge.

At first they can't see it. Then Tori finds it with his torch. The twisted Christmas-red and winter-white circle of flowers shimmers as it floats. Momentarily, it stops, caught in a submerged tangle of fallen branches. Then, as if it has taken on its own life, the wreath pushes through into the silvery liquid darkness. Effortlessly, it catches the flow and floats past Tori and Frances. The train has vanished, safely heading north, taking Beverley and a full load of passengers to the end of their journey.

Frances can hardly breathe. Her skin is tingling and her knees are shaking. She clings to Tori as the flowers float around a bend in the river and disappear.

He puts his arm around her and holds her close, kissing her damp cheek. 'Your sister's wairua, her soul, it's free, Frances. You've finally let her go.'

Frances feels as though a piece of her very soul is unravelling. 'Valerie!' she sobs. Tori grips her more tightly until he feels her surrender to his strength.

Although the land around the weeping waters continues to cool as the midnight hour approaches, a warm joyful flow courses through her body like a thread of red mercury. She smiles at Tori. 'My sister is safe now, but I know a part of her will always stay with me. You've taught me that. Thank you.'

Frances delves into her pocket until she feels the golden bracelet. She caresses it and, for the first time, smiles inwardly as she touches the soft links and tiny heart.

Tori reaches for her and she goes to him willingly. Arm in arm they turn back towards the mountain. In the night, it soars above them, seeming to melt into the black sky.

'Te ha o taku maunga, ko taku manawa,' he whispers to her. 'That means, the breath of the mountain is in my heart. And you are there with it.'

They see it at the same time — a white curling cloud of steam rising from the summit, lit by the moon — and their hearts quicken as if picking up the beat of the earth.

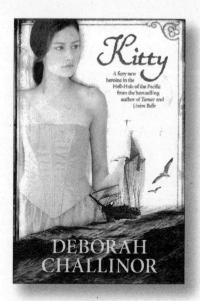

Kitty

When 18-year-old Kitty Carlisle's father dies in 1838, her mother is left with little more than the possibility of her beautiful daughter making a good marriage. But when Kitty is compromised by an unscrupulous adventurer, her reputation is destroyed. In disgrace, she is banished to the colonies with her dour missionary uncle and his long-suffering wife.

In the untamed Bay of Islands, missionaries struggle to establish Victorian England across the harbour from the infamous whaling port of Kororareka, Hell-Hole of the Pacific. There Kitty falls in love with Rian Farrell, an aloof and irreverent sea captain, but discovers he has secrets of his own. When shocking events force her to flee the Bay of Islands, her independent heart leads her into a web of illicit sexual liaison, betrayal and death.

HarperCollinsPublishers

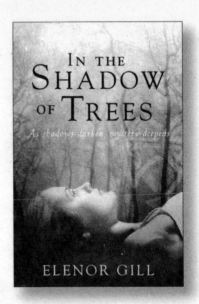

In the Shadow of Trees

Regan is an acclaimed sculptor, renowned for her sensuous work in wood. When her relationship with the much younger Jason Sullivan ends abruptly, Regan retreats to an isolated cottage to prepare for a new exhibition.

Almost at once she begins to fall under the spell of the trees — recurring dreams and inexplicable lapses in time inspire her, yet leave her exhausted and strangely disturbed. As she immerses herself in her work, a surprising new relationship begins to develop with Liam, the estate handyman sent to repair the cottage.

But as he watches the shadows deepen around Regan, Liam becomes increasingly concerned. When they discover the bizarre fate of generations of Sullivan women, his concern turns to fear. But Liam has secrets of his own, secrets that threaten his new bond with Regan, a bond that may be her only chance to escape the gathering shadows.

HarperCollins*Publishers*

Union Belle

When the first effects of the 1951 waterfront workers' strike ripple through the country, Ellen McCabe — wife, mother, union supporter — is happy with her life in Pukemiro, a small coal-mining town. Even when her husband's union lays down their tools in support and the strain of making ends meet begins to wear her down, she's ready to play her part in the lean months ahead.

But when Jack Vaughan comes to town, something inside her shifts. Jack is handsome, a charismatic war veteran — and a friend of her husband's. Suddenly everything changes, with irrevocable consequences, as the turmoil and divided loyalties swirling through the town threaten to tear her apart.

Union Belle is a story of love, duty and passion played out against the backdrop of the infamous strike that turned friends into enemies, shattered communities and almost brought New Zealand to its knees.

HarperCollins*Publishers*